The Rainbow Option

Judge Block woke up feeling cold. He didn't know it, but he was deep in the Sierra Nevada Mountains.

The tall man spoke. "Here's the deal, Judge. This is a Course In Reality. It's not optional, because reality is not optional.

"You issued an injunction last Tuesday blocking the high-yield seeds that would end the starvation in Africa. That was your 'answer.' For the first time, the answers you impose on others, others who are guilty of no crime, you will have to live with yourself. Live with your answers.

"There is your cabin for shelter. You have your blanket. Here's a down parka. We're leaving you with enough food for ten weeks, if you confine yourself to one can of food per day. If you want more, we've left you some seeds, conventional seeds, which you can plant. You'll find out for yourself how hard it is to grow your own food."

*　*　*　*　*　*

An arrogant federal judge must survive in the wilderness, where he painfully learns to grow his own food … and the humility to ask for help from a Higher Power.

A Shoshone Indian youth becomes the leader of a band of ARK survivors, after he invents a way for them to evade the predator drones hunting them.

The government infects its own citizens with a deadly virus. A small group of Davids race to develop a cure. Can they succeed before the government Goliaths kill millions of people?

As gangs and hunger stalk the nation, small groups of resisters survive in the ARK locations. Can America have a new birth of freedom? One brave woman and one brave man point the way, with …
The Rainbow Option.

The Rainbow Option is the suspense-filled sequel to *The Noah Option.*

Praise for Michael McCarthy's thriller *The Noah Option*:

"Once I got a feel for the characters I couldn't wait to see what was going to happen next! At halfway through, I was so hooked I'd stay up later every night."

~ Angelique Smith, Camden, S.C.

"It took until page 2 to become totally immersed."

~ Susan Cannon, N.C.

"Trust me; you won't be able to put it down! The characters are compelling, and the story is inspiring."

~ Don Smith, The Don Smith Show *www.DonSmithShow.com*

"Mr. McCarthy has written a delightful tale about what happens when Government runs amuck."

~ William Thrift, Arkansas

"This is a story of successful people whose work challenges the control of a world turned increasingly dystopian by a government ..."

~ Jack Joyner, Georgia

"The Noah Option" ought to be on every High School reading list. ... Buy it. Read it. You will be glad you did."

~ Pam Danz, N.C.

"... a fast paced page turner [that] keeps the reader on edge.

~ Jaynie Whitcomb, Florida

"... an action thriller with techy support ... The big and powerful against the little guy is a timeless tale. Good Show!"

~ Nancy Kosling

Books by Michael McCarthy

Fiction
The Noah Option

Business Non-Fiction
You Made My Day (with Janis Allen)
Sustain Your Gains ~ The People Side of Lean – Six Sigma

MICHAEL McCARTHY

WESTBOW
PRESS®
A DIVISION OF THOMAS NELSON
& ZONDERVAN

WestBow Press books may be ordered through booksellers or by contacting:

WestBow Press
A Division of Thomas Nelson & Zondervan
1663 Liberty Drive
Bloomington, IN 47403
www.westbowpress.com
1 (866) 928-1240

www.TheNoahOption.com

Cover design by Kathy Peterson / Advertising PLUS. adplus@mac.com

ISBN: 978-1-4908-6907-0 (sc)
ISBN: 978-1-4908-6908-7 (e)

Library of Congress Control Number: 2015901937

Print information available on the last page.

WestBow Press rev. date: 3/18/2015

Dedication:

To Tyrone S. Woods and Glen Doherty, two American heroes.
They stood up instead of standing down in Benghazi.
They fought and died to defend their fellow Americans.

Tell them in Sparta, passer-by,
That here, obedient to our word, we lie.

The epitaph written by Simonides for the 300 Spartans
who died in 480 B.C. defending the pass at Thermopylae
against a Persian army of one million.

May we all stand up to defend our God-given freedoms declared
over 200 years ago, so that this nation, conceived in liberty,
shall not perish from the earth.

Michael McCarthy
August 2014

PART ONE.
LIVE WITH YOUR ANSWERS

"The democracy will cease to exist when you take away from those who are willing to work and give to those who would not."

Thomas Jefferson

"… testing whether that nation, or any nation so conceived and so dedicated, can long endure."

Abraham Lincoln, *The Gettysburg Address*

CHAPTER ONE

Federal Judge Barry Block opened the refrigerator and grabbed a bottle of beer. It was warm. *What happened?* he thought. Feeling the milk cartons, they were warm also. Everything had spoiled. *Odd, the power was on to open the garage door.* He went to the light switch and flipped it. Nothing.

"Arjana! What's going on?" No answer. Taped to the refrigerator door was a note.

Barry, the power is has been off for hours. I called the power company. Gone to the deli for take-out. Back by 6:45. ~ Arjana.

He looked at his watch. 6 p.m. He would have to wait for supper.

Cursing, he went back to the kitchen. Picking up the phone, he started to call the power company. The line was dead. He took out his cell. It was dead too. *And I just recharged it in the car on the way home. What's going on?*

He decided to go to the neighbor's house to use their phone. When he opened the front door, he saw a typed page taped to it. Judge Block read:

The time has come to LIVE WITH YOUR ANSWERS. You must now learn to live with the answers you force on others.

What kind of a joke is this, he thought. He frowned, crumpled the paper and kicked it aside.

He started to walk next door. Then he saw the power company truck pull up, a crew cab with four doors. Grunting with relief, he changed direction and walked over to it. Three men in power company uniforms got out.

"Why does it take three of you to do a simple repair job?" began the judge in a loud and angry voice.

The tallest man spoke. "Union rules, Judge. Two for safety and one more just in case."

"Just in case of what?" asked the judge.

"Just in case we encounter a ruthless narcissist armed with arbitrary government power like you," said the tall man. One man slipped behind the judge and clamped a chloroformed cloth over his nose. The other one hoisted the judge in a fireman's carry as he lost consciousness.

"Time to live with your answers, Judge," said the tall man. They placed Judge Block in the back seat of the truck. The tall man uncrumpled the page kicked aside by the judge and taped it back on the door. They drove away, unnoticed by the neighbors watching the CBC Nightly News in their living rooms.

* * * * * *

Kathy Coeur-Saignant on the CBC* Evening News breathlessly read, "Here in the U.S. a legal injunction against distribution of so-called super-seeds is good news for anyone concerned about the health of the planet. *Central Broadcast Collective*

"In San Francisco, Judge Barry Block of the Federal 9th Circuit Court granted an emergency injunction to halt the distribution of the super-seeds sold under the brand name Carver's Legacy.

"For the story, we go to our planetary green justice correspondent, Abby Trammel. Abby?" Abby stood before the courthouse.

"Kathy, these are the seeds invented by Dr. Grace Washington of Tuskegee University. She won the Nobel Prize two years ago for her groundbreaking research in plant genetics. Independent agencies have verified that her crop seeds yield four times more food than conventional seeds, on just one-tenth of the land and with only one-tenth of the water currently used for similar crops.

"However, for years a private company paid the salaries of the researchers who developed these seeds. This arouses suspicion that they may want to sell these seeds instead of giving them away for free.

"The company, Nutritional Abundance Industries, was set to ship emergency supplies of these seeds to Botswana, where severe crop blight has brought the population to near starvation. These seeds are resistant to blight and mature quickly. These seeds can end the starvation threat in Botswana.

"Dr. Aaron Smith, professor of sociology at Vassar College, offered a word of caution to us."

A balding man with a grey beard appeared on the screen.

"Abby, the consensus of ethical sociologists is that this increased food supply will feed more people around the globe. Our planet simply cannot sustain more people. We need fewer people on the planet, not more. These seeds are irresponsible and a threat to the ecology of the planet. They must be outlawed."

Abby reappeared, microphone in hand, standing on the courthouse steps.

"Kathy, today Mr. Samuel Solipsis, chief counsel for the Pristine Influence on Society Foundation (PRIS), presented arguments in Federal Court for an immediate emergency injunction to stop distribution of these seeds, including the shipments to Botswana. The injunction further calls for destruction of all of the super-seeds. Let's listen."

The screen cut to a courtroom scene where Samuel Solipsis stood before Judge Block.

"Your Honor, these "Franken-food" crop seeds are known to deform children and mutilate animals who eat them. PRIS asks for immediate relief in the form of an injunction forbidding sale or release of these seeds in any form, and the destruction of all warehoused supplies of these seeds, to be witnessed and verified by an observer from PRIS."

Mr. Blunt, counsel for Nutritional Abundance Industries, rose. "Your Honor, there is no evidence that the Carver's Legacy brand of bio-engineered seeds either deform children or mutilate animals. Furthermore, counsel for PRIS has not submitted any evidence supporting this notion. They ask us to take their word for it."

Judge Block peered over his half-frame reading glasses at Blunt. "Mr. Blunt, this court holds higher standards than the merely legal statutes passed by Congress. For our precedents and standards we adhere to international law and the moral law that the needs of the many outweigh the needs of the few. Can you offer definitive and authoritative proof that these foods won't mutilate animals? Or won't deform children?"

"Your Honor, you will see in our brief before you medical studies showing that grain grown from these seeds is safe for human consumption."

"What about the mutilation of animals?"

"Your Honor, we have no studies about animals, because these grains are not intended for animal consumption. However, you have before you a deposition from nine professors of veterinary science summarizing the research findings that if a given food is safe for human consumption, it is safe for animal consumption."

"Not good enough, counselor. I hereby find for the plaintiff. Nutritional Abundance Industries will cease and desist from selling or distributing these seeds immediately, and they will destroy these seeds in the presence of a witness to be supplied by PRIS. Mr. Solipsis?"

"Thank you your Honor. We will file the name of our witness with the court in the morning."

The screen cut back to Abby on the courthouse steps.

"Kathy, although there may be deaths due to starvation in Botswana, the consensus of progressive minded advocates of justice for the planet is that a few hundreds of thousands dead is a small price to pay for the greater good – a healthier, less populated planet. Back to you, Kathy."

* * * * * *

Judge Block woke up feeling cold. He didn't know it, but he was deep in the Sierra Nevada Mountains. Before him was a small stream. Behind him was an old log cabin, nearly invisible under the trees in the darkness. Three men wearing goose-down parkas sat on logs around a campfire, hands extended toward the fire. Shivering, Judge Block got to his feet. He was wearing only the suit he had worn to the office that day. He went to the fire and extended his hands to warm himself.

"Good evening Judge," said the tall man. "Blanket?" He held out a woolen blanket. Block took it without a word and wrapped it around himself.

"Where am I?"

"That's for us to know and you to find out," one of the men said.

"Ever been a boy scout, Judge?" the third man asked. Block shook his head. "Too bad. Have a seat." He sat down on a log and looked at them across the fire.

The tall man spoke. "Here's the deal, Judge. This is a *Course In Reality*. It's not optional, because reality is not optional. You issued an injunction today blocking the high-yield seeds that would end the starvation in Africa. That was your "answer," your legal answer, even though there is not one law, not one precedent, not one article in the US Constitution that supports that position. You cited a higher standard, international law, although jurisprudence does not admit any standards not in the U.S. Constitution or U.S. legal code. You unilaterally made up your own standard instead of adhering to laws passed our elected representatives in Congress. Your standard, your answer, was that 'the needs of the many outweigh the needs of the few.' You never considered the rights of the few, or of the many, because you decided that you alone had the right to decide who has rights.

"Very well. Now you will learn to live with that answer, *your answer*. The rights of millions of third-world subsistence farmers to freely decide to buy enhanced seeds, or not, outweigh your need to abuse your power and exceed your legal authority. You will now have to live as they do, as a refugee, and *eat like they do*, on their meager subsistence diet. For the first time, the answers you impose on others, others who are guilty of no crime, you will have to live with yourself. Live with your answers.

"This *Course in Reality* lasts ten weeks. You will live here through your own efforts. Then we will bring you out of the woods. Guards are posted at a one-day's march in every direction, so if you try to escape, you will be captured and returned. We have given out a story that you are visiting your in-laws in Albania for ten weeks. Your wife Arjana is in fact on her way to visit relatives in Albania. She was told that you're in de-tox. She was delighted to hear it. So there will be no search for you.

"There's your cabin for shelter. You have your blanket. Here's a down parka. We're leaving you with enough food for ten weeks – if you confine yourself to one can of food per day. If you want more, we've left you some seeds, *conventional seeds*, which you can plant. You'll find out how much work it takes to grow your own food. It's early April, so if you plant immediately, you will have vegetables to eat by late May. Of course, these seeds will require you to water them by hand, pick insects off the sprouts before the vegetable is ruined, and mulch them with leaves for fertilizer. Then you will eat a bit better, with a fresh food supplement to your canned goods. If your gums begin to bleed, it means you need fresh vegetables for vitamin C. You'll find out for yourself how much work it takes to grow your own food.

"You have a shovel to garden with, and an axe to cut firewood. There is a grill, a spit, and a fry pan for your cooking in the cabin fireplace. You have only one day's worth of firewood, so you will have to begin cutting firewood first thing in the morning. Burns calories. Good exercise for you. Except that it burns more calories than you will get from your one can of food a day. If you eat more than one can a day, you will run out of food before the end of the two months and starve. Your choice. You also have a bow and three arrows, if you would like to hunt for a food supplement. There's a knife for gutting and skinning any game you shoot.

"There are also some books you can read by firelight if you wish. The Wilderness Survival Guide, the Bible, Milton Friedman, Thomas Sowell, Walter Williams, Ayn Rand, the Federalist Papers, and the U.S. Constitution.

"Subsistence living, for a man who forced subsistence living on others. Live with your own answers. Any questions?"

The judge looked terrified. "This isn't safe! What if I'm injured and need medical help?"

"There's a first-aid kit in the cabin with the same supplies that any family in rural Botswana has. Not much. Good luck, Judge. You'll need it. One other thing helps."

"What?"

"Prayer. If you're humble enough to ask for God's help, you may get it. But often, His help comes in a way you didn't expect."

With that, the three men stood up and walked away. The judge stared numbly into the flames of the campfire.

* * * * * *

Three days later, Judge Barry Block was still in the denial stage of his predicament. He kept thinking, *A Course in Reality? What are they talking about? Living with your answers? Don't they know I give the answers? I'm a federal judge!* He couldn't believe he was really abandoned to live on his own in the woods, and kept hoping that someone would show up to rescue him.

He did nothing for the first three days. He had burned up his one-day supply of firewood the first night in the cabin fireplace with a big roaring fire. Since then, he had chopped no firewood. He lay curled in a fetal position at night under his blanket in the cabin, shivering and listening to owl hoots and coyote calls. Once he thought he heard a panther scream. During the day, he had sat staring at the ashes of the campfire, feeling sorry for himself. *Why me? Who are these people? This is not fair! If I get out of here alive, I'll see that they rot in jail!*

On day four, he had had enough of being cold all night. He tramped around in the woods with the axe, looking for fallen wood. He found plenty, but he had to chop it into lengths he could carry. He gathered wood all day long. That night, he built a tiny fire in the fireplace and moved his blanket to sleep as close to the fire as he could. Several times in the night he woke up cold and put more wood on the fire, but only a little.

On the morning of day five he had plenty of wood left to build up the fire and heat his can of food. He ate half and set the remainder of the can on the rough wooden mantelpiece. He began digging and planting his garden that morning. In the afternoon, he went in search of more firewood. In the evening, he picked up the half-full can, intending to heat it on the fire. It was covered with ants. He shrugged and put it on the grate over the fire anyway. *Extra protein,* he thought.

On the afternoon of day seven, he decided he was ready to practice with the bow and arrow. Only three arrows! He spent an hour firing arrows at a stump. Finally he managed to hit the stump on three out of five tries. Now he decided to try for a rabbit. He had seen a lot of them in the woods. When startled, they zigged and zagged in spurts of speed that he could never hope to follow and lead with his aim. He would have to sneak up on a rabbit that was standing still. Suddenly, he saw one. Carefully, he stepped closer. A twig snapped under his foot. The rabbit ran off. He cursed.

He threw down the bow in a temper tantrum. "I'm a federal judge!" he screamed. He kicked at a downed tree trunk. "Ow!" he yelled, hopping on one foot. Finally he sat down on it. After three minutes of deep breathing, he started thinking about his situation. *I can't overrule a rabbit as if I'm the judge of the forest. This is reality, not my courtroom. An injunction won't make this tree into firewood. Only me and an axe. A ruling and a gavel won't put a rabbit to roast on the spit. Only me and the bow and arrow. Get to work, Barry.*

He quietly began to look for another rabbit.

By day eight, Judge Barry Block was a mass of blisters: blisters on his feet, blisters on his hands. And sore! Sore legs from walking. Sore arms and back from chopping wood and spading the garden. Sore legs from walking back and forth from the stream with small cans of water to water his planted seeds. He had so far opened and eaten thirteen cans of food. He couldn't help himself. He was so hungry! Taking stock, he realized he would be fasting for the last five days of his exile. Unless ... he could get these seeds to grow, or catch fish and game. Or find edible wild plants. Or all of the above.

By day ten, the relative quiet and loneliness of the woods began to bring him some small measure of quiet in his mind. Instead of the constant *why me, why me, why me,* his thoughts began to follow the sequence of the task at hand. *There's a downed limb. Chop it into two-foot sections that I can carry easily. There's another. Chop.* At night, he used the sharpening stone left for him to sharpen the axe blade.

The repetition of the manual work of digging and chopping and hoeing began to take on a rhythm as his muscles grew stronger and less sore. Without realizing it, he was acquiring the spiritual discipline known to monks as working meditation. He took satisfaction in the solid *chunk* sound of the axe biting into the wood, and the solid resistance he felt in his arms as it hit.

Chapter Two

Judge Block settled into a routine in his *Course in Reality* in the woods. In the morning, weed, spade, and water the garden. After lunch, search out firewood and split it for the evening fire. At twilight, when the rabbits were more active, practice stalking them.

On day twelve, he got one. He gutted it as best he could and roasted it on a spit over the fire. After eating a small portion that night, he raised the spit and left it to smoke the rest of the night. According to his Wilderness Survival Guide, smoked meat would last longer. He disciplined himself to eat sparingly, and made the rabbit his only food for two days.

On the third day after that, he got another rabbit. He grunted in satisfaction when the arrow struck its target. He became aware of his own feeling of satisfaction and then lowered the bow, thinking, *am I taking satisfaction in killing things?*

He sat down on a log and thought about it. *No, I don't pull the wings off flies or look for things to kill for the fun of it. I'm taking satisfaction in my own growing competence at surviving in the woods.* He got up and retrieved the rabbit and headed back to the cabin, whistling. Another two days of food without opening cans. He had made up for four of the five cans that he had consumed above his budget of one can per day for the ten weeks.

Suddenly, he stopped. He had an epiphany. *When I ate those five cans, I was borrowing against my own future. Except that out here, there is nobody else to pay back what I borrowed. I borrowed from myself, and it was up to me to pay myself back, or else starve the last five days. This is what the government does with deficit spending, except that they evade the issue by assuming that the next generation will pay the debt.*

Now, I see why that's wrong. Out here, I have to work to earn the extra food to pay myself back. I had to painfully learn to use a bow and arrow, and then learn to stalk rabbits, and then figure out the best time of day to hunt, and then spend that time each day hunting. This rabbit is the fruit of my labor.

He started walking back to the cabin. He gutted the rabbit and hung it up inside the cabin. *I'll cook it tomorrow morning,* he thought. Amazingly, he wasn't hungry. He stoked the fire and went to bed.

The next morning he built up the fire and found the spit. Then he looked where he had hung the rabbit. It was gone!

He nearly panicked. *What could have happened to it?* Then he saw the note on the mantelpiece. "Hi Judge. We needed food and didn't want to hunt today, so we took your rabbit. There are four of us, and only one of you, so our needs outweighed yours. Your friendly guards."

Blast! It's not fair! They have access to food from the outside world and I don't. I worked hard to get that rabbit and they just took it!

He slumped, realizing that now he was still three cans down on his food budget. He sighed and opened a can for breakfast. After breakfast, he sat on a log at the campfire pit and tried to come to terms with his loss.

I tried, I learned, I worked, and now this. All my effort and it still wasn't enough. No matter how good I get at this, I can't do everything that's needed. I give up. His shoulders slumped and his head drooped.

Suddenly, his head popped up. He had another epiphany. *That's right. I can't do everything. The tall guy said to pray and to ask for help. Ask God for help. I've never believed in God, but I need help from someone or something bigger than myself. I'm going to try.*

Judge Barry Block knelt down in the dirt in his filthy clothes and folded his hands together. *Lord God, I've never believed in you before, so I'm not sure what to say. I can't do everything I need to do to survive. I can't do it by myself. I'm stuck and I need help. I need Your help, and I ask You to give me help to survive out here. I hope there's something in this universe bigger and wiser and more powerful than me, Who cares enough to take an interest in me. I'm calling that something God and I'm asking You, God, for help. Thanks for listening.*

He rose up. Oddly, he felt better. He began to tend the garden. That evening, he got another rabbit. This time, he cooked it that night and let the remainder smoke. He blocked the door with the heavy wooden table before he went to bed.

* * * * * *

On day eighteen of his coursework in the woods, Judge Block woke up with a start early in the morning. It was still dark. A crashing, crunching noise had woken him. He felt rain on his face. He threw back his blanket and stood up. Lightning flashed, revealing a hole in the roof where a large tree branch had fallen. For protection from the rain, he moved his blanket under the large table and tried to get back to sleep.

When it was daylight, he surveyed the damage. A large pine branch had punctured the roof. There were no materials to repair the cedar shake roof. He looked at his surroundings. *Aha! I think I see a way to improvise a repair.*

When he made his foraging trek for firewood, he looked for low-hanging pine boughs with lots of pine needles. He brought some back with each load of firewood. When he judged he had enough, he dragged out the table and bench from inside the cabin. He placed the table next to the cabin wall, and then the bench on top of the table. Next he piled all the pine boughs on top of the bench. He climbed up and stood on the bench and threw the boughs onto the roof.

He was high enough to pull himself up and shimmy his way onto the roof. He then pulled out the branch that had caused the damage, and made a kind of thatch of pine boughs over the hole. He used pieces of firewood to weigh it down.

Back on the ground, he surveyed his work. *Funny,* he thought. *I take as much satisfaction with this work as I do with legal work. Maybe more, because it's tangible. I can see the results, and they're pretty good, for a repair without proper materials or tools.* Whistling, he took his bow and arrows and went hunting. He got his rabbit.

When he returned to the cabin, he found three filleted trout, a package of butter, and a filet knife on his table with a note. "Judge, The Lord helps those who help themselves, and so do we. After we saw how you went to work and repaired your own roof, we thought we'd lend a hand. These fillets can be cooked on your grill, or fried with the butter. There's a fishing rod in the corner with three hooked flies. Best spot is a pool about 300 yards downstream. Best time is early morning. The knife is sharp, so be careful. ~ Your Guards."

Stunned, he sat down. Tears came to his eyes, as he remembered what the tall man had said, "If you ask for help, the Lord will give it to you. But it will come in a way that you didn't expect."

Thank you, God. I'm grateful for this help. He wiped his eyes and got up and built a fire. Then he spread butter in the pan and on the trout filets. After they were cooked, he set aside two filets for the next day.

He took a bite. *Umm,* he thought. *Best I've ever had.* He sat on the hearth and continued his reading in the Thomas Sowell book, by firelight.

*　*　*　*　*　*

On day fifty-five of his *Course in Reality* in the forest, some of Barry Block's green beans, new potatoes, and green onions were ready to pick and eat. On day fifty-six, some tomatoes were ripe enough to pick. He picked enough for four meals. He now had plenty of food to last him until day seventy. On day fifty-seven, he returned after his trek for firewood to find a bottle of beer, a shaker of salt, and some cut-up steak. And another note.

"Congratulations! Your gardening work is paying off. This meat, plus your vegetables, will make a great beef stew in your fry pan. Enjoy the beer. ~ Your guards." Barry smiled, shook some salt on his palm and licked it. *Mmm.*

*　*　*　*　*　*

On day seventy, Barry Block was fit, tanned, and self-reliant. He was healthy. He was forty pounds lighter and down to what his doctor would call his ideal body weight for his age.

His muscles were toned and he was sleeping like a baby, without alcohol. He woke up early, caught six trout, filleted them, and began frying all six. He was just removing the first fillet when his five guards showed up, including the tall man.

"Gentlemen, you're just in time for a hot breakfast. Welcome, and sit down!"

The tall man smiled. "Why thank you, Judge. You have now graduated from your *Course in Reality*. We brought coffee and biscuits." He held up a large thermos. Another man held up a bag from a fast food restaurant. They sat down and began to eat in fellowship.

After breakfast, one of the guards handed a small backpack to Barry. "Here's a change of clothes. There's some soap in there, in case you want to wash up at the creek. A towel, too."

Barry smiled and said, "Thanks." He hoisted the pack and went down to the creek. He returned refreshed and smelling better.

The tall man produced a small mirror. "Judge, did any of these squirrels tell you that you look like Abraham Lincoln now that you have a beard and are skinnier?"

Barry looked at himself in the mirror. "Just don't invite me to any theatre performances!" They all laughed.

Barry looked around at each of their faces. "Fellas? Unless you're in a hurry, I want to talk a while before we go. This time in the woods has changed me, perhaps more than you expected. Got a few minutes?" They all nodded, and sat back down on the logs around the fire.

Barry began, "First of all, I now know firsthand how hard it is to raise your own food …." He talked for a long time about his experiences and what he had learned from his *Course in Reality*. He was a changed man; changed by living with his answers. "I've grown up. I was living in the real world that I couldn't order around with an abstract legal ruling. Talk wouldn't make a seed grow, I had to do the work to water it and mulch it."

On the drive back to San Francisco, Barry Block continued his conversation with the five men. "Guys, I know you can't trust me yet, but I want to become a member of the Constitutional Resistance Movement. I want to help roll back this governmental madness that I helped create."

The five men looked at one another and said nothing. "We'll see," said the tall man.

 # CHAPTER THREE

AFTER DROPPING THE JUDGE BACK AT HIS HOUSE, THE FIVE MEN WENT back to an apartment they used as a safe house. Once inside, they popped a frozen pizza in the oven and sat down at the kitchen table. The tall man took out his phone and brought up a screen. After ten seconds of thumbing the touch screen, he looked up.

"Spy block is now on, covering our cell phones and scrambling all signals, including sound waves, coming from this room. We can talk safely now."

"Is that like Maxwell Smart's 'cone of silence'?" teased an older man.

"What's that?" asked one of the younger men.

"Never mind. BYT."

"BYT?"

"Before your time. It's a generational thing. You'll understand when you're older."

The tall man spoke. "So, what about the judge? Can we trust him?"

The older man shook his head. "Too soon to tell. I say we keep him under surveillance to see what he does with his new-found information about us. Informing on us would be a great way for him to score brownie points with the Fed overlords. And since he's a Federal Judge, technically he is one of the Feds."

One of the younger men nodded. "I agree. Easy for him to say he wants in. Let's see what he does over the next several weeks."

The tall man looked around the table. "Agreed?" They all nodded. "Next item: the increasing petty tyrannies and secret police actions. How are we going to respond?"

The fourth man said, "The number of controls and things to comply with have stepped up. We're seeing these petty tyrannies in schools and homes every week. Remember that guy arrested last week because he allowed his twelve year old son to push a lawn mower? The charge was child abuse and child labor."

The fifth man added, "And Homeland Security is getting bolder and more visible in their Federal Fear and Intimidation Raids on citizens' homes. The raids still aren't reported by the media, but the neighbors are talking. The silence by the media when whole neighborhoods know it's happening makes it all the more intimidating. Which, of course, is their goal."

The tall man said, "We can't be everywhere, but if we can intervene in a few cases, word will get around. It will give people hope. Which they need right now."

The others all chorused "I'm in." One of them removed the pizza from the oven, sliced it, and put it on the table. They all pulled their chairs closer and reached for a slice.

"We may be alerted to a raid via some of our friends who keep their oaths." They ate for a while.

"And we can probably do some outing and social shaming of the petty tyrants in the schools with my new Swamp Fox app."

They all looked at the tall man. "Swamp Fox? What's that?"

He grinned a dazzling smile full of white teeth and pulled out his phone. "Let me show you." They all leaned in closer.

* * * * * *

Audrey Barnes sat on her couch watching television. A tray with a bowl of chips sat on the cushion beside her. "Ha!" she exclaimed. "Fat chance!" On the table on the other side of her a framed photo showed a bride in white with a young man in the dress blues of the Marine Corps. In her fifties now, Audrey still missed her husband. He had died nine years ago in Afghanistan.

On the television, Bill O'Reilly had just asked, "Will government ever cut their own budget instead of taxing us more?" Muttering to herself, Audrey took a sip of iced tea from a glass glistening with condensation.

There was a sharp knock on the door. Audrey made a face and reached for the remote control. After muting the sound, she heaved herself up from the couch and walked to the front door. She thought, *Who could this be at 9 at night?*

She switched on the front porch light and looked out the peephole. Two people in brown uniforms with black ties stood there, one male, one female. Wrinkling her brow, Audrey muttered "What the … ?" Out loud, she said, "It's nine fifteen at night. Who is it?"

The female agent made a fist with her left hand and pounded on the door with the heel of her hand. Three sharp blows.

"Open up! Federal agents!"

"Show me your identification," Audrey shouted. Three more sharp blows. Audrey went to the phone and called 911. "This is Audrey Barnes at 327 Maple Street. There are two people pounding on my front door. They say they are Federal agents, but they won't show me any identification." The 911 dispatcher said, "We'll have a sheriff's car there in five minutes. Don't open the door."

Just then the front door slammed open. The male agent had kicked the door down. Audrey dropped the phone, ran to her bedroom and locked the door. She pulled her Sig Sauer handgun from her bedside drawer and operated the slide to chamber a round. She sat on the floor with her back to the wall and aimed her handgun at the locked door.

Three sharp blows on the bedroom door. "Federal Agents! Open up."

"You have not identified yourself, "Audrey shouted back. "Police are on the way. Either slide your ID under the door or leave!"

Three more hard knocks on the bedroom door. "If you don't open up, we'll kick down this door too." Just then, sirens were heard. The two agents looked at each other, cursed, and holstered their weapons. They pulled out their identification wallets as they made their way back to the front door.

Squinting in the beam of bright flashlights, the two agents held their IDs in front of them. Two sheriff's deputies were standing behind the open doors of their police cruiser, aiming their handguns with one hand and a flashlight with the other.

"Homeland Security! Agents Wall and VanJones," said the female brown shirt.

One of the deputies called it in. "They check out OK," came back from the dispatcher in a static tinged radio voice. The deputies lowered their weapons and their flashlights.

The taller deputy asked, "What's up, guys? We had no notice that you were operating in our county, so we rolled when the citizen called 911."

"Then your sheriff is a little behind," the female agent said sharply. "Yesterday's presidential executive order 10-290 directs that Homeland Security is the ranking police agency anywhere in the US. We even out-rank the FBI. And we don't need to notify anyone where we're operating."

The taller deputy shrugged. "It's just a professional courtesy." He looked hard at the female agent. "And it might prevent you from being shot accidentally."

Then he reached into the cruiser and pulled out a microphone and keyed it to the loudspeaker on the overhead light bar of the car. Blue lights continued to flash.

"Mrs. Barnes? Sheriff's deputies are here. You are safe. You can come out now."

After a moment, Audrey appeared at the doorway, blinking in the light and holding her Sig Sauer pointing down.

The deputies pulled their weapons again. The two brown-shirted agents took a shooting stance with their own weapons. Over the loud speaker the tall deputy shouted, "Mrs. Barnes! Put the weapon on the ground. We are the sheriff's deputies you called."

As Audrey bent down to place her gun on the ground, the female agent shouted, "Put your weapon down, or I'll put you down!" Audrey let go of her gun and slowly stood up, tears in her eyes.

The female agent rushed up and pushed Audrey against the wall. She handcuffed her and said, "You are under arrest for threatening a federal agent, and other crimes against the Federal register of regulations." She marched Audrey down the porch steps towards a black SUV.

Audrey gave a stricken look to the tall deputy. "Officer! I didn't do anything wrong. I called you for protection." The female agent pushed her head down into the back seat of the SUV.

"Now hold on, Agent ... Wall?" the deputy said. "VanJones!" she snapped back.

"This woman did not know you were Federal Agents. You didn't show her your identification, so she called 911. She's done nothing wrong. Why were you here after nine at night anyway?"

The male agent crossed his arms and shook his head. "You just don't get it, do you?"

The female agent marched up and got in the tall deputy's face. Or tried to. She was a head shorter.

"First of all, this is none of your business. This is Federal business. Second, she should have opened up when we knocked. We're no longer required to show identification to citizens, and they no longer have the right to ask for our identification. Third, she has a gun in her possession, which was outlawed by another presidential executive order yesterday. Fourth, she was holding a gun while in the presence of Federal agents, which was also outlawed yesterday. Fifth, she has been accessing suspicious and subversive web sites and has purchased Tea Party bumper stickers. She is an enemy of the State."

"So purchasing Tea Party bumper stickers is now a federal crime?"

"No, but it gives us probable cause to investigate to see if she is a part of any terrorist plot against the state. Not that it's any of your concern." She glared at him.

He smiled down at her. "Hey, we're all on the same team here. If there's any home grown terrorist plot in my county, I want to know about it and help take it down."

She took a step back. "If we need your help, we'll issue orders telling you what to do. Now back off. You do know that it's a crime to interfere with a Federal agent in pursuance of her duties?"

He breathed out deeply, to help control his temper. "You just won't take yes for an answer, will you? I'm trying to be supportive here."

Arrogant Federal swaggering bully, he thought. *Made an agent last week and now she thinks she can order around anyone in the country. Trouble is, she can. Busybodies with power, always a dangerous combination. She's always wanted to tell people what to do, and now she has unlimited power*

20

to back up her personal demands. It used to be called abuse of power. Now it's called Federal discretionary power.

Agent VanJones stood behind the open door of the SUV. "Like I said, when we want support, we'll order you to give the support we require." She slammed the door and drove off.

Another innocent citizen carted off, and for what? To send a message. To spread fear and intimidation in the community. To make once free citizens docile sheep.

"Another FFIR," he said to his partner.

"FFIR?" His partner raised an eyebrow.

"Federal Fear and Intimidation Raid."

"Oh, right."

"Oh well. RUC." He pulled out yellow crime scene tape and began to remount the door and seal it as best he could.

His partner was looking at him. "Render unto Caesar?"

He stopped his work, turned and faced his partner. "That which is Caesar's."

His partner raised his hand, palm out, as if he were being sworn in for a court case.

"I took an oath."

The tall deputy smiled and raised his own hand palm out. "To protect and defend the Constitution of the United States."

"Against all enemies, foreign and domestic." His partner smiled back.

His smile faded into a grim look. He glanced in the direction the SUV had gone. "Against all enemies, foreign and domestic."

"Glenn, I suspected, and hoped, but I wasn't sure enough to try an RUC. Glad to know you, Keeper."

They clasped hands, as if for an arm wrestle. "Glad to know my partner will keep his oaths."

"How can we help that poor woman?"

"She did nothing wrong under the Constitution of the United States. I know a few other Oath Keepers and I have a way of contacting the Constitutional Resistance Movement. We'll get her out of this somehow. In the meantime ..." He got behind the wheel and reached up to the dashboard.

"What?"

"I activated the dashboard cam as soon as we pulled up. Standard operating procedure. How about we show the world the arrogance of Agents Wall and VanJones via an upload to FreedomToobz.ARK?"

"Good idea! I'm sure it will go viral, especially with those two nasty Federal viruses as the stars of the show." He winked at his partner.

# CHAPTER FOUR

"CITIZEN AUDREY BARNES, DO YOU KNOW WHY WE CAME TO QUESTION you?" She was in a Homeland Security interrogation house. The address was unlisted to the public, the media or local law enforcement.

Audrey had recovered some of her composure. "No, but I know why you came at 9 o'clock at night and why you refused to show identification."

Agent VanJones smirked. "Oh, so you think you know something about us?"

Audrey answered calmly, "You come at night without ID in order to instill fear and uncertainty among my neighbors and the rest of the town. You want us to live in fear of that nighttime knock on the door. You want us to live in fear of men, not of laws. You want us obey you, not the law."

VanJones smirked again. "The talking points of the CRM and the Tea Parties. Typical."

Suddenly she grabbed Audrey by her blouse and jerked her forward. She thrust her angry face within inches of Audrey's.

"Who told you to say that? Who are you working for? Who are the other members of your cell? Talk!" She violently pushed Audrey back against the chair, nearly tipping it over. Then she backhanded Audrey. Blood dribbled from her nose.

Just then both agents' cell phones make a bing noise indicating they had text messages.

With an annoyed look on her face, Agent VanJones looked at the screen on her phone.

Then she looked puzzled and showed her screen to her partner. "What do you make of this?" she asked. He glanced at her screen, then said, "I got the same thing. 'Tekel?' What do you suppose that means? A new code from headquarters?"

Wiping blood from her upper lip with the back of her hand, Audrey smiled and said, "It's a code alright, but from a different Headquarters."

The door burst open and a man with a red, white, and blue Constitutional Resistance Movement patch pinned to his chest stepped into the room with a compressed air dart gun. He shot a tranquilizer dart into both agents while they were reaching for their side arms. He grabbed the wrist of the closest agent, peeled it from the handgun and positioned her between him and the second agent. Wavering, Agent Wall managed to squeeze off one round before the powerful tranquilizer rendered him unconscious. The bullet tore through Agent VanJones's calf. She screamed before passing out herself.

"Ms. Barnes? Are you OK?" Two more men with CRM insignia entered the room and knelt on either side of her.

"Yes. Just a nose bleed." She stood up, a little shaky. The two men supported her on both sides.

The first CRM commando knelt down, extended Agent Wall's right arm and locked the elbow, then broke it across his knee. They could all hear a sharp crack as the humerus broke.

"No more backhanding or holding weapons for him for a while," he said grimly, lowering the arm back to the floor.

"Can one of you get a bandage on her leg? Looks like a through and through."

After staunching the bleeding and bandaging the leg wound, he said, "She already has a leg wound, so I'll just do a 'Reacher' on her." Flipping open a knife from his pocket, he sliced the thumb web on the Agent VanJones' right hand. "She won't be able to hold a weapon for a while. Bandage her hand too, would you?"

The other CRM commando swiftly stopped the bleeding and stood up. "Done."

The first commando nodded. "Let's get Ms. Barnes out of here."

He cautiously stepped into the corridor, looked both ways, and then motioned the other two to follow, supporting Audrey Barnes between them. Fifteen minutes later they were ten miles away.

* * * * * *

"Ms. Barnes, you're safe for the moment. They were intending to make an example of you, and so we thought it best to rescue you. That's the good news."

From her seat, Audrey looked up at the face of the first CRM commando, who was clearly in charge. He was a tall black man. "And the bad news?"

"You can't go back. They'll arrest you if you do, and make more serious charges against you. You will be treated more harshly than before. And we probably won't be able to rescue you a second time."

Taking a deep breath, she looked into the distance and murmured, "There I was, just another middle-aged widow watching television alone at home. Just me and my bowl of chips, minding my own business. Then Homeland Security charges in and my life changes in an instant. What did I do to deserve this?"

"According to Agent VanJones, you purchased some Tea Party bumper stickers. As of yesterday's presidential order 10-290, that is probable cause to investigate you for subversive activities against the state."

"So, bumper stickers are now criminalized? I bought those a month ago. I never even put them on my car." She took another deep breath. "So what are my options?"

"We can get you out of the country on the Underground Railroad, or you can go underground with the Constitutional Resistance Movement. If you stay, they'll televise you in a show trial. Since you helped us rescue you, you could get the death penalty or life in prison for treason against the state. At the very least, they'll send you to one of their internment labor camps, the so-called 'American Prosperity Camps.' Hard labor for the rest of your life."

"Can I retrieve anything from my house?"

"No. They'll be watching it now. But someone who likes to keep his oaths sent this to you." He handed her a framed photograph. It was her wedding picture with Bill, her personal Marine Corps hero.

Tears rolled down her cheeks. "Thank you for this." She caressed the photo with her fingers. She whispered, "Bill, what would you do?"

Still looking at the picture, she smiled a wistful smile. Then she looked up at the commando. Her mouth set into a firm line. "I was a medical corpsman in the Navy when I met Bill. Can CRM use an old-fashioned field medic?"

He smiled back at her. "Sure can."

She stood up, her posture ramrod straight. "Let's roll."

* * * * * *

Agent VanJones woke up in a hospital room with a doctor standing over her. "Where am I?" she mumbled.

"You've been wounded, but you're safe now. We treated you for a gunshot wound in the leg and a cut on your hand."

Agent VanJones moved her leg. Her face twisted in pain. She held up her bandaged hand.

"The good news is that you're healing nicely," said the doctor.

"And the bad?" she snarled.

"It will be six weeks before you can handle a firearm again, and it will be awkward with the scar tissue on the web of your hand. And I'm afraid you'll have a slight limp when you walk. The bullet was a 'through and through,' but it nicked a nerve."

"And you were too incompetent to repair it!" She shouted, her face contorted in anger.

"Agent VanJones," the doctor replied, involuntarily stepping back, "you had state of the art medical care, but there are some things even modern medicine can't do. One of them is regenerating nerve cells."

"You'd better be right about that, or I'll see to it that you spend the rest of your career treating frostbite in Nome, Alaska!"

Shaking his head, the doctor left the room thinking, *Self-righteous arrogance! Made a Homeland Security Agent barely three months ago, and now she thinks she knows how to practice medicine better than I do. Basic training for Agents must include arrogance, abusive threats, and petty tyranny. Well, she can control me, but she can't regenerate her own nerve cells.*

Brows lowered, Agent Maudire VanJones held her eyes in a fixed stare at her leg under the sheet. Whenever she moved it, pain flared.

A nurse came in. "The doctor has prescribed this medication for your pain." She held out a medicine cup with a pill in it.

VanJones knocked the cup out of her hand. "NO! No pain medication! Every time I hurt it will remind me of the people who did this to me! And every time I hurt I'll think about the ways I'll make them hurt. So no, nursie, don't try to take away my pain. I want it. I'll use it. And I'll make sure others feel my pain too!"

She grasped the wrist of the nurse and twisted. The nurse cried out in pain. VanJones released her wrist and smiled for the first time since she woke up. A twisted smile of satisfaction. She had reasserted her control over another human being.

"Agent VanJones, you frighten me!" the nurse blurted out, shrinking back and rubbing her wrist.

VanJones fixed her glare on the nurse. Her mouth twisted. "I'm glad."

 **CHAPTER FIVE**

In his office, Judge Block adjusted his computer monitor to avoid the glare of the morning sun. Sipping his coffee, he began reading an email sent to all federal judges.

> To: All Federal Judiciary
> From: President Fletcher, The White House
> Subject: Executive Order 6336 re: Federal Court Decisions
>
> It has come to our attention that many decisions handed down by Federal Judges favor the constitutional rights of the individual over the prerogatives and authority of the government. This has resulted in a hodge-podge of lawsuits and appeals that slow down the smooth functioning of the executive branch.
>
> All members of the Federal Judiciary are therefore directed and required to make your decisions in favor of the government whether the government is the defendant or the plaintiff. Evidence, the presumption of innocence, and so-called "constitutional" grounds are to be disregarded whenever they do not support the government's case.

A version of the historical "divine right of kings" is to be operative here. In order to rule effectively, Our authority must be supreme and unquestioned. The landmark case *American Catholic Bishops vs. the United States* established once and for all the supremacy of the government over churches and so-called individual conscience. Any so-called constitutional rights that conflict with our pronouncements or regulations will be null and void as a matter of regulation under this Executive Order.

As a matter of regulation, mused Judge Block, *not as a matter of law.* He took another sip of coffee and looked out the window. *So, we are now a nation of men and not of laws. One man. The President. It's his way or the highway. The Executive Branch now gives orders to the Judicial Branch. So much for the Constitution.*

Turning back to the monitor, he forwarded the email to a recipient with the suffix .Ark.

Thought you'd like to know the latest, he typed.

Logging off, he donned his judicial robe and walked down to his courtroom. Passing his law clerk, he noticed her date-stamping an incoming document. *They don't need judges to try cases anymore. Just a rubber stamp reading: Government wins, citizens lose.*

*   *   *   *   *   *

That night, the Judge's phone rang. "Care for a cup of coffee and an extra can of stew?"

"Love to." The Judge recognized the voice and the reference.

"The Starbucks two blocks west of you. Eight fifteen."

Judge Block scanned the room as he entered. Noting the tall man at a window table, he ordered at the counter. He wrapped both hands around the paper cup, enjoying the warmth. The tall man stood up as he approached.

"Outside."

Propping one foot on a chair, the tall man put his coffee on the table outside. Judge Block did the same. No one else was there in the evening chill.

"Got your email. They're getting more blatant." He took a sip of coffee.

The judge nodded. "Yes. No pretence of following the Constitution. "Sooo, when you're not chaperoning students in the forest, you're reading emails from obscure federal judges."

The street light shone on the lower half of the tall man's face, shaded even at night by the ubiquitous ball cap.

"Wilderness education is a hobby of mine. Spotting salvageable talent is another. Last month, you said you wanted to help. Things are more dangerous now. Are you still willing?"

"Yes." The judge nodded and looked him in the eye. "I'm in."

He looked down at his coffee cup. "Arjana drained my bank account from wherever she is in Albania. She's filed for divorce. I have no personal ties to worry about now."

The tall man put his hand on the Judge's shoulder. "I'm sorry to hear that."

"Don't be. I'm not." The Judge took another sip of coffee.

"Judge, here's how Constitutional Resistance Movement members will identify themselves to you." He took out a piece of chalk and drew a symbol on the metal table top. "Then you will give this counter-sign." He drew something within the first symbol.

Judge Block stared at the symbols, transfixed. "A symbol of the first rule of law, and not of men. Ingenious," he breathed. The other man rubbed it out with his paper napkin.

The judge took a sip of his coffee. "I have to ask, is revolution the goal of the CRM?"

"Not revolution, restoration – of the Constitution and the principles America was founded on. Restoring and limiting the role of government to the enumerated powers ratified in 1787: protection of the rights of individuals and adjudication of disputes. The principles that once made America the most prosperous nation on earth."

"That's a tall order. Do you think such a small group can make any difference?"

"Two thousand years ago twelve people changed the world, even after their Leader was arrested and executed. But we might not succeed. Then our mission shifts to preservation. Preservation of Americans who believe in the principles of America. We will preserve and protect small communities of freedom-minded people, like Noah preserved and protected two of every species from the flood. Like Noah, we will retreat into lifeboat communities, Arks if you will, and stay there until this flood of government coercion and control subsides."

"Reminds me of the monks in the medieval monasteries, preserving books and classical learning behind high walls from the barbarians who were burning down civilization."

The judge looked over at a poster on the coffee shop window. It read: "Burn this racist Constitution! Help Occupy San Francisco burn copies of the greedy capitalist constitution of the U.S.! Friday night at 8!"

"And the barbarians have returned. The first city they sacked was Detroit. San Francisco is next. I'm sure you heard about the Google bus that the Occupy San Francisco people fire-bombed last week. Six software engineers dead and twelve severely burned."

He thumbed his phone screen, and then handed it to the tall man. "Look at the official post on the Occupy SF website."

The tall man read, "The People's justice against the evil geeks who make money off the rest of us! Apps and software should be free!"

"As if software just magically appears from nowhere." The judge frowned.

The tall man shrugged. "My colleagues and I will be in good company then, fighting the good fight. And the monks had to wait for centuries. Do you still want in?"

"I took an oath. I now know the true meaning of that oath." The judge stood at attention and raised his right hand. "I, Barry Block, do solemnly swear that I will support and defend the Constitution of the United States against all enemies, foreign and domestic, that I will bear true faith and allegiance to the same; that I take this obligation freely, without any mental reservations or purpose of evasion;" he paused, then added, "and to this purpose I pledge my life, my fortune, and my sacred honor. So help me God."

The tall man also stood at attention and raised his right hand. "So help me God."

"Thank you, Judge. Too many have 'stood down.' You just stood up. And I'm proud to stand with you." He shook the judge's hand. "One more thing. The CRM is committed to not initiating violence. We will defend ourselves if attacked, and we will defend American citizens from attack when we can. Our methods are stealth, sabotage of the government's tyrannies, both large and petty, exposing what the corrupt politicians are doing, and forcing the power elites to live with their answers."

"You certainly forced me to live with my answers. And it worked. It was truly a *Course in Reality*. I learned to see reality. How work, not talk, is needed to live in the real world. And how you can't cheat reality."

The tall man reached into his pocket. "This government will learn that it can't cheat reality either. Here's a cell phone, identical to your own. May I see yours?"

The judge took his phone from his jacket pocket. The tall man did something on his own screen.

"There, this is now a clone of your phone. Apps, contacts, everything. But it has an encryption mode and a special app. Watch this." Again he scrolled through some screens and entered code words.

"Now it's yours. If anybody else picks it up and scrolls through, they'll see nothing unusual. Even a forensic IT person won't find anything. Code name for our special app: Swamp Fox. It plays like a game if anyone else finds it. Give me your old phone."

They exchanged phones. "Just keep us informed for now, Judge. Send all messages via this phone. We'll be in touch when we need you." He took another sip of coffee.

"You'll never know when we might call on you. We borrowed our motto from the Coast Guard: Semper Paratus."

"Always ready." The Judge smiled at him. "I will be."

"Vaya con Dios, my friend." The tall man turned and walked off into the gathering fog.

Chapter Six

Janie Tyler walked with her third grade classmates down the school hallway. At the door to the cafeteria, her teacher looked closely at each small child as they entered. She noticed the girl's brown paper lunch bag and put her hand on Janie's shoulder.

"Janie, honey, you go to that line over against the wall."

Clutching her brown lunch bag, Janie blinked under her long black bangs. She looked at the other children lined up before a table with their lunch bags and boxes. A man in a brown uniform with a badge on his chest sat behind the table. Another man in uniform stood beside him. The seated man absently tapped a fingernail against his badge, making a clicking noise. The badge read "FDA Nutritional Enforcement." The icon on the badge prominently featured a watchful eye above a crossed spoon and fork. When Janie's turn came, the man sitting at the table looked at her sternly.

"Take the food out of your bag and place it on the table."

Janie nervously did as she was told. The man unwrapped the waxed paper from her sandwich.

"Peanut butter and jelly! What kind of mother do you have? Is she a moron mom? This does not conform to the Federal School Lunch Nutrition Protocols Act! Young lady, take this Non-Nutritious Lunch Warning Form NNLW66.6 home to your mother. The other officer will pin it on you to make sure you don't lose it. If this happens again, you and your mother will be sent to in-school suspension for re-education on the federal requirements for your lunch. This non-nutritious lunch is hereby confiscated."

Wrinkling his nose in disgust, he swept the sandwich into a large garbage can next to the table.

"Go to the cafeteria lunch line and get a tray. Your mother will be billed for the lunch. Next!"

The standing man in uniform put his big hand on her small shoulder. "Hold still."

He used a safety pin to attach a bright pink form NNLW66.6 to her blouse. "OK, you may go."

Blinking back tears, she walked to the end of the cafeteria line. Two girls and one boy in the line looked back at her.

"Pink freak! Pink freak! Pink freak!" they chanted.

Janie began sobbing.

"Loser lunch! Loser lunch! Loser lunch!" they shrieked.

"Moron mom! Moron mom! Moron mom!" they continued.

"My mom is not a moron! Yours is!" She kicked the shin of the girl closest to her.

The principal appeared and gripped her by the shoulder. "Young lady, violence is not tolerated here." She waved a teacher aide over. "Take her to the in-school suspension room."

Janie's teacher approached the principal. "Was that necessary? Of course the child is upset after this public taunting by the other children. It's cruel."

The principal narrowed her eyes. "Mrs. Prentice, you know very well that public taunting is the federally mandated and accepted educational protocol for Behavior Modification for Political Correctness. Children and parents subjected to public humiliation are much easier to control. Remember, behavior and belief control is the primary mission of all schools now that we are under direct federal control. The National School Superintendent in Washington reaffirmed this just yesterday. Didn't you read your mandatory email notices yesterday after classes?"

Mrs. Prentice looked down subserviently. "It must have slipped my mind."

The principal glanced over at Mr. Pitts, the FDA Nutritional Enforcement Officer. He was watching them. She turned back to stare again at the teacher and thought, *I must make a note of non-conformance in the political loyalty section of Mrs. Prentice's annual performance review. They'll be checking up on me.*

*   *   *   *   *   *

FDA Nutrition Enforcement Officer Fred Pitts left the elementary school that day feeling satisfied. He had reached his quota of "home lunch deficiency enforcement confrontations" for the day and logged them in on his FDA "Enforcement App" on his smart phone. His supervisor would be pleased.

He drove home to the adjoining county, whistling to himself. Most federal officials and "enforcers" like him made it a practice not to live in the county where they did their enforcement work. Their work engendered too many hard feelings, and the children they practiced their "enforcement" on might belong to their next door neighbors. It didn't make for cordial exchanges over the backyard fence.

He stopped for gas. At the pump, he inserted his Federal Gasoline Ration Card first. That identified who was purchasing the gas, so that no one could exceed the number of gallons they had been allotted by the Federal Energy Rationing Board in Washington, D.C. Then he inserted his FDA Nutritional Enforcement Officer Exemption Privilege Card, which gave an automatic override of the personal ration limit on gasoline. As a federal employee, he was given the privilege of unlimited gallons, unavailable to ordinary citizens. *Some animals are more equal than others*, he thought with satisfaction.

Then he inserted his Federal Confiscation of Private Property for Federal Business Card, which would give him the gasoline for free. The station owner looked out the window at his black SUV. That legal theft of her property meant two more meals of beanie-weenies for her family.

As Fred pumped his gas, another man pulled up on the other side of the pump. As he drove in, he noted the Federal license plate on Fred's black SUV. He pulled out his cell phone and touched an app called "Swamp Fox." He rapidly tapped through several selections. Then he pocketed his phone and got out to pump his own gas. He was tall.

Fred decided to pick up some milk and bread in the convenience store inside. Leaving his SUV blocking the pump, he swaggered in.

As the door closed behind him, his cell phone began shrieking at high volume.

"Federal parasite alert! Federal parasite alert! This person is a Federal agent paid with your tax money to enforce petty tyrannies on his fellow citizens!" Then the message repeated, "Federal parasite alert!.."

Fred jumped when the shrieking began, and then looked around to see where it was coming from. Finally, he realized it was his own cell phone. Digging it out of his pocket, he frantically tried to shut it off. Every button he pushed amplified the sound more.

"Federal parasite alert! Federal parasite alert! ..." the shrieking continued, louder.

Outside, the tall man pumping his gas smiled. A half-dozen other shoppers in the store turned to stare at Fred in his uniform. They frowned at him.

"What are you looking at?" Fred shouted. He put his hand on his gun, holstered at his side. He took a defiant stance, glaring at the people staring at him. Just then, the shrieking changed to a "klaxon" sound.

"AH-OOO-GAH! AH-OOO-GAH! WARNING! WARNING! This person is identified as an FDA Nutrition Enforcer, who terrorizes your children at school each day. He inspects their lunch bags and touches their sandwiches with his dirty fingers! He confiscates the brown bag lunches made by mothers!"

The other shoppers continued to stare at Fred. They didn't say a word. Fred decided to brazen it out. He put his bread and milk on the counter.

"I'm paying and leaving. NOW!" he snarled at the owner, frozen there staring at him.

The tall man outside replaced the pump nozzle and pressed another button on his cell phone screen. The owner inside began the motions of ringing up the sale. She stopped and stared at the screen of her cash register.

"What is your PROBLEM?" said Fred, yelling to be heard over the shriek of his cell phone.

"The screen is frozen. I can't ring anything up!" replied the woman helplessly.

"WHAT? WHAT? SPEAK UP!" Fred yelled. Suddenly he threw

his cell phone on the floor and stomped on it. The shrieking stopped. Outside, the tall man began tapping on his own cell phone again.

The woman took a quick step back. "I said the screen is frozen. I can't ring anything up!"

Fred's face got redder. "You're lying! I can have you arrested for harassing a federal officer! Do it!"

Swiveling the screen around toward Fred, the woman replied "See for yourself! It's not my fault!"

Fred looked scared for the first time. He turned to face the other shoppers, still frowning at him.

"This is a set up! You are all conspiring against the federal government! Treason is punishable by death! You're all in on it! I'm taking my bread and milk and leaving!" He grabbed the milk and bread and fled out the door.

The tall man watched as Fred screeched his tires and sped off. He nodded and thought, *The bigger they swagger, the more cowardly they retreat.*

As he got back into his car, the tall man began singing, "Swamp Fox, Swamp Fox, tail on his hat... nobody knows where the Swamp Fox at; Swamp Fox, Swamp Fox, hiding in the glen, He'll ride away to fight again. Got no money, got no beds, got no roof above our heads; got no shelter when it rains, All we've got is Yankee brains!"

* * * * * *

When he pulled into his driveway, Fred turned off the engine and sat, breathing heavily. *What in the world was that? What just happened? And HOW did it happen?*

After a few minutes, his breathing returned to normal. He gathered the milk and bread and went into the house. His wife Molly rushed into the room as the door closed.

"Fred! Thank God you're home! Something awful happened!"

Fred collapsed into a chair, feeling weak. *Now what?*

"Bill Contly next door called me, saying 'What's this about Fred being a child terrorizer?' I said, Bill what in the world are you talking about? He said he got an email alert with a link to the sheriff's map of convicted child molesters. When he clicked on it, he said there were new pins in the map with the legend, CT, Child Terrorizers. He said our house had a pin on it. The pin said Child Terrorizer, Fred Pitts! Fred, what's going on?"

"Molly, I don't know what's going on. Let me get to the computer and see for myself."

Sure enough, there was the CT pin on his house and his name: Fred Pitts. The map legend for CT read: *Child Terrorizer: This person intimidates your children at school, making them feel like criminals for bringing a home-packed lunch. They also interrogate your children about their parent's habits: does your mom recycle, do they share toilet flushes, does your Dad say anything bad about the government? Their job is to bully small children.*

Just then, the phone rang. "Fred? This is Bill. Is it true that you terrorize children at school? I've seen you come home in your uniform, and I knew you worked for the FDA, but I thought you inspected food processing plants."

"Bill, I just try to make sure school children get the proper nutrition. It's a good thing. There's nothing bad about it."

"My children have told me about these bullying Food Gestapo agents in the school cafeteria, poking into their lunch boxes! And wearing guns! I know what you do. You should be ashamed of yourself, bullying little children! I don't want uniformed brown shirt thugs intimidating my children!"

"Now Bill, you and I are friends, but you're starting to sound like an anti-government traitor. You don't want me to have to report you, do you?"

"You cowardly bully, you'll have to report everyone on the block! And if you don't return my crescent wrench I'll file theft charges against you!" The line went dead and the doorbell rang.

Fred went to the front door. Molly stood behind him. Four other couples were there, all from the neighborhood. Fred stood speechless.

"Fred, we are putting you on notice that if you bully any of our children, we'll have you arrested! Are you some twisted psycho, picking on little children?"

Fred's face reddened. "Who do you think you are? Do you know who I am? I'm a federal officer, enforcing federal rules and regulations! Threatening me is a federal crime! I'll see you all in jail!"

One of the men was bigger than Fred. He stepped forward "We are not threatening you Fred, but we are *telling* you: stay away from our children. And tell your co-worker bullies to stay away too." They all turned and left.

Molly was pale. "Fred, these people were our friends. I can't live with these accusing stares every time I step out the door. Fred, you have to DO something!"

"What do you expect from me?" Fred's face was sullen.

Molly ignored this warning sign. "I expect you to make peace with our neighbors, or move us out of this neighborhood, THAT'S what I expect!"

"You expect! You expect! I can't get a Federal Relocation Permit just because you don't like the way the neighbors look at you!"

"Fred, I'm thinking about our children too. No child in the neighborhood will play with them now. You HAVE to DO something!"

"The only thing I HAVE to do is shut you up." He viciously backhanded her face. She fell backwards to the floor from the force of the blow. There were red welts on her cheek where his big fingers had struck her.

She lay there, looking up at him through tears. *He really is a bully*, she thought. *Maybe I should take the kids and move to one of those battered women's shelters.*

The next morning, all four tires on Fred's government SUV were flat.

"Molly! Where is that tire inflator? My tires are flat."

"Fred, you borrowed that from Bill next door. I returned it last month."

Cursing, Fred phoned for a tow truck. He was an hour and a half late getting to work.

Chapter Seven

Judge Block took off his tie, put on a windbreaker and left his office at the 9th Circuit Court of Appeals. It was lunchtime on a sunny day. He took Bus 14 to Justin Herman Plaza. He hummed to himself as he strolled up to a food truck and bought a hot dog. He sat on a bench and looked at the latest tent city erected by "Occupy San Francisco."

One of the protesters emerged from his $800 backpacking tent and adjusted a placard that hung from his tent pole. He stumbled a little; still hung over from last night's partying with his fellow occupiers. He opened a plastic-wrapped backpackers' gourmet food item and began eating it like a sandwich. His placard read: WE ARE THE **99%**! REDISTRIBUTE THE WEALTH OF THE **1%**!

Then he ambled unsteadily toward the hot dog truck in his $300 hiking boots and $200 SPF 60 outdoor shirt. Watching, Judge Block moved to the other end of the bench in order to hear better.

The hot dog truck owner asked, "What'll it be?"

The expensively dressed protester replied, "You are exploiting defenseless pigs and cows with these disgusting unhealthy hot dogs you sell! You should be serving healthy food and giving it away for free. You don't deserve to be here! Leave!"

The truck owner was dressed in jeans and a t-shirt. He calmly looked over the expensive "outfitter" hiking gear the protester was wearing. Then he noticed the backpacker food item he was eating.

"I'm willing to have an open mind. What's that you're eating?"

"Prosciutto jerky. Very healthy. Very sustainable. Very low resource consumption."

"May I see the package?"

"Certainly."

The young cart owner studied the package, looking at both sides. Then he began reading, "Prosciutto jerky. Processed from pampered maiale in the Tuscany region of Italy, fed on the finest high intensity farmed corn, oats, and our secret seasoning: Montepulciano d'Abruzzo wine and grapes. Imported to the U.S. by High End Marketing Incorporated. Contains one serving. Price: $45."

Looking up at the protester, the cart owner said "Sounds like food for the 1% to me."

"I am NOT part of the one percent! That just happens to be sold at the Sustainable Foods Market where I shop. Sustainable Foods Market contributes 5% of their profits to the Pristine Influence on Society Foundation to build a better earth."

Looking back down at the package, the cart owner asked, "Do you know what prosciutto is? Or maiale?"

The young protester looked confused. "My girlfriend made me go vegan. She said prosciutto is made from compressed soy fiber."

"I hate to break the news to you, but prosciutto is ham, and maiale is pig. You're eating pork, buddy."

His eyes widened as he looked at the thin pink strips in his hand. "What! That can't be. You're just repeating talking points from the FACTS News Network."

The truck owner handed the package back to him. "Read it for yourself."

"No! My girlfriend said it was soy fiber, so that's what it is. Screw you!"

The young man gave him the finger, then turned away and walked back toward his tent.

Thoroughly amused, Judge Block approached the truck owner.

"I admire the way you attempted to educate that young man about everyday reality, like reading the label."

"I did the best I could with what I had to work with."

Judge Block laughed at this. Then he stooped over and used his finger to trace out a symbol in the sandy soil in front of the food trailer. It looked like this:

The truck owner quickly looked around. Seeing no one watching them, he came from inside the trailer and stooped over. He drew two numbers inside the symbol:

His voice pitched low, Judge Block said, "A nation of laws," The truck owner softly spoke the counter-sign: "and not of men."

The lunch crowd was drifting away, going back to their offices. Since no one was close enough to hear, the truck owner continued, "I'm new to the CRM. Where did this symbol come from?"

Judge Block quietly replied, "The early Christians were persecuted by the Roman Empire and had to go underground. They identified themselves to each other by drawing the ichthus symbol, which means fish in Greek." Here he drew it in the soil:

"In the Greek spelling of ichthus, ΙΧΘ Υ Σ, the letters stood for Jesus Christ, Son of God, Savior. We in the Constitutional Resistance Movement devised our own symbol, an icon of the two tablets given to Moses, containing the Ten Commandments. This is the earliest instance of a nation governing itself by laws and not by the changeable whims of a king."

The truck owner grunted. "Makes sense. I learned the Ten Commandments in Sunday school. Before Sunday School was made illegal." He looked carefully at Judge Block, memorizing his face. "What's up?"

Judge Block rubbed out the symbols with his shoe. "We need a new app."

"I'm listening."

"We need an app that will allow us to pair with any Federal cell phone, track its whereabouts and eavesdrop on conversations."

"That's doable. I'll pass the word."

"When it's ready, put it out as a download on .ARK with the usual encryption. Code name: Swamp Fox 2.0. Swamp Fox 1.0 is an unqualified success, by the way. Our first beta test was to 'out' some of the food Gestapo agents terrorizing school children and their mothers. Quite satisfying."

"We aim to please."

"How soon?"

"Two weeks, maybe less."

"Amazing. Vaya con Dios."

Chapter Eight

Two nights later, the Judge was at home to watch the President give a speech intended to reassure the nation. The country and the economic markets were in turmoil after it was leaked in the media that the government had been spying on the computers of all American businesses. *And I know the spying was done without warrants*, reflected the Judge, *because I'm one of the panel of judges that rule on such warrant requests. So much for the Fourth Amendment. More rule without law.* Millions of businesses had moved their money and their computer records offshore. The crawler at the bottom of the screen read "Tune in at 8 p.m. for the Concerns & Reassurance Address by the President." Sometimes it was just the acronym. The President began speaking.

"Ladies and Gentlepersons, my fellow Americans, and my fellow citizens of the planet, I come before you today in a time of grave economic crisis. Recent events have led some businesspeople to take certain actions to protect themselves. Let me both reassure them and warn them. I reassure them that under my administration your private and proprietary business data will be kept confidential. We only review and monitor the business transactions of American businesses, small and large, because, as I've always said, we have your best interests at heart, and we know what is best for you.

"I warn all Americans that moving your money without authorization from the Treasury Department is a violation of my new executive order 3678, issued this morning, and made retroactive to last week. I've always said that your money is held in trust for future generations. Let me be clear: I am now that future generation and I am the one who holds your money in trust ..."

The screen flickered for a minute, and the face of a tall black man came on the air, replacing that of the President. "My fellow Americans, this is not a presidential teleprompter malfunction ..."

Judge Block gasped. It was the man who had kidnapped him into his *Course in Reality*, the man who had recruited him into the Constitutional Resistance Movement, the man who had given him the secret phone apps. The judge felt as if he was in physical shock. He numbly listened.

"In the New Testament, John 8:32, Jesus said: 'And ye shall know the truth, the truth shall make you free.' ... The truth shall make you free, but first it will make you miserable. Unfortunately, you are beginning to learn the truths about current events and corruption within your own government and these truths will make you miserable. ..."

The judge was using the encrypted mode on his phone to text a message to the man on the screen. His voice continued from the television, " ... go to this web site to start your journey to truth and freedom: www.thetruthwillmakeyoufree.Ark. You can also go to channel 1776 on your television."

Judge Block was so excited he sprang out of his chair and began pacing.

The tall man knelt. "Heavenly Father, help our nation in this hour of need." He opened his eyes and looked into the camera. "Thank you, and may God bless America."

The President reappeared on the screen. "... I know what is in your best interests, and I will tell you what your best interests are. ..." The judge was jumping up and down.

"Moving on to other matters, we have today signed seventeen new executive orders, and this means that We will no longer allow Americans to do the following seventeen things ..."

The Judge was frantically entering '1776' into his cable vision remote. There he was! The tall black man from the forest. The man who had recruited him into the Constitutional Resistance Movement.

"My fellow Americans, my name is Isaiah Mercury. If you haven't seen the surveillance video smuggled out of the Treasury Department, go to the link shown on this page...the government's explanations are self-contradictory lies, as you have seen. They admit that they are snooping on your private data, '*for your own good*' as if we are children and they're our parents.

"I speak now to all Americans: working men and women, tinkerers, inventors, entrepreneurs, and plain old independent contrarian cusses who like to run their own lives their own way. Running your own life your own way *is the American way.* ...

"Several years ago, some friends and I could see that there was a rising flood of government corruption and coercion starting to drown the hardworking families of America... We started to connect the dots, and the dots revealed that the various special interest groups, all have one 'special interest' in common ... *they want power and control over you and how you live your life.*

"So, my friends and I planned a way to protect ourselves ... My wife, the Nobel Prize-winning botanist Dr. Grace Washington, came to the same conclusion and the same idea independently. She invented the perfect name for it: The Noah Option."

Grace joined Isaiah on the screen. Then the camera focused on her alone.

"My fellow Americans, you recently saw me in a televised show trial in Washington, D.C., on phony trumped-up charges. My crime? Feeding the hungry people of Africa, India, and Asia with the enhanced seeds I invented. The government prosecutor attempted to blackmail me in the pretrial conference."

Grace paused and held up a picture of Noah's Ark to the camera.

"Those of you who went to Sunday School will remember the story of Noah. God sent a flood, but decided to save Noah and his family. So He instructed them on how to construct an ark and bring two of every animal in it, male and female, so they could survive the flood and then repopulate the earth and start fresh. After the flood, God sent a rainbow in the clouds as a sign of his promise that He would never do it again, and that it was safe to start over.

"We decided that we would find or create little "Arks," places where honest people ... could live and be safe from this flood of corruption, coercion and control.

"I'm not going to tell you where these places are, but if you really want to come to one of Noah's Arks, keep coming to these web pages … and look for clues. When you've figured it out, just get out. Don't tell anyone. Close up shop and come. Disappear. … You can rebuild anything with one tool: your mind.

"One requirement, though. Don't come to an Ark if you like to control other people, tell them how to live their lives, and dream up and enforce a bunch of rules on other people. In the Arks, one of our principles is *Mind Your Own Business.*"

The camera switched back to Isaiah.

"I've moved to New Zealand and set up my business here. We will wait for this flood of corruption and power-hunger to subside. And while we wait, we will build a new world for ourselves, as Noah and his family did. Maybe we'll never come back.

"I speak again to all American tinkerers, inventors, entrepreneurs, everyday hard-working men and women, and plain old independent contrarian cusses who like to do things your own way. I say, be proud of what you do. Be proud that your hard work, your inventions and the services of your businesses, large and small, make life better for everyone.

"Grace and I have retreated into an Ark, … someday this flood will subside.

"When that dove flies onto the windowsill of my Ark with an advertising flyer for green olives in her beak, then I'll know it's safe again for people to engage in capitalism … buying and selling the best we have created to offer each other, without being treated like criminals or children or slaves. Then, as Dr. Martin Luther King told us we would, we will all shout together, … in the words of the old spiritual, 'Free at last, free at last, thank God Almighty, we are free at last.'"

The screen went black. Judge Block switched back to CBC. Kathy Coeur-Saignant was red in the face and shrill … "this is the most dangerous terror threat to America since 9/11. This man Isaiah Mercury, the supposed software genius, is said to have exploited underpaid and overworked computer programmers, members of a minority race, to build up the ill-gotten profits of his company, Promethean Software International. He now poses a serious cyber-threat to the security of the United States. I know all politically correct thinking Americans call upon the President to use the full might of American diplomatic pressure to force New Zealand to extradite this criminal back to the United States to face criminal prosecution for his terrorist cyber-hacking into the President's television speech."

Her voice dropped an octave lower, for dramatic effect. "If the president's own words, spoken from the president's own teleprompter, in the president's own television show aren't safe, then none of us is safe."

And I never made the connection, thought Judge Block. *He always wore a ball cap and working clothes. I've seen his picture on the business pages, but there he was usually wearing a suit and tie. Well known in the software world of the San Francisco Bay area, and yet anonymous in overalls.*

The genius who invented the best-selling Invisible Hand software to run small businesses on cell phones, smart or not. The tall black man. The man in uniform in an electric company truck. The man in the woods. The mystery man meeting me in coffee shops … was Isaiah Mercury.

CHAPTER NINE

CARL WHITE RAN HIS FINGERS OVER FIVE ENVELOPES ON HIS DESK, thinking, hesitating. Then he pushed them aside and began rereading seven "regulatory compliance demand" notifications from seven different government agencies. The federal EPA demanding that no grease or oil from employee's hands should be washed down the clean-up sink drain. Potential pollution of sewage water. The state Department of Health and Human Safety demanding that he personally supervise all employees as they washed their hands at least three times a day, and before every break when food or beverages might be consumed, to be sure they washed off all grease and oil. Potential toxicity from grease or oil on the employees' hands might contaminate their coffee and doughnuts.

Personally supervise. He snorted. *As if I'm their Mama.* He looked at the third legal document.

"You are hereby commanded and required," it read, "to make reasonable accommodation to all persons in your employ with the disability of illiteracy. You must read out loud to them all portions of their rights under the newly revised and expanded Collective Health Care Executive Order, with particular attention to the sections outlining their unlimited rights to erectile dysfunction drugs, abortions during any trimester, cosmetic surgical make-overs, cosmetic tattoos, cosmetic tattoo removal, sex-change operations and sex-change reversal operations.

"In order to not embarrass any individual with the disability of illiteracy, you must read all two thousand pages of the law to all employees gathered in a group, whether illiterate or not (on the clock, paid time). In order to make sure nobody forgets their many healthcare rights, you are required to read the law to them each quarter of the year. Failure to do so constitutes a violation carrying a fine of $25,000 and/or not less than six weeks in federal prison for the named owner or manager of the business."

I run an auto shop, not a healthcare clinic. And since the public government schools can't be bothered to teach reading while they are busy teaching sensitivity towards the poor snail darters and the evil humans who oppress them, I have to read to the people they 'graduate.'

That's it. I'm convinced.

He pulled the five envelopes back in front of him. They contained a month's severance pay each and a personal note from him. *Sorry guys, I've had enough. I'm going ARK.* He put the envelopes into each employee's mail slot. *Good thing my cousin in Texas knows how to contact a 'coyote' to smuggle me and my family into Mexico.*

He started to lock the door behind him. Then he laughed. *Am I trying to protect my property? The thieves all have badges and government job titles now.* He taped a piece of cardboard to the door. With a magic marker, he wrote: *Gone 2 by 2.*

*　*　*　*　*　*

Doctor Farley listened as the Federal Mandate Audit and Enforcement Agent read a list of violations to him. His single-physician practice had been audited for the past eight days by this federal auditor, who wore a badge and carried a gun.

"Failure to maintain free-vend condom machines in the restrooms, failure to offer free narcotics to any patient who requests them, failure to file Revocation of Collective Healthcare Benefits forms for patients with long-term chronic diseases or debilitating conditions..."

They want me to be their death panel. They want me to enforce their regulations about who gets healthcare and who dies from lack of healthcare. Revocation equals a slow death. I took an oath: First, do no harm.

As the auditor droned on with his list of violations, Doctor Farley looked at his diploma from a School of Medicine hanging on the wall.

Four years of pre-med, four years of med school, three years of residency, and for what? So this politically connected community organizer with a fourth grade education can tell me how to practice medicine? No thanks. Those ARK people are right.

That afternoon, after his nursing assistant had gone home, he sent an email on 24-hour delay to his patients: *Since all medical treatments are determined by interpretations of Federal law, you don't need me anymore. You need a lawyer. I'll keep you in my prayers. I've gone 2 by 2.*

Then he taped a hand-printed sign to his clinic door: *Gone ARK.*

* * * * * *

Tim Harrison sighed as he removed yet another 'forbidden' product from the shelves of his hardware store. He looked at the label. Wax-N-Feed. Wood furniture conditioner and polish with real beeswax. *What's wrong with furniture polish?* he wondered.

Tim pulled the Federal recall notice from his back pocket and re-read it. "In compliance with the Federal Court judgment in the lawsuit PRIS versus The EPA and All Furniture Polish Manufacturers in the United States, all furniture products containing beeswax are hereby prohibited and are to be removed from all store shelves immediately. PRIS (Pristine Influence on Society Foundation) has asserted that the harvesting of beeswax constitutes a disturbance of the natural balance of the environment and a violation of the property rights of bees. Under the new Federal ruling (Executive Order 7894) providing that any lawsuit concerning environmental damage or social justice requires no evidence, this summary judgment is immediately granted.

"Store owners and distributors will note that they are required to dispose of these products within three days without sending it to a landfill. Landfill disposal carries a fine of $33,000 and/or not less than six weeks in prison. Failure to remove and dispose of these products within three days carries a fine of $33,000 and/or not less than six weeks in prison. This court notes that the only Federally approved waste disposal firm for this type of product is Holder Limited, who may be contacted at Disposal@WaxLaw.com. Their minimum fee for disposal within the three day deadline is $33,000, payable by bank draft. Their

Certificate of Proper Disposal is the only one recognized by this Court and the EPA.

Tim snorted. *So what they really want is $33,000, since nobody can comply in three days without using this crony-capitalist company. Which happens to be owned by the Attorney General's brother-in-law. You can't win. You have to do what they say ...*

The paper slipped from his fingers and fluttered to the floor. He stood, transfixed, staring at the shelf in front of him. *You have to do what they say ...* Suddenly a bit dizzy, he reached out to steady himself by holding onto the shelf.

One of his employees saw him sway and called out. "Tim? You OK?"

He shook his head to clear it. Then he straightened up. "Yeah. I'm OK."

"Thought maybe you were having a stroke or something. You worried me."

"No. Not a stroke. An epiphany." *You have to do what they say ... No! You don't! You can quit and ... go ARK!* He strode to his back office. Grabbing a piece of paper and a Sharpie, he printed "Had enough. Gone ARK." Then he drew an icon:

Walking quickly to the front door of his hardware store, he taped up the sign. Then he went home to pack. Customers gawked at the sign.

*   *   *   *   *   *

By week's end, hundreds of thousands of small businesses across the nation had shut down and the owners disappeared. The unemployment rate ticked up from 14 percent to 18 percent. Thousands of photos and videos of the Ark icons and "2 x 2" signs taped on doors and gates of closed businesses were posted to FreedomToobz.Ark and other social media sites. Local television news began showing the signs and reporting on the closings and the disappearances. Network news ignored it.

Just as everyone had mentally dated events as "before 9/11 or after 9/11," now everyone began referring to "N plus". The date of the The Noah Option telecast, plus the number of days.

By the end of the month, N+30, word along the Mexican border was that the coyotes could now pick up some extra money going the other way: smuggling Americans into Mexico. Some of the old pre-civil war Underground Railroad routes into Canada were reactivated by the Constitutional Resistance Movement. Like those who smuggled slaves to freedom, they smuggled Americans out of the country and into ARK locations. In northern border states, hunting and fishing guides put up hand-painted "2x2" signs. This was code, meaning they would smuggle you across the border into Canada.

There were rumored to be several Ark locations within the United States, but no one could confirm this.

Bumper stickers and graffiti began appearing: "Pray for the Arks," "Lord, send the Dove of Capitalism," "My son/daughter is an Ark-Angel," "2x2 — Who's next?" and "Pray for a Rainbow."

Chapter Ten

The white van rolled to a stop in Bill Herman's driveway. His wife Sue called out from the kitchen, "Bill, there are some people unloading suitcases in the driveway. Were you expecting visitors?" The decal on the van door read "Community Action." The logo showed an upraised fist.

There was a loud knock on the door. "No honey, I wasn't expecting anyone. Would you get that?"

Sue opened the door. Before she could speak, a woman in a brown shirt and black tie demanded "Are you Citizen Sue Herman?" Behind her stood two couples and six children. Two of them were toddlers. All of them had suitcases on the ground beside them.

Sue was a petite woman in her seventies. The woman in the brown shirt was stocky and limped a little. Sue put her left hand to her chest in an unconscious defensive gesture.

"Yes, I'm Sue Herman. May I help you?"

The woman thrust a piece of paper at her and stepped past her into the house. "Special Agent VanJones of Homeland Security, on temporary duty with Community Action Corps. Citizen Herman, by order of the federalized Community Action Corps, your home is hereby condemned and occupied for the common welfare. The county tax rolls list this home as eighteen hundred square feet for only two occupants. That constitutes social injustice when so many are homeless. You will now share this living space with these two families."

Bill Herman, a frail retired man in his eighties, came into the room. "What's this about condemning my house?" he quavered.

The two couples carried their suitcases past Bill and into the bedrooms. The toddlers began pushing magazines off the coffee table in the living room. The older children stood in front of the open refrigerator, drinking from cartons and bottles.

The woman in the brown shirt spoke derisively to Bill. "YOUR house? There is no YOUR anything anymore. This is the people's house. You are the greedy 1%, hoarding too much house for your merely personal use. We are the 99% that you have stolen from."

Bill spoke up more strongly. "Now just you hold on a minute. This is America. Private property can only be condemned for public use, like a bridge or a highway. Putting squatters into my house is not like building a bridge. This is illegal!"

The stocky woman in brown stepped up to put her face in front of Bill's nose and poked him in the chest with her index finger. She winced and rubbed the web of her hand. There was a red scar there.

"Now you listen, old man. Social justice involves more than bridges or highways. The Supreme Court has ruled that the takings clause of the Constitution includes taking property for the greater good of the community. The board of directors of the county Community Action has decided that it is unfair and unjust for two people to live in a three bedroom house that can house three families."

Sue returned from the back of the house and interrupted shrilly. "Bill, one of the couples is putting their clothes in our bedroom closet!"

"The needs of the people come first," the stocky woman told her. "The largest bedroom goes to the couple with the youngest toddler who needs to sleep in the room with them. Move your stuff to the smallest bedroom in the house. The other children will sleep here in the living room."

Sue stared horrified as urine ran down the leg of one toddler onto her living room rug.

"Young woman, I am a lawyer by training," said Bill. "Who is on this board and who elected them?"

The woman in the brown shirt snorted and went to the refrigerator. She pulled out a bottle of beer and took a swig.

"Old man, you are now responsible for keeping all alcoholic products out of the hands of the children living here. The penalty for the first violation is six months in jail."

"Ma'am, I asked you a question. Who is on this board and who elected them?"

"Old man, I don't have to answer any of your questions, but I'll humor you just this once. Question me again and you are guilty of interfering with a Special Agent of Homeland Security, on loan to Community Action, an offense punishable by six months in jail."

She took another drink of beer. "The board is not elected, it is appointed by officials of the Federal Social Justice Administration. It has the power to confiscate property and money in the name of social justice for the 99%. It also has the power to compel service in the name of social justice and the common good."

With a stunned look on his face, Bill sat down. One of the children turned on his large screen television to a punk rock music channel and turned up the volume. Bill winced, as if in pain from the volume.

The stocky woman settled into the chair next to Bill and put her muddy boots on the coffee table. She spoke loudly over the music pounding out from the TV.

"As a Special Agent of Homeland Security on loan to Community Action, I hereby compel your service for the common good. You are the designated cook for this social housing unit. You are to cook three meals a day seven days a week for the twelve people living here. Failure to do so constitutes an offense punishable by six months in jail."

Bill looked up helplessly. "What?"

"You heard me. Start cooking. Now!" The Agent jerked Bill to his feet and shoved him toward the kitchen. Bill stumbled and nearly fell. His wife Sue ran forward to support him.

"Bill is eighty-six years old! He doesn't have the stamina to cook all day long! Why are you doing this to us? We voted for this administration. We contributed money to all of the social justice organizations for over forty years. We have always believed in social justice!"

The Special Agent sneered, "Donating money you stole from the people! Writing checks was too easy a way for you to support social justice, all the while living in the luxury you denied to the 99%. Now you will support social justice with your personal labor. You, Citizen

Sue, will be the dishwasher and cook's assistant for this housing unit. You wanted social justice? Now you will learn what social justice really is. Being eighty-six years old is no excuse. Citizen Bill has eighty-six years of selfish consumption to make up for with his personal labor for the people. You too. Get to work woman!"

One of the children, a tall teen-ager, tugged on Sue's arm. He was eating a piece of the cake she had baked yesterday. "Lady, what's for supper? I'm hungry."

Sue looked down. Tears ran down her genteel face. "But we always supported social justice," she whispered to herself.

Chapter Eleven

Grace walked into the house. *A day of productive work*, she thought, *leaves me tired but satisfied*. Sighing, she dropped her purse on the kitchen counter. "Isaiah? I'm home. Where are you?"

"Here. The living room." His voice was low and slow.

Her heels made a staccato as she made a beeline to him. "Sweetheart? What is it? You sound sick."

"I feel sick. Have you watched the news?" He was sitting on the couch.

"No. I just got home. I rarely listen to radio or TV when I'm at work."

"Listen to this." He pushed the play button on the DVR he had paused. The local Christchurch, New Zealand news anchor was speaking.

"The President of the United States announced today that the government has confiscated all private retirement accounts and bank accounts. Panic broke out as citizens made a run on the banks to withdraw their money."

The news footage showed crowds lining up at the doors of banks. One woman was crying. "I don't have any money for groceries for my children! All of my money is in the bank. I trusted the bank. I trusted the President! How am I going to feed my children?"

The news anchor returned. "That woman represents millions of U.S. citizens who can't access their own money to buy food and pay their bills. Here is the announcement from U.S. President Barry Fletcher."

The footage showed the President standing at his podium. "My fellow Americans, in this hour of grave crisis, I have acted to protect the solvency of your government. Taxes have not been enough to cover our spending for the past twenty years, and yesterday the Chinese Premier announced that his government would no longer purchase US Treasury Bonds. When I ordered Federal Reserve Chairman Weimar to print enough currency to cover the shortfall, the dollar dropped so low on the international markets that Saudi Arabia, the United Arab Emirates, and Canada refused to sell us oil and natural gas unless we paid with gold."

He lifted his head in his trademark "look down his nose at you" pose.

"As you know, traitors and terrorist agents have sabotaged our programs for wind and solar power. Those manipulators have somehow increased greenhouse gases, thereby changing the climate enough that the sun doesn't shine every day for our solar power farms, and the wind doesn't blow every day for our wind power farms. Since I closed all coal mines and nuclear power plants, oil and gas are our major source for electricity. Since I took control of all electric utilities, we have had to ration electricity to eight hours a day for the collective good. We need the oil and gas until we can stop the traitors and harvest our own wind and solar power.

"As a temporary defensive measure, I have told our oil partners that I would rescind the money-printing order and pay our bills with money donated by our citizens by presidential executive order. They have agreed to accept currency for half, and gold from Fort Knox for the other half. All private bank accounts and retirement accounts are immediately nationalized for the good of the country.

"I know that this is a hardship for many, but I've always said I would ask you to make sacrifices for the good of the many. We can all tighten our belts for a while, and this austerity will help the First Lady's program to fight obesity in America. I know you'll support her in this.

"To ensure that the shared sacrifice will be fair, I've issued an executive order directing the local IRS offices to begin food rationing via food stamp debit cards sent to every citizen. All grocery stores are hereby nationalized and ordered not to accept cash or credit or debit cards. Only food stamp cards will be accepted. In this way, no greedy rich person can buy more food than any other American. You are all equal in the eyes of the government, and the government is here to force everyone to be equal.

"And so I say to all Americans, be happy in your hunger, for this is the sacrifice you've been waiting for."

Grace sank into a chair. "Now I feel a bit queasy myself. He has just made everyone in America dependent on the government for their daily bread. If there is any bread."

Isaiah held her gaze for a long time, then whispered, "Grace, I've got to go back. I've got to do something to help."

"No!" She lunged from her chair and fell to her knees in front of him, burying her face in his chest. He could feel her body heaving with sobs.

"Isaiah, you can't go! They'll kill you! You know they'll kill you!"

They held each other a long time. Finally her breathing began to be deep and regular. He whispered "I couldn't live with myself if I didn't do something. I have to do something."

"I know," she said in a low voice. "That's the man I fell in love with and married. He does something." She quivered a little in his arms.

"Isaiah?" She whispered. "If you go, I go too."

"I know. That's the woman I fell in love with. When there is a problem, she does something about it."

He cupped her chin in his hand. "But Grace, we'll have to travel separately. We're too well-known now. Being seen together will be a dead give-away. Being apart is an additional sacrifice we'll have to make."

She felt as if her heart was being squeezed. "I'm still afraid."

"I know." He caressed her hair with his left hand and reached to clasp her hand with his right. He brought her hand to his face and kissed the palm, cupping her fingers around his cheek. This gesture always made him feel warm and connected to her.

Releasing her hand, he closed his eyes. "God of Abraham, Isaac, and Jacob, hear our prayer. We know that all things are in your hands. You delivered Noah from the flood. You delivered Your people from bondage in Egypt. You sent Your Son Jesus to heal the sick, feed the multitudes and raise the dead. Lord, give us the wisdom to know the right thing to do, and the strength and courage to do it."

Grace lifted her face and looked into his eyes. "Amen." She smiled, then put her head on his chest again. She had a faraway look in her eyes. "Amen, brother man, amen."

She closed her eyes. *Lord, please protect this man of mine. He is precious to me. Please hear my prayer, but ... Thy Will be done. Help me to accept that ... Thy Will be done.*

CHAPTER TWELVE

THE TALL MAN SLIPPED INTO THE CORRIDOR OF THE FEDERAL Courthouse and entered the restroom. Inside a toilet stall, he removed a judicial robe from his backpack and donned it. Checking himself in the mirror, he adjusted his necktie, then put on a pair of black framed eyeglasses. *Worked for Clark Kent.* Satisfied, he stepped back into the corridor and walked up the stairs to the second floor.

He paused outside the door with "Judge Block" painted on the glass. He looked at his wristwatch. Five-thirty p.m. Government employees, including the Judge's secretary and law clerks, left at five. He opened the door and entered. Reaching into his pocket, he activated a special app he had prepared for this occasion. Walking past the leather upholstered couch and chairs in the outer office, he tapped on the glass of the inner office door.

"Come," said a voice from within.

He opened the door and walked in, standing before the judge's heavy oak desk. "Hello Judge."

"You! I wasn't sure I'd ever see you again. Especially after you interrupted the President's televised speech with one of your own! Your face is now known all over the nation. Everyone knows you're a wanted man. It's dangerous for you to be here."

"You might not have ever seen me again. But, as you legal types say, exigent circumstances."

"You were safe in New Zealand. Why did you risk re-entering the country?"

"Yes, Ark Pacific, as we call it, is a safe and comfortable enough base of operations. But, I've been following developments here. The breakdown of the rule of law. The roving gangs terrorizing innocent families. The food shortages. Starvation in some cities. Martial law, with troops herding citizens at gunpoint like inmates in a prison camp. The power outages and brown-outs. Children beaten for their school lunches. Millions of innocent families living like refugees. Actually, they are refugees. Refugees from this man-made disaster of total government tyranny. Petty local tyranny and savage national tyranny."

The tall man stopped and bowed his head. "Dear God, You gave us the most free, most prosperous country in 5,000 years of human history and what did we do? We threw it away for a mess of pottage." A tear trickled down his cheek.

"Judge, I couldn't stay away. It would be like walking away from an injured person at a terrible automobile accident. You know the man will probably die, but you have to try to help him anyway. You have to try. At least ease his suffering if you can. It's the right thing to do."

The tall man strode to the window and looked at the street below. His face was impassive, but his eyes were sad. "If this country has to disintegrate under the contradictions of this government, I want to ease the suffering of innocent working families if I can. I also want to give them the means to fight back against the tyrannies, petty and large."

The judge looked nervous. "Is it wise to speak this openly?"

The tall man smiled. "As soon as I walked into your office I activated a masking app on my cell phone. It blocks all surveillance devices, including the spyware on your computer and smart phone that allows government agents to see through your camera lenses and overhear what everyone says. I must give them credit for that. They didn't have to install their own surveillance devices. They are called cell phones and computers. We buy them ourselves and install them in our homes and carry them around with us. We paid for and installed the government's surveillance equipment. The one time the government figured out how to run one of its programs without spending more money. Ingenious. You may speak freely."

The judge exhaled. Some tension drained from his face. "Well then, I guess I can call you by name, Isaiah. You are just one man. What can you hope to accomplish by yourself?"

"Me alone? Not much. But if I can place the right tools in the hands of the Constitutional Resistance Movement, the ARK people, and the many millions of ordinary American citizens who have had enough, then we'll have leverage. Like Archimedes, I can move the world if I can find a place to stand."

"Well you know Archimedes spoke figuratively, since you can't stand anywhere except on this world. I still don't see what one man can do." The judge shrugged.

Isaiah smiled one of his biggest smiles. "Oh ye of little faith! I do have a place to stand. I stand on the shoulders of patriots like you, Judge, and millions of other believers in constitutional government and free markets. And here is my lever."

He placed his phone on the judge's desk. "Place your phone next to mine, Judge, while I synch you up with some apps created especially for you and the CRM. We are about to go viral."

With a puzzled look, the Judge placed his phone next to Isaiah's. "Go viral with what?"

"Behold *David's Sling*, my code name for a new suite of apps that will help the CRM and ARK dwellers communicate, locate government enforcer types, block government surveillance, hack their messages, counter-spy on them using their own spy software, and insert some functions into their phones, computers, and other devices that will … let's just say it will make them unhappy."

The judge whistled. "If it can do all that, it is some sling indeed."

"Just as the sling magnifies kinetic force through the power of leverage, these apps will magnify and multiply the kinds of monkey wrenches we can throw into every attempt by the government to use force against its own citizens. We won't meet force with force, we will simply neutralize their force and turn it against them, like judo. We will deny the bullies their ability to push us around. Without a workforce of coerced slaves, they won't accomplish much. Without slave labor, I seriously doubt they'll be able to feed themselves, much less lord it over the rest of us."

"Well, that much I do understand." The judge looked down thoughtfully. "I can attest from painful personal experience, I didn't even know how to grow a tomato, much less grow enough food to sustain me for any extended time." He looked up at Isaiah. "Any hints about how these apps are going to work this magic against our enemies? We're like the French Resistance in World War II. We're behind enemy lines and can't work openly."

Isaiah chuckled. "Not to worry. My specialty is non-violent sabotage and 'outing' of the enemy government bureaucrats. My biggest and best weapon is the truth. Shining a light to reveal the truth of who they are and what they are attempting to do is often the best way to fight them."

Just then the Judge's phone made a sound like a land line makes when the phone is left off the hook. "What's that?" asked the judge.

"My signal that the synch-up and transfer is complete. If anybody asks, you can say 'did I forget to hang up that last call? Now bring your phone over to the window."

Judge Block joined Isaiah at the window. Isaiah stood beside him. "Find the 'Near Here' app. Scroll down through the categories for bars and pharmacies, etc., down to 'pest control'. Among the termite control and other services, you'll see 'Locate Vermin' with the roach icon. Touch that."

When he did, the Judge saw a map app showing his current location in the Federal 9th Court of Appeals building, the courtyard below him, and the street beyond. The courtyard was sprinkled with green dots, interspersed with a dozen roach icons.

"What do the dots and roaches signify?" asked the Judge.

"Watch," said Isaiah. He pulled up the window sash. They felt cool evening air and heard the sounds of traffic from the street beyond the courtyard. "Touch the word 'out' in the lower right hand corner of the screen."

He touched it. Immediately a dozen phones in the pockets of people in the courtyard below began blaring out an announcement in speakerphone mode. Startled, the Judge looked out the window at the scene below.

"Attention, everyone! I am a government bureaucrat! Each day I create and enforce stupid rules and regulations to make your lives more difficult. I am a petty tyrant! I love to tell you how to run your life, how to raise your children, and even how you should treat your pets. I find ways to tax your hard-earned income and waste it on my silly whims, do-gooder projects and extravagances! Take my picture with your phone NOW and show it to all your friends so they'll know who I am and what I do to everyone around me! Stay away from me, because I will inform on you and find ways to order you around!"

A dozen people frantically dug through their pockets and purses to find their phones. A dozen people frantically stabbed at touch-screens to try to turn off the blaring voice. It didn't work. The message began repeating, magically synchronized so that all twelve phones broadcast the message together, making a surround sound effect. The voice was perfectly clear anywhere in the courtyard.

As the message continued for the second time, other pedestrians began to give the twelve a wide berth and muttered curses under their breath. Some did snap pictures with their own phones, and then turned and walked briskly away. The twelve began to quickly scatter away from the public square.

"Look," said Isaiah, "they are like cockroaches scattering in a basement when the light is turned on. We just turned a light on them."

"Wow!" said Judge Block. "I can do that? At what range?"

Isaiah reached over and touched the 'out' button. Immediately the message was silenced. Isaiah pulled the window down. The twelve scattering people slowed their pace and slunk away, looking fearfully over their shoulders. The intimidators were not used to being shamed and intimidated themselves.

"A one block radius, roughly. It pings all phones within that range, checks the owners against a database of known government bullies, and then begins the message from their speakerphones. You can even change the message, if you wish. I trust you and other CRM members to remember that we don't use force unless in defense of our own safety and that of our families. I don't want anyone to use this to incite violence against them. Just use it for social shaming and identifying who your enemies are, so that you can protect yourselves from them. The signal can't be traced back to you, incidentally."

"Isaiah, this is powerful. When they have no facts or arguments for whatever hare-brained scheme they want to impose on us, they distract the public from their lack of arguments by shaming us and calling us racists and power mongers, greedy oppressors of the poor, global warming deniers and evil polluters of the planet. It's about time they have to live publicly with the truth about what they do every day for a living."

"Amen, brother, amen."

"Like you said in your broadcast, 'The truth will make you free, but first it will make you miserable.'" He hugged Isaiah.

Isaiah pressed his palms together in prayer and bowed his head. "Lord, give us the strength and the courage to fight the good fight, and the perseverance to finish the race."

Judge Block reached out and put his hand on Isaiah's arm. "Amen, brother, amen."

Chapter Thirteen

In the faint light of early dawn, thirty armed agents of the joint EPA/FDA Search and Destroy Division Command switched off the safeties on their assault weapons. The squad leader reached up to tighten the strap on his combat helmet. Then he keyed his helmet radio three times. The shadowy figures climbed over fences and moved into positions surrounding their objective.

A light came on in the farmhouse kitchen. Through a part in the gingham curtains, Squad One could see a woman turning on the coffee and placing a frying pan on the stove. She put on a yellow apron. Soon, the agent closest to the window could smell bacon frying. His mouth watered. *I sure could go for bacon right about now*, thought the agent.

A small girl came down the stairs into the kitchen.

"Good Morning, sleepy head. Here's a glass of orange juice for you." Her mother tousled her daughter's blond hair affectionately. The girl looked to be about nine years old. She was dressed in blue jeans and a plaid shirt. She hugged her mother around the waist and pressed her head against her. Then she took a drink from the juice glass.

"Janie, you left the feed bucket on the porch last night. Take it with you when you go to feed the goats."

"OK Mom." The girl took a canvas jacket from a peg near the door and put it on. As soon as the door slammed behind her, the goats began bleating. They knew breakfast was on the way.

"I'm coming, girls. I'm coming, Liza Jane," she called out to the goats. She and her mother and dad called the nanny goats 'girls.' They all had names. Liza Jane was her favorite, a white goat with a black patch on her forehead. She was due to deliver a kid any day now. Janie could hardly wait to see the baby goat. Daddy had promised that it would be hers. *My very own goat*, she breathed.

In the kitchen, a man came down the stairs. He stretched his arms over his head, yawned, and then kissed his wife. "Did you sleep well?"

"Yes. You?"

"Fair to middling. I have a busy day today. I promised Janie I'd build her a shed that looks like a schoolhouse for her to play in with her pet goat."

He poured himself a cup of coffee. Then he opened the refrigerator and removed a plastic container. He poured some goat's milk into his coffee.

The agent looking into the window keyed his mike. "Go, go, go!"

Agents in black combat garb kicked open the farmhouse door and ran in, pointing their weapons at the farm wife and her husband. Too surprised to react, the farmer stood there with the coffee cup in his right hand, staring. His wife screamed and dropped a plate, which smashed into pieces on the floor.

"Hands up! You're under arrest for violating FDA Food Processing Regulation 6.FDA.66. On the floor! ON THE FLOOR!" The squad leader viciously kicked the woman in the back as she slowly knelt down in preparation for lying on the floor. The force of the kick sent her sprawling.

Instantly, her husband sprang up and punched the squad leader in the jaw. They fell to the floor and rolled over, struggling.

"You coward! You bully! You kicked her when she was down! If you touch my wife again I'll kill you!"

Two other agents dragged him off the squad leader and held the man between them. The squad leader picked up his weapon and fired twice. The farmer slumped.

"You heard him. He was going to kill me. Frisk him for weapons."

The wife began screaming and sobbing. "Why? Why?"

*   *   *   *   *   *

Janie had just opened the gate to the goat pen when she heard her mother scream. As she turned, an agent grabbed her arm. She screamed and thrashed, dropping the bucket. He attempted to place his hand over her mouth.

"Aaahh! She bit me! The little brat bit me!" He released his grip, and she ran toward the house, screaming. "Daddy! Mom! Someone tried to grab me! Help!"

Just then, she heard shots from inside the house. She screamed again, "Daddy! Daddy come get …"

A burst of automatic weapons fire cut off her last word. Three bullets went through her heart and lungs. She fell forward.

The agent ran up to the body. With his boot, he turned her over.

Another agent ran up and looked down at the small body. She looked up at the sky, with morning sun lighting the clouds. Her blond hair fanned around her head in a golden halo. Blood soaked her plaid shirt. Her lips moved, "Come get … me." Her eyes froze in the fixed stare of death.

The first agent looked at him and sucked on the bite marks on his hand. "She bit me," he spat out.

The second agent looked troubled. "Why did you shoot her? She's just a little girl, for heaven's sake!"

"She was calling for her father to come get his guns. You know how these farmers are. Gun nuts."

"Bud, I heard her. She was calling for her dad to come get *her*. You shot and killed a little girl for nothing." He paused and whispered, looking down at her, "Nothing."

Bud grabbed him by his vest with both hands and shook him angrily. "Listen, man. You heard her calling for her father to come get his *guns*. That's what we both heard! You got that? Guns!"

His squad mate saw the rage in his eyes and heard the paranoia in his voice. He knew how easy it was for friendly fire "accidents" to happen while on a raid. *Be careful,* he thought. *He's a rage-aholic.*

"Yeah, man, right. Guns. Calling to get guns. That's what we heard." Bud released him and looked back down at the small body. Then he sat down and began to carve a notch on his rifle stock. There were nine notches there already.

*　*　*　*　*　*

Ten big black government SUVs drove into the farmyard. A squat woman in tactical fatigues got out of the first vehicle, limping a little. The squad leader came forward and saluted.

"Report!" she snapped. She thrust her chin forward pugnaciously.

"The area is secure. Two suspect casualties. One minor injury to our forces."

"And the evidence?" the woman raised one eyebrow.

"Secure. In the kitchen." He gestured toward the house.

She began striding toward the house. "Our minor injury? What was it?"

The unit leader kept pace beside her, "The little girl bit one of my men. Didn't even break the skin."

She nodded as she entered the farmhouse. "Very good. Where is the evidence?"

The unit leader pointed. "The plastic jug on the counter top. Raw goat's milk. Unpasteurized. No FDA seal of permission, taxation, and inspection."

The farm wife was seated on a stool, her head down, sobbing. Armed agents with assault rifles stood on both sides of her. She looked up at the woman in the fatigues.

"Is that what this is all about? *Goat's milk?*" She looked incredulous. "You killed my husband over *goat's milk?* Where is my daughter? What have you done with her?" She screamed, "WHO ARE YOU?"

The woman in fatigues pulled a folded document from her jacket pocket. "I'm Special Agent Maudire VanJones, commanding this joint FDA/EPA Search and Destroy Division Unit." Unfolding the document, she read, "This search, arrest, and confiscate warrant authorizes us to arrest you for the crime of producing, selling, and/or consuming non-approved food products. FDA Food Processing Regulation 6.FDA.66 specifically prohibits this."

"WE MILK GOATS! We drink the milk. What's wrong with that?"

Looking down and reading again, the Special Agent in Charge intoned, "Eating or drinking anything not approved, taxed, and inspected by the FDA is a federal crime punishable by imprisonment of not less than one year and a fine of $50,000."

Folding up the warrant, she looked at the plastic container. "I don't see an FDA tax stamp on this container of goat's milk."

"For this you smashed your way into my home and killed my husband? A tax stamp?"

"He resisted arrest."

"He defended me when one of your goons kicked me in the back! Look!" She turned to show the muddy boot print on the back of her blouse.

"So, you resisted arrest too." The woman turned to the unit leader. "Add that to the charges."

Two agents dragged the little girl's body into the room and dropped it beside her father's body. The wife screamed again and threw herself on the body, clutching it.

"My baby! You killed my baby! You killed my little girl!" She sobbed uncontrollably, rocking back and forth with the small body in her arms.

The Special Agent in Charge looked impassive. "Collateral damage. Take her away. Schedule television time for the show trial. This case will frighten more citizens and bring them into line. Every publicized raid like this intimidates millions of Americans from doing anything without our permission. They have to learn who is in control."

"Yes ma'am." The squad leader nodded at her men. They dragged the sobbing wife out. Her yellow apron had the bright red blood of her husband and daughter smeared on it.

The agent who had watched through the kitchen window went to the stove. He ate a piece of bacon from the platter there. *Yum. Good bacon.* He picked up another piece and popped it into his mouth.

Chapter Fourteen

Diana Nomenski looked out her corner office windows and smiled a small tight smile of satisfaction. From here on the 44th floor she could see three buildings that had housed businesses she had shut down. Her eyes hardened. *Capitalist pigs! Defecating on the planet. To the slaughterhouse you go.* She unconsciously clenched her fists and grimaced out the window at the Chicago skyline.

Turning back to her desk, her eyes fell on the annual report for PRIS, the Pristine Influence on Society Foundation. She was the Executive Director of PRIS. She flipped it open to the page with the title PCB: Purging of Capitalist Businesses. Running her finger down the page, she stopped at the section called PCB Scorecard. She allowed herself a small smile.

Sixteen thousand businesses shut down by PRIS lawsuits for the "crime" of exceeding their carbon allowances. Carbon allowances set so low that just walking into the building and flipping on one light switch put you over the limit. Carbon allowances that PRIS had rammed through Congress without one public hearing. Carbon allowances that PRIS would selectively enforce to punish its enemies and reward its friends. It was the Chicago way.

Sixteen thousand businesses shut down so far. Four million jobs lost. Four million people out of work. Four million people and their families forcibly relocated to the government-run "American Prosperity Camps" for re-education and ecologically correct agricultural work therapy.

Diana smiled her tight smile again. *Let the vermin learn what ecologically correct work is. Let them get their hands dirty and their backs sore. Let them die at the age of forty, the pre-industrial life span, worn out from physical work. No carbon-spewing labor-saving machinery for them! Let them die early and purge the planet of their undeserving little lives and give it back to the snail darter and the river minnows, who deserve to inherit the earth.*

Letting her fingers caress the page, she closed her eyes and parted her lips. She felt pleasure as she thought about the millions now suffering because of her politically correct attack projects run through PRIS. *Stupid proletarians too dumb to know they were polluting the planet every time they went to work. Well, let them suffer. And their children. Serves them right.*

Her intercom buzzed. Frowning, she picked it up. "Yes?"

"Ms. Nomenski, your EarthPurge project team is here."

"Send them in."

She set her lips in a grim line. *Time to ramp up the project to a global scale. Time to rid Gaia of the vermin infesting her once-pristine beauty. Time for project EarthPurge.*

*   *   *   *   *   *

She looked around the conference table at her EarthPurge project team. Diana picked up the remote control and snapped on the large flat screen television mounted at one end of the conference room.

ZNN reporter Loup Blitzen was introducing a retrospective on the blight that had ravaged Botswana one year ago. The footage that followed showed the gaunt bodies of mothers and skeletal children with bulging bellies. "This was the situation one year ago in Botswana. Fortunately, humanitarian groups in the USA, primarily the Pristine Influence on Society, managed to get blight-free seeds through to the desperate farmers. The crops from these seeds saved the population from the worst famine since the 1930s starvation in the Ukraine under Soviet Dictator Joseph Stalin."

Diana clicked the pause button for the DVR. The image of small children with bloated bellies remained on the screen. Then she looked around the conference table again.

"We managed to spin our way out of that one, thanks to our friends in the media. We actually tried to help along our favorite Horseman of the Apocalypse – Starvation – by preventing those seeds from entering Botswana. It was that enemy of the planet – Dr. Grace Washington – and her corporate lackey, Minerva Stone of Nutritional Abundance Industries – who managed to evade our court-ordered destruction of their super seeds. They pulled that corny "Noah Option" stunt by escaping to their so-called "ARK" in New Zealand. Then they played the hero by shipping the seeds to Botswana from New Zealand. That ended the blight and the starvation. Fortunately our media friends like Loup retold the story to give us credit us for the seeds."

She glared at the people around the table. "That was a target of opportunity, and we missed our chance. Next time, when we release our own genetically modified virus on the world, we will stomp on this infestation of homo-sapiens like roaches. Roaches have a better claim to the planet than most people. Our GM virus will reduce planetary population by two billion people. That will leave just one billion to go, to reach our goal of a 40% reduction in world population. And that's just for starters."

One young woman kept staring at the small children on the screen. She had a blank look on her face.

Diana picked up the papers in front of her and began tapping them against the table top to straighten them up. Without looking up, she said "I expect a status report on Phase Two of Project EarthPurge by this time next week. We can't let up. They're making babies while we sleep. We have to get rid of massive numbers of people. Dismissed."

As the others stood and began to file out, the young woman continued to stare at the image on the TV screen. Diana looked up sharply.

"Hughes-McLauren, what's the matter with you? I said dismissed. There's work to be done."

The young woman looked at her helplessly. "It's … it's just that I never visualized these suffering babies and toddlers when we began the project to reduce population through a virus. They're in pain. They're the same age as my children."

Diana snorted. "So? What about the suffering of the snail darters?

They are sentient too, you know. It's been proved that they feel pain no less than human beings. What about them?"

Ms. Hughes-McLauren looked down. "I know, I know that. It's just hard to look at the suffering on those small children's faces. Before, it was just an abstraction about what numbers the planet could sustain. Looking into the face of a child is personal."

Diana put down her papers and walked over to the seated woman. Looking down at her, she shouted "Those children are part of the problem! They have no right to be here! In a properly run world, the parents would have had to apply for permission from the authorities to have a child! China! China has the right idea. One child per couple. All others aborted. The only mistake China is making is allowing parents to select boy babies and aborting the girls. A government run by women would be sensible enough to require that the boys be aborted, not the girls."

The woman looked up. Tears ran down her face. She wailed, "I know. I know I'm wrong. I just can't stop thinking about my own children."

Diana stopped shouting, but her voice was still harsh. "How old are your children?"

"The baby is six months, and Felix is four."

"Who authorized you to have children? I certainly didn't. All members of PRIS are required to apply for UN Agenda 21 Population Sustainability Permits before they are allowed to have children. Where is your Population Permit blue wallet card? It had better say "two!""

Ms. Hughes-McLauren's face had a look of panic. "I didn't know! I never got one! My husband is not a member of PRIS. We never discussed it. Oh Ms. Nomenski, surely you can make an exception for me?"

Diana calculated. *Best not to frighten her any further. She might try to take the children and run.* She softened her voice.

"Of course, of course. I'll start the necessary paperwork. I'll need you to bring in the children to our PRIS doctor to certify that they're in good health and have no genetic disorders. You can do that next Tuesday. Just bring them with you to the office."

The woman clasped one of Diana's hands in both of hers. "Oh, Ms.

Nomenski, thank you, thank you. You are a true friend. I'll bring both children in on Tuesday."

Nomenski watched her walk out. *I am a true friend … to the Earth.* When the door closed, Diana pulled out her phone and touched a number.

"Dr. Dreen, a Mrs. Hughes-McLauren will be bringing two small children to you next Tuesday. See to it that you prescribe the six week slow acting euthanasia poison for both of them. Say nothing to the mother. She was thoughtless enough to get pregnant twice without obtaining the Population Permits. Make it look like a genetic disorder. After it's over I may tell her the truth, and publicize it to make an example of her foolish oversight. We can't let a good bad example go to waste." She paused. "Be sure to mark their charts for organ harvesting. We can't let good organs go to waste either."

"Yes, Ms. Nomenski."

Tapping the "end call" button on her phone, she looked out the window again. *The fundamental transformation of America and re-education of Americans is a never-ending task. No rest for the righteous elite.* She shrugged and turned back to her papers.

Chapter Fifteen

In his office, Dr. Dreen looked at the phone he had just hung up. Next to it was a photo of his wife and two children. A boy and a girl. He thought they looked happy, smiling … trusting … who? Him. They trusted him to be a good father. To care for them, provide for them, protect them. He shivered, thinking about the instructions he had just been given.

On his computer screen, he found the folder called "office parties." Opening it, he found the folder marked "Winter Solstice Party." PRIS did not celebrate Christmas. He scrolled through the pictures until he found "Hughes-McLauren family" and opened it.

A baby and a boy. About four months and four. Sonia Hughes-McLauren and her husband Bill. The boy had a mop of curly brown hair. He was holding a doll representing Gaia, the earth goddess. Bill had an open, easy smile. He cradled the baby in one arm and his other arm was around Sonia. The boy held his mother's hand. The all-American family.

He looked back at the photo of his own wife and children. Very similar. He closed his eyes and thought back, remembering. To a time when he was about eight years old, in a Christmas pageant at his family's church. His mother had made him a shepherd costume from an old sheet. He walked up to a crèche scene and knelt beside a papier machè sheep. Clutching his shepherd's crook, he looked down at a plaster baby Jesus in a manger. The yellow straw had been real.

Different days, before the Hate Crime of Christianity regulations had been proclaimed, back when Christian religions could be practiced openly. Before the religion of love had been decreed by the government to be a religion of hate, and outlawed as a hate crime. Why was that? He tried to remember, then shook his head and opened his eyes. The regime issued so many regulations each week, sometimes contradicting those of the previous week. He had stopped trying to understand the reasons given for the endless regulations, or even to keep up with them all.

That night, he tucked his children in their small beds and kissed them on the forehead. Returning to his own bedroom, he quickly fell into a deep sleep beside his wife. He dreamed he was in a barn with animals. An ox and a donkey. In his dream, he laid down his shepherd's crooked staff and went to sleep. He dreamed.

A person appeared in this dream within a dream. It was a man, dressed as a shepherd, just as he had been dressed as a little boy at his church Christmas pageant. The man's face shone with light. He spoke to John Dreen in a voice at once resonant and yet gentle. The voice seemed to penetrate his body like a tingling vibration. "Take the children to a place of safety. Find an Ark of safety where life is still sacred. Do not return until those who threaten the lives of children are no more."

He awoke with a start. He sat up and looked at his bedside clock. Midnight. "John?" his wife asked in a sleepy voice. "Are you OK?" He leaned over and kissed her cheek.

"Just a vivid dream. Go back to sleep." She turned over and was still. He quietly got out of bed and walked, barefoot, to his children's bedrooms. He stood in each bedroom for a long five minutes, listening to their breathing and watching them stir. After re-tucking each of them, he padded downstairs to his study.

Closing the door, he sat at his desk and turned on the lamp. *What Nomenski is asking is wrong. I can't do it.* He stared at the phone for ten minutes. Then he called the Hughes-McLaren home. "Hello?" came a sleepy voice.

"Sonia? This is Dr. Dreen, John Dreen. I'm sorry to wake you, but this is a life and death matter. I'm taking Mary and the children away, to one of those ARK places. You should bring your children and Bill and come with us. Why? Today Diana Nomenski ordered me to administer a slow acting poison to your children when you bring them to see me next Tuesday."

He paused. "What? Yes I'm serious. You know that woman is in love with death. How do I know? Have you ever looked into her eyes? They're cold and lifeless, like a doll's eyes. They hypnotize you, like snake eyes."

He took a deep breath. "Sonia, she's evil. Deep-down evil. And she has enough friends in this regime to do whatever she wants. Including murdering your children. And mine, if she gets half an excuse."

"We can all go in my RV. I have a permit for it, and for my family and colleagues, for medical duties. I'll pick you up at 5 a.m. this morning. Pack light. Where? I'm not sure. We'll head west. I have extra gas tanks I installed long ago. We'll get far away from Chicago."

Putting the phone down, he held his head in his hands. *Guide me, Lord. I haven't prayed since I was a kid. Guide me and give me the courage to shepherd these children to safety. Amen.*

He stood up. *I've got packing to do*, he thought.

*   *   *   *   *   *

Thirteen hundred miles later, they pulled into the Wind River Indian Reservation trading post. Frederick Blackhawk greeted them at the counter. "What can I do for you folks?"

John Dreen looked at him with a steady gaze. "We're looking for asylum in an ARK community. We heard there might be one hereabouts?"

Frederick looked back just as steadily. "Depends. Do you aim to mind your own business?"

Sonia stepped forward, her arm around her son's shoulders. "We've learned that it's wrong to try to mind other people's business. Seemed OK to run other people's lives, until they started running ours. Then they didn't want to just run our lives. They treated our lives as their property. They wanted to kill these children. Still do. My children and I are nobody's property. And nobody is our property."

Frederick's face remained stern. "Do you have any skills to offer the community? Can you earn your own way? We're mostly farmers here."

"I'm a doctor," John said. "I've brought medical supplies with me. And shovels and hoes. I'm no farmer, but I can learn. Sonia and Bill are registered nurses. My wife Judy was raised on a dairy farm. We're two families, and we aim to carry our own weight."

Frederick smiled. "Welcome to ARK Shoshone. You'll be safe here, the good Lord willing and the drones don't find us."

Sonia began crying. She looked at her husband Bill, then at John and Judy Dreen. She sobbed, "And the Lord remembered Noah. And the Lord remembered us."

* * * * * *

Diana Nomenski threw her phone at her head of security. It struck him in the eye and caused immediate bleeding. He shouted out in pain and clutched at his eye. "My eye, my eye! You've cut my eye!" He bent over in pain. The others at the conference table were silent, shocked.

"If your worthless eye had been on the job, you would have been watching Dr. Dreen and Hughes-McLauren slipping out of town! Burnfield! Call 911 for an EMT! Mephis! Get this worthless lump of homo-sapiens flesh out of my sight. NOW!"

Someone took the man by the arm and guided him out of the room.

She glared at the rest of the EarthPurge team. "I hope for your sakes that no one else knew about this little escape. As of now this project is a matter of national security.

"Next month I'll be presenting our project to an inter-agency meeting in Hawaii. Homeland Security, FDA, EPA, HSS, the UN Council on a Sustainable Planet, the Green Coalition, and PRIS will be conferring about ways to help cleanse the planet of surplus population. In the meantime, I've offered our EarthPurge Virus to the Homeland Security Counter-Revolutionary Search and Destroy Command.

"I've want to introduce Maudire VanJones, the Deputy Director for the Western Region Domestic Search and Destroy Division of Homeland Security. I've invited her to sit in on this briefing.

"Madame Deputy Director, welcome to PRIS! And congratulations on your promotion up from the Joint EPA/FDA Search and Destroy Command."

Diana started clapping as a stocky woman entered and made her way to the front of the room. Dressed in a brown uniform and carrying a holstered side-arm, she walked with a slight limp. All of the Earthpurge team dutifully rose and clapped enthusiastically.

After VanJones acknowledged their applause with a nod, she sat down next to Diana. Diana sat, then spoke sharply.

"Very well. EarthPurge Team, report!"

The team leader, sitting to the right of the Deputy Director, straightened his papers and cleared his throat. "As of today, the EarthPurge Virus is ready to go operational. We have the virus ready for dispersion by spraying. Enough to contaminate the food rations of 40 million people. In three weeks, we will have enough to purge an additional 80 million. That's forty percent of the population of the U.S. Or wherever we choose to disperse it."

VanJones asked, "How long does it take for the virus to work?"

A woman in a white lab coat answered, "Seven to eight days for symptoms to appear. Then an additional twelve to eighteen days to produce death. Our data predicts an 80% kill rate among those infected with the virus. For children, 100%."

Diana Nomenski rubbed her hands together, then clasped them in satisfaction. "Tell the Deputy Director about the contagion factor we've built in."

Nodding, the woman continued, "That's one of the nice features of this virus. It's not contagious. Once it kills the host, it dies with the host. You can only acquire the virus by eating contaminated food. So, we can target the population we want to purge, contaminate their food, and not worry that the virus will splash back on us."

Deputy Director VanJones grunted and said, "That's good, but there's always a glitch factor. What if a non-targeted person eats contaminated food accidentally? Is there a cure?" She unconsciously rubbed the scar on the web of her right hand.

Diana answered. "Unfortunately, no. But that turns out to be another nice feature of this genetically modified virus. There is no permanent cure, but we do have an antidote. It only works for two weeks at a time. All infected people have to take the antidote every two weeks for the rest of their lives. And we control the antidote, so we can control whoever we wish – with the power of life and death. Just like the people's government already controls those who speak out by denying them healthcare. This method just works a little faster. Within three weeks."

This time the Deputy Director smiled a tight smile. "That is an advantage."

Diana stood up. "Madame Deputy Director, if we may?" Maudire VanJones nodded.

Activating a smart-board display, Diana began to scroll through presentation slides. "We have thought of several advantages this virus will give the Search and Destroy Division: One, this allows you to take out the traitors who resist our control in an indirect, stealthy manner. You won't have to worry about bystanders filming you with their phones when you arrest or kill people – and then posting it on the internet.

"Two, since the delivery is through food, you can blame either the super-seed food crops created by the fugitive Grace Washington, or you can blame the unsanitary living conditions in these so-called ARK hide-outs. Either way, your agency won't be suspected."

The woman in the white lab coat asked, "Weren't all the super-seeds on US soil destroyed? Wouldn't that make it hard to blame deaths on them?"

Diana hissed, "Who gave you permission to speak? Your specialty is biological warfare, not propaganda! Remember your place!" The woman looked down, terrified.

"Ever since the great communications expert Joseph Goebbels plied his trade, we have known the power of the Big Lie. Even if obviously untrue, repeat it often enough, and soon everybody agrees that it is something 'everybody knows is true.'" Diana was almost shouting. "Few will remember that the seeds were destroyed, and even they will be convinced after three hundred media repetitions of the Big Lie in three weeks. And the media will cooperate."

Deputy Director VanJones nodded. "You may be sure, the media *will* cooperate."

Diana tapped on the board. "Three. In the current food shortage, this administration has many extra mouths to feed in the American Prosperity Camps where you have put the unemployed and the ARK people you have managed to capture. Why not purge them with the virus and then blame your enemies, the renegade Constitutional Resistance Movement and the cowardly ARK dwellers?"

The Deputy Director stood. "Ms. Nomenski, well done! EarthPurge

Team, well done! You have created a useful tool, and several promising scenarios for using this tool. You will all be remembered for being valuable servants of the state when we have finished the fundamental transformation of America!"

Like an orchestra conductor, Diana bowed, then with a sweep of her arm directed the EarthPurge Team to rise and take a bow. Diana thought, *not only will this be part of the fundamental transformation of America, it will be a sweeping purge of the vermin homo sapiens infesting our dear Gaia mother earth.* She did not consider herself a member of homo sapiens, but a higher, more enlightened ruling species: *homo intelligentsia.*

 # Chapter Sixteen

Several weeks later, Judge Block returned to Justin Herman Plaza for another lunch alfresco in the warm spring sunshine. Waiting until no one else was in line, he strolled up to the hot dog vendor's catering truck.

"I'll have one hot dog with mustard and a bottle of water."

Looking up, the vendor winked at him. "One Swamp Fox special, coming up."

After placing the order on the counter, the vendor leaned on his elbows, his hands holding a white towel. Judge Block took a bite of his hot dog and smiled at the vendor. "Best I've ever had."

"We aim to please."

"Here's another lunch order for you. We'd like an upgraded app, one that will allow us to pair with any Federal cell phone, track its whereabouts, do the usual eavesdropping on their phone calls and conversations, but also insert voice and text messages that seem to originate from inside Federal agencies. The insertions and tracking must be untraceable. Ideally, it will allow us to map all of the Federal phones, computers, and other devices on their network and perform these kinds of operations on all their devices simultaneously."

"Can do. It'll take longer. Maybe three-four weeks."

"That works. The usual distribution and encryption on dot ARK."

The vendor grinned, "David's Sling 2.0. You want mustard with that?"

"No, just pepper relish. Lots and lots of pepper relish. We want to make things very hot for the Feds."

"Can do. How are our friends in the other Arks?"

"Waiting, preparing, and praying. Helping us and praying for us. Waiting for that rainbow."

"Amen brother. Vaya con Dios."

* * * * * *

Judge Block sauntered over to the tent city of the "Occupy San Francisco" protest partiers. Two were sitting on a park bench they had liberated and dragged to their tent site. One strummed on a guitar while the other took a swig from a bottle of wine in a brown bag.

The young man holding the wine bottle was the same one who had argued with the hot dog vendor several weeks ago. Looking up at the Judge, he smiled and drawled "Wat-up, dude?"

Holding out his hand, Judge Block asked, "May I have a drink?"

"Ab-so-freaking-lutely right you can have a drink! Here you are, my man!"

Taking a swallow, the Judge pulled the bottle out of the bag and looked at the label appreciatively. "Very fine. Meteor Vineyard Perseid Cabernet Sauvignon 2007. This costs nearly $100 a bottle. An expensive vintage for a 99 percenter, no?"

The young man suddenly looked scared. "Aww, how should I know? I found it in the trash barrel over there."

Judge Block pulled a receipt from the brown bag. "So you are not Alexander Sorosander III?" he asked, reading from the slip of paper.

"Nooo ..." began the young man, when his companion cut in, "But that's you, man. Alex Sorosander. Sorosander ... the third? I never knew you were the third, man. Say! I get it! This means your father is Alexander Sorosander II, the big Wall Street hedge fund octopus with his tentacles around everybody's money! The one percent of one percenters! One of the richest dudes in the world! Dude! That makes you the inheritor of billions!"

"Noo ..." the young man said again, but his companion shoved him face down on the ground and sat on him.

He reached into Alexander's jeans pocket and took his wallet. He took out a high end credit card and read "Alexander Sorosander III. So! It's true!"

He began shouting, "HEY EVERYBODY! We got a ONE PERCENTER hiding among us! Hey man, where is MY bailout? I could use a hundred thousand, at least. Come on, you can afford it! Ask your old man for your big fat 1% allowance!"

Hung-over Occupiers began crawling out of tents. One girl screamed, "HOSTAGE! Take him hostage! Instant media op, right in our laps. We've taken a back seat to those New York Occupy people for too long. This is our big chance to hit the front page of every paper, blog, and web news aggregator in the country! The son of Alexander Sorosander II, taken freaking hostage by Occupy San Francisco! The ransom we want is control of the entire fascist country!"

The erstwhile singer pulled young Alexander up. "Hostage! Great media idea. I've got him!" He held Alexander by the arm.

Alexander looked up at him in a panic. "But, but, I'm one of you! I've been here with you from the start, nearly four months now. I protest with you. I party with you. I'm one of you!"

Another occupier shouted, "Not a hostage, an example! If he's the One Percent of the One Percent, let's crucify him! I have hammer and nails and lumber here from making our protest signs last week. Let's make an example of him! I have gold spray paint. We'll crucify him on a cross of gold, just like his old man does to us! CRUCIFY HIM!"

The refrain was taken up, "Crucify him! Crucify him!"

Judge Block took off his windbreaker and stepped close to Alexander. "If you want to live, do what I say." Alexander looked into his eyes and nodded weakly.

Gripping his ball point pen, Judge Block drove the point into the back of the guitarist's hand. "AAAHHH!" he screamed, releasing his grip on Alexander's arm. Wrapping the windbreaker around Alexander, he said "Pull up the hood, then walk with me. Fast."

"My hand, my hand!" shouted the guitarist. While everyone looked at the upraised hand, Judge Block and Alexander quickly walked away. They ducked behind the hot dog catering truck. Judge Block knocked on the door.

When the vendor cracked open the door, Judge Block said, "In the name of the rule of law, I ask sanctuary for this young man. I'll alert nearby CRM folks to run interference."

"Done. Get in." The vendor pulled out a trash can from under a counter. "Under there." Alexander crawled in. He placed the trash can in front of him.

Police cars were already pulling up in response to the 911 call placed by Judge Block on an encrypted channel. There was a confusion of blue uniforms and protesters shouting at one another in the plaza.

A van with a housepainter's logo pulled up on the street behind the catering truck. The driver rolled down the passenger window and called to Judge Block, "Somebody call for a taxi?"

Judge Block pulled Alexander out of hiding and hustled him over to the van. The driver slid the panel door open. "Stay down back there until I tell you," said the driver.

"You'll hear from me," said Judge Block, sliding the door closed. The van pulled into traffic.

*   *   *   *   *   *

Alexander was hidden at a CRM safe house. During supper, he whined to the painter, "This is not fair at all! I'm an occupier. I marched and protested with them. I threw bottles and rocks at the police with them. I sat down at the sit-in protest at the Bank of America with them. Why did they turn on me?"

"We've not been properly introduced. My name is Thomas." He held out his hand.

"But why did they turn on me?" Alexander ignored the outstretched hand.

"Because your daddy's rich. I guess rich people don't have much use for manners." The painter returned to sharpening a hunting knife on a whetstone.

"But that's not my fault! You can't pick your parents! It's not fair, I tell you!"

"Life's not fair, brother. Deep down, you know it. Deep down, your friends know it too. Your daddy has given a lot of money to the Occupy Movement, and they know it."

"Yeah, that's another thing! You'd think they'd be grateful that my dad gave major money to fund this movement. I even kept it a secret that he was my dad. I didn't want anybody to think I was lording it over them because of his big donations."

"No, brother, they aren't grateful. They resent him for it. Now they want to punish him for it."

"But that makes no sense! Why would they resent him?"

"Because he, and their own parents, have given them something for nothing. They've never had to work for anything. When you give somebody something for nothing, you make them good for nothing. Deep down, they know they're good for nothing and they hate themselves. And because they evade personal responsibility for what they've become, they look for someone else to blame. So they blame your dad. I disagree with the progressive causes your dad supports, but he does have a skill: he knows how to make money investing. They resent his competence and want to tear him down."

"That's nonsense! They've all been to college like me. They are good for something! They have degrees!"

"Not one of those people has a skill that anybody would pay them for. That includes you. They studied things like 'post-modern feminist Marxist critiques of the fascist capitalist agri-business in America.' Poseurs talking to one another, pretending to know something important."

"But that IS important! I took that class at Yale."

"I know. We've checked you out. Now that you passed the course, what can you do?"

"I can tell grocery shoppers why they shouldn't buy from the big companies like Kraft and Kellogg who make a profit from producing food that ought to be free for everyone."

"If they don't buy from those companies, how will they get their food?"

"By urban farming and sharing their harvests at the urban whole foods co-op."

"Ever do any urban farming?"

"No, but it's the politically correct, green and sustainable way to get your food."

"But you don't do it *yourself.* Know how to do it? Ever tend a garden?"

"No. Never had the chance to learn. But I'm doing my part by being a part of Occupy San Francisco."

"Then this is your lucky day. Since you can't be an Occupier anymore, you can learn how to grow a garden."

"Sorry, not my thing." He was ladling out a second helping of beef stew into his bowl.

"Around here, if you eat, gardening is your thing. If it's not your thing, then you don't eat." The painter put down the knife and took the ladle away from Alexander. "Eating's a thing of the past for you until *you learn where food comes from.*" He removed Alexander's plate and scraped it into the trash.

"Hey! I wasn't finished eating."

"You are now."

Just then Judge Block came in the back door. He was wearing a flannel shirt, jeans, and hunting boots.

"I've been listening with my remote app. I do believe young Alexander is ready for *A Course in Reality.*"

The painter said, "I agree. Ready to go?"

"Yes. Alexander, we're going on a road trip. Get in the van."

Alexander looked puzzled. "But I want to go back to my tent at the Occupy site."

Looking at the painter, Judge Block said, "Shall we show him?"

Nodding, the painter turned on the television. Kathy Coeur-Saignant was reporting on CBC News, "The martyrs at Occupy San Francisco continue to protest the removal of Wall Street heir Alexander Sorosander III from them. Let's listen." The camera showed a bonfire burning in the center of the tent city and a crowd of occupiers chanting, "We want Alexander the Third! We want Alexander the Third! Crucify him! Crucify him!"

They were passing around items.

"Hey!" said Alexander. "That's my stuff they are passing around! That's my $600 sleeping bag!"

"Looters doing what they do best, stealing other people's property," said the painter.

The picture shifted back to Kathy at her news desk. "We sent our roving reporter Abby Trammel out to San Francisco to cover this story. Abby interviewed one of the Occupiers."

The picture shifted to Abby sticking a microphone in the face of the Occupier who had started the crucifixion idea. He said, "Alexander Sorosander III was a double agent for the capitalist greed conspiracy in this country. He pretended to be one of us while he collected intelligence about our secret plans."

"What secret plans?" interrupted Abby.

"Like our plan to hold a sit-down strike in the lobby of Merrill-Lynch. They rob money from the rest of us, and don't even serve locally grown foods in their cafeteria!"

"So what will you do to him if he's returned?"

"He's a traitor, and treason is punishable by death. We will crucify him on a cross of gold for all the world to see. Unless his father agrees to every one of our demands."

Abby looked down at a piece of paper. "I see that you have 75 demands. Would you tell us one or two of the most important demands?"

"Well, Abby, they're all important, from free abortions for middle school students to free arugula for the poor. I guess the biggest demand is for an end to world hunger."

The next shot showed Abby facing the camera with the bonfire visible over her shoulder.

"This is Abby Trammel, reporting live from Occupy San Francisco. Back to you Kathy."

"Thanks Abby." Kathy made the 'anchor quarter turn' with her head to face into the next camera, then continued, "Those brave protesters have a good cause and a good point. Someone has to be held responsible, and Alexander Sorosander the Third certainly deserves it. Crucifixion is too good for him. That's it for tonight for the Corporate Broadcasting Collective, where we report what's good for you to know, when we think it is good for you to know it. Remember, CBC has earned the Federal Broadcasting Oversight Bureau seal of approval for politically correct redacted reporting. Good night, comrades."

Snapping off the television, the painter turned to Alexander. "Still want to go back?"

Alexander shook his head uncertainly, "No. No, I guess not. But where can I go? Occupy San Francisco is the only thing I've done since college."

The Judge put his hand on Alexander's shoulder. "Come with us. We have some things to show you, and you have some things to learn."

He looked at the Judge suspiciously, "What if you want to kill me just like the others?"

"If I wanted you dead, I'd have left you with your friends who were ready to crucify you."

"OK. Where are we going?"

"You'll find out. It's a surprise. Trust me." The three got in the van. They drove off into the night.

Chapter Seventeen

Alexander Sorosander III stood in the clearing in the woods, looking blankly at the axe in his hand.

He doesn't have a clue, thought the Judge. *Well, neither did I.*

"That's an axe," explained the Judge.

"I know what it is," Alexander said with a sullen look on his face. "I just don't know what you expect me to do with it."

"We don't expect you to do anything with it." The Judge exchanged a look with the painter. "Here, let me show you how it works." Taking the axe, he set a round of wood on the stump. Swinging the axe, he split the wood neatly in two. Then he split one of the halves.

"This is a good size to burn in your fireplace. To keep you warm at night and to cook your food. That is, if you want to keep warm at night and if you want to cook your food. That part is up to you." The judge handed the axe back.

"What do you mean, warm at night? Isn't this dump heated?" Alexander jerked his head toward the log cabin.

"It doesn't heat itself. It's heated if you cut wood, split wood, split kindling, build a fire, light a fire, and tend it. Again, up to you."

"But, but, I was never in the Boy Scouts. I'll freeze tonight. I don't know how to do any of that stuff! " He shook his head and took a step back.

"Then you'd better learn." Thomas the painter took a step back and pointed at the cabin. "There are instructions in a survival guide book in there. Learn or shiver."

"Remember, your canned food won't be enough calories for your ten weeks in the woods gathering firewood to keep warm. This is the part where you learn where food comes from." The Judge softened his voice a little. "I learned and survived. You will too."

"I'll die before I ever learn this," the young man wailed. He put on his best pitiful face and turned to the Judge. "Won't you stay and help me for a few days?"

"Then you wouldn't learn." The Judge's voice turned brisk again. "Time for us to go."

"If you get desperate, there's one more thing you can do," the painter said.

"What?"

"Pray. Ask for help." The painter smiled.

"Won't *you* stay and help me?" Alexander switched on his pitiful face again at the first sign of compassion. It had worked for him his entire life.

"Nope. If I did that, I wouldn't be helping." The painter's smile vanished. He got behind the wheel of his van. He and the Judge drove away.

Darkness was falling fast. Alexander could hear tree frogs. He shivered and looked around at the forest. Then he looked at the axe in the stump and his face assumed a stubborn pout. *They can all go jump.* He began looking for the parka they said was in the cabin.

* * * * * *

He burned up all the firewood the first night. After shivering through the second night, he began using the axe. By day seven his hands were a mass of blisters, but he had firewood every night. On day eight he found a pair of gloves on the stump next to the axe. A note read: *Thought you could use these. – Thomas.*

He put them on gratefully and began hoeing in the garden he had begun planting. Even with gloves, his hands hurt. He dropped the hoe. *No sense in this. Save the hurt for chopping firewood. I've still got plenty of food.* He was already running a deficit on his canned food budget. He ate three cans a day, even though he had been warned that he only had one can a day to last the 70 days of his *Course in Reality* in the woods.

Well, they won't let me starve. They'll bail me out. Thomas gave me gloves already. He'll give me more stuff when I need it.

* * * * * *

When the canned food ran out on day 22, Alexander woke up with a smile on his face. Like a child at Christmas, he walked out to the stump, expecting to find a gift of food. There was nothing.

This isn't fair! I'm not a farmer. They can't expect me to survive by myself. After all, it takes a village. His stomach growled.

By day 24, he was ravenous. He began practicing with the bow and arrow. He planted the rest of his seeds. *They'll never grow in time*, he thought grimly.

On day 25, he found a leaf on the stump with a note. *Find a picture of this in your survival guide. It will tell you what to do. – Thomas.*

The plant had an edible root, according to the survival guide. He took the leaf with him when he went for firewood that morning. He looked carefully at the forest floor. *Aha!* He spotted one and used the axe to help dig out the roots. He was down on all fours, digging with his hands. The morning dew wet his pants legs and coat sleeves. He bit into a root immediately, even though the guide said they tasted better boiled. It was faintly bitter. He ate it all. He began digging for another.

Judge Block was watching him through binoculars. Suddenly, an image flashed into his mind. Someone down on all fours, getting wet with the dew. He lowered the binoculars and thought. *I read about this last night in the Bible. The fourth book of Daniel.* "… and they shall make thee to eat grass as oxen, and they shall wet thee with the dew of heaven, …" *Well, there he is, rich kid, grubbing for roots on all fours and wet with the dew. He does not know that God is God.*

Judge Block handed the binoculars to Thomas the painter. As he watched Alexander, Thomas thought, *he's down on all fours, digging like a badger. Are we being too hard on him? He waited too long to plant his vegetables. They'll never ripen in time. Maybe I should give him more cans of food?*

Standing up, Alexander put another root in his pocket. Then, grunting, he shouldered the axe and began his daily search for firewood. That afternoon he continued hoeing and watering the garden.

Thomas passed the binoculars back to Judge Block. The judge smiled with satisfaction and thought, *the boy has guts. Took him longer, but he's learning. Might even become salvageable talent. Dear Lord, bless this boy and prepare him for what's to come. You were right, Bob Dylan. There's a hard rain a'gonna fall. But not the one you were forecasting.*

Part Two.
The Collapse

"Half the harm that is done in this world
is due to people who want to feel important."
T. S. Eliot, *The Cocktail Party*

"It is as if it were necessary, before a reign of justice appears,
for everyone to suffer a cruel retribution
– some for their evilness, and some for their lack of understanding."

Bastiat, *The Law*

"There are only two kinds of people in the end:
those who say to God, 'Thy will be done,'
and those to whom God says, in the end, 'Thy will be done.'
All that are in Hell, choose it."

— C.S. Lewis, *The Great Divorce*

I heard the sound of a thunder, it roared out a warnin'
I heard the roar of a wave that could drown the whole world ...
And it's a hard rain, rain's a-gonna fall.

Bob Dylan. *A hard rain's a'gonna fall*

Chapter Eighteen

N PLUS 60. THERE WERE CRITICAL SHORTAGES OF HARVESTING contractors and crews and equipment in the Midwest. The next year would be a hungry year. Thirty-five percent of scheduled airline flights were cancelled due to the shutdown of a number of aircraft maintenance companies. Too many skilled harvesting contractors and aircraft mechanics had "gone ARK."

*　*　*　*　*　*

N plus 90. Sixty percent of American towns were experiencing periodic brownouts and outages due to interruptions in fuel deliveries to power plants. Families couldn't keep food in their refrigerators for very long. Fuel train engineers and dispatchers were "going Ark." Food processing and canning plants were producing less due to maintenance technicians disappearing. Plus, there was less food from the harvests.

The United States of America was about to face something it had never faced in its entire history: a food shortage. The complex supply chains now had many missing links. The missing links were people with know-how.

Government thugs had broken the fingers of the invisible hand of capitalism. The visible steel fist of government central planning was smashing the invisible hand of decentralized free markets that had worked so well.

Government apparachniks were busily forcing the same kinds of government controls that were perfectly designed to produce the famines and mass starvation in Soviet Russia in the 1920s. Ironically, the USA "breadbasket to the world" that had fed hungry Russians in the 1950s and 60s was now adopting the same economic and political system that had produced those grain shortages in Russia.

Rumors flew thick about secret ARK locations within the United States.

*   *   *   *   *   *

The thin Shoshone teenager walked past green fields of soybeans. As he approached a farmhouse he slowed and looked in all directions. He held his hands up in front of him so that an observer could see that he held no weapons. He stopped in front of the porch.

"Hello, the house?" he called out. "My name is Joseph Wakini. I'm looking for work. I heard that the Young family is looking for a farmhand." He waited.

He heard a scraping noise and noticed two holes opening in the metal door. A gun barrel protruded from the lower hole. A voice came from the upper hole.

"Bend down and pick up that rock with both hands. Don't drop it until I say so, or you'll get shot."

Joseph squatted and grasped a rock as big as a loaf of bread with both hands. It was heavy enough to require both hands to lift it. He slowly rose up with the rock. He heard deadbolts clicking open. The door cracked open and a rifle barrel poked out. Then a man cautiously emerged behind the rifle. He scanned his surroundings 180 degrees, then looked Joseph up and down.

"Where did you hear about the work?"

"Frederick Blackhawk at the trading post told me. Said you needed help with the harvest and your cattle."

"OK. Just stand there with the rock until I check. Sarah! Call Frederick Blackhawk and verify that he sent this young man. What did you say your name was?"

"Joseph Wakini."

"Sarah? You get that?"

A softer voice answered "I got it. Wait a minute."

Joseph shifted his weight from one foot to the other. His long black hair was pulled back from his lean reddish-brown face and secured with a leather thong on the nape of his neck.

"John, Frederick says he's OK."

The man lowered the rifle barrel and took his finger off the trigger. "OK, you can drop the rock. Sorry, but with the marauders around we have to be careful about strangers."

Joseph dropped the rock. "I understand. I want work. I worked on my grandfather's place until he died. I was too young to work the farm by myself, so I hired myself out. That was two years ago. Work is hard come by these days."

"My name is John Young." A woman in a gingham farm dress stepped out of the house. She had a holster belted around the dress. She kept her right hand on the butt of the pistol. "This is my wife Sarah. Come up here and have a seat."

Joseph sat on an old weathered ladder-back chair at a wooden table on the porch. Sarah looked at his work boots. They were worn and scuffed. Her eyes appraised him like she was sizing up a young steer at the sale barn. "You hungry?"

"Yes ma'am. Nearly always hungry."

"You can get rations from the WIC office in town, you know."

He snorted. "The compassion-pushers? No thanks. You see how their holier-than-thou compassion has destroyed my people. Now we are mostly drunks, lay-abouts, and drug addicts. Those government people who," – here he made air-quotes – "only want to help," he wrinkled his nose in disgust, "helped my people learn to be helpless and good for nothing."

"I have some oatmeal left over from breakfast." Sarah went back into the house, leaving the door open.

John leaned his rifle against the house and met Joseph's eyes. "You're pretty wise for someone so young."

Joseph did not look away. "My grandfather taught me to earn my own way. He wouldn't take any of the hand-outs offered by the government. He farmed his own land and made a living from his crops. He home-schooled me and I learned farming from him."

Sarah returned with a bowl of oatmeal and a glass of milk. "Go ahead," she said. "We already ate."

He bowed his head and clasped his hands. "Lord, I thank you for your blessings and this meal provided by these good people. Amen." He picked up the spoon and began to eat.

Sarah said, "Are you a Christian?"

Joseph nodded. "My grandfather took me to Mass every Sunday at St. Stephens Catholic Mission Church."

Sarah spoke slowly, "We are Mormon, but we respect all people of faith, Christian, Jewish, or otherwise. I heard what you said about how your grandfather raised you. Sounds like a good man."

Joseph drank down the last of the milk. "He was a good man. Stubborn and independent. Our surname, Wakini, is the name of a black bear in a Shoshone story. In the story a grey grizzly bear, Wakinu, rudely stuck his paw in where the black bear Wakini was feeding on an ant hill. There was a great fight, and Wakini overpowered the strong grey grizzly Wakinu. Wakini was in the right, for no animal may ever touch another's prey. Wakini had found and worked for his own food. Wakinu tried to take what belonged to another."

He paused and wiped off a milk moustache with his shirt sleeve. "Too many Wakinus around nowadays. I'm proud of my family name Wakini. We earn our own way."

John looked at Sarah, who nodded. John said, "You're hired. You can sleep in the bunkhouse and eat with us. Supper is at six, breakfast at five. You know anything about tractor repair?"

Joseph stood and rolled up his sleeves. "Since I was nine. Lead the way."

*   *   *   *   *   *

Three weeks later Joseph was working on another tractor. This one had broken down in the middle of John Young's wheat field. Squatting beside one of the front wheels, he was brushing off mud and matted grass in order to see better. He suspected that the old axle bearings needed to be repacked with axle grease. Sweat trickled down his forehead as he worked.

He heard a whistle and an answering bark from somewhere behind him. Slowly standing up, he shaded his eyes from the strong glare and looked at the edge of the field. Three head of cattle came through the open gate, herded by a mongrel cattle dog. Someone in a straw cowboy hat was leaning down from the saddle to close the gate behind.

Joseph walked to the other side of the tractor and pulled a Remington 22 rifle from a scabbard attached to the tractor frame. He chambered a round, then cradled it casually across his body. The tractor was between him and the approaching horseman. The rider's straw brim was pulled low, making it difficult to see a face.

When the rider was 150 feet away, Joseph frowned and called out "That's close enough, stranger. This is John and Sarah Young's land, and I work for them. Who might you be, and why are your cattle on their land?"

The rider pulled up and studied him for a moment. Joseph saw the straw hat turn left, revealing a sunburned cheek. A new whistle sounded toward the dog. Immediately the dog ran in front of the cattle and froze them with one bark. Then the dog sat, panting, and looked back at the rider, as if to say, "What next?"

"I'm Cathy Peterson." Joseph was surprised to hear a clear strong female contralto. "Sarah Young bought these cattle from my dad, Paul Peterson. Our place is northwest of here. I'm delivering them."

Joseph's frown softened a little, then tightened again. "Hold there while I check." He reached into a pocket for a walkie-talkie. "Mrs. Young? Joseph here, in the north wheat field." He cocked his head to listen, but kept his eyes on the rider.

"Sarah here. What's up, Joseph?"

"Got a Ms. Cathy Peterson here with three head of cattle. Claims you bought them from her Dad. Please confirm."

"That's right. Does her hat have a red bandana for a band? Riding a pinto pony?"

"Yes and yes."

"That's her. Let her come up and talk to me."

He held up the walkie-talkie unit, waved it back and forth, and called, "Mrs. Young says come talk to her."

The rider nodded and trotted up to the tractor. Dismounting, she looped her reins around the tractor's hitch. Pushing her hat back on her head with one gloved hand, she stuck out the other and said, "Pleased to meet you. You must be Joseph Wakini."

Blond bangs dropped from under the straw hat and framed a rosy freckled face adorned by red lips and the whitest teeth he had ever seen. The rest of her hair fell to her shoulders. Blushing, he just stood there, holding the walkie-talkie in his left hand and the rifle in his right.

She just smiled at him, holding her gloved hand out. Suddenly, the walkie-talkie crackled. "I bet that boy is just gawking. Cathy, you're the prettiest thing he's seen in three weeks, except for our newborn calf."

Joseph looked down, embarrassed. "Put down the rifle and shake her hand, Joseph," crackled the voice on the walkie-talkie. With a start, he put down the rifle and reached out to shake the proffered hand.

"Finally! Thought I'd be here till next spring!" Cathy's eyes were twinkling.

"I'm … I'm Joseph Wakini," he stammered.

"I knew it! The only boy my age within 20 miles, and too shy to say much! Just my luck, I guess." Her cornflower blue eyes crinkled in mischief. Holding out her hand, she added, "May I speak to Mrs. Young?"

Jerking his head up again, he said "Oh! Right! Here." He handed the walkie-talkie unit to her.

"Hello Mrs. Young, Cathy here. Where do you want me to pasture these steers?"

"Hi Cathy. You can put them in the corral next to the barn for now. We'll be wanting to brand them before we put them out to pasture. The local rustlers just snip off the ear tags nowadays, so that's no good anymore."

"Yes Ma'am. Barn corral. Got it."

"Cathy? One more thing."

"Ma'am?"

"Bring Joseph in with you. Otherwise, he'll stand there stunned and we'll have to send Kemosabe to herd him in like a lost steer. Let me talk to him."

Grinning, she handed the unit to Joseph, who was blushing again. "Ma'am?"

"Joseph, it's nearly lunch time and you'll probably need some parts to get that old tractor running anyway. Ride in with Cathy. I'll have lunch on the table and you can call in to the trading post for the parts you need."

"Yes Ma'am." He looked up to see that Cathy had already remounted. Still grinning, she reached out a gloved hand for him and took her boot out of one stirrup.

"Wait." He unbuckled the rifle scabbard, put the rifle in it, and slung it over his shoulder. Then he pulled himself up and sat behind her.

"Hold on to my waist," she said, then kicked her pinto into a trot.

You don't have to ask me twice, he thought. He could smell her hair. Lavender.

"Who's Kemosabe?" he asked.

"The dog."

"Oh."

Herded in by the dog? Oh! Now I get it. He blushed again, glad the girl couldn't see his face tucked behind her corn-shuck yellow hair.

Chapter Nineteen

In the bright farmhouse kitchen, sunlight fell on the table where Sarah Young had hot ham and cheese sandwiches and cold water waiting for them. After Cathy and Joseph sat down, Sarah reached for Joseph's hand. They all bowed their heads.

"Dear Father," Sarah spoke. "We thank You for our daily bread and Your many blessings. Bless this boy and girl and keep them safe. Bless John and bring him home safely to me. Amen."

They all took big bites of the sandwiches. "Umm, Mrs. Young, you sure do make a good thick sandwich," beamed Cathy.

"Yep," nodded Joseph.

"Doesn't say much, does he?" Cathy remarked. Joseph blushed again. He couldn't think of anything to say back. Desperate, he took another big bite of his sandwich. Nobody expected you to speak with your mouth full.

"Well, Cathy, you know what they say," remarked Mrs. Young. Cathy looked up at her. "What?"

"Still waters run deep." Mrs. Young winked at Cathy and took another bite herself.

Women! Thought Joseph. *Always got to have the first and the last word. She is pretty, though.* He sneaked a quick glance at Cathy. She was looking right at him. He quickly looked down again.

*   *   *   *   *   *

As the spring wore into summer, Cathy found excuses to ride over at least once a week to "see how them steers are getting on." She would bring cookies or brownies she had baked. She always rode by the field where she knew Joseph was working.

For his part, Joseph managed to find a reason to drive to the trading post for parts and supplies once a week himself. He always stopped by the Peterson place to inquire "if they needed anything from town." Somehow they always did, and nothing would do but that Cathy had to ride to town with him "to be sure to get the right brand of the stuff mother wants."

Her mother June always smiled when Cathy said this. "That's right. Cathy knows exactly what I want." Then she would wink at her husband Paul, who winked back.

As the two young people were driving away, Paul would take June's hand and squeeze it. "Young love, mother. Young love."

June smiled. "Sarah Young says Joseph's a hard worker and honest as the day is long. Cathy may have struck it lucky meeting this young man." June thought, *Dear Lord, bless this young couple. Give my Cathy a good person to fall in love with. Amen.*

* * * * * *

On one of these trips to the trading post, Cathy had a list of medical supplies to buy.

Frederick Blackhawk placed the items in a basket Cathy had brought. It had been years since paper or plastic shopping bags were available.

After the first five items, Frederick Blackhawk shook his head. "I can't help you with these last three items, Cathy. The companies that made these medicines have gone out of business. Maybe some of the scientists and chemists that made them are in some of the other ARK locations. Your dad may be able to send out word on the underground grapevine, but communication is slow and spotty."

"Thanks Mr. Blackhawk." Cathy lifted the basket and walked back to the truck. Her usually smiling face was sad. She sat close to the passenger side window and stared into the distance.

"Cathy?" Joseph's voice was quiet and tentative.

She looked back at him. Still no smile.

"Cathy, what is it? You look sad and serious. What's going on?"

"Oh Joseph, it's my grandmother." Suddenly sobs wracked her body in wave after wave of anguish. She covered her eyes with one hand.

"Oh Cathy! Cathy." He stopped the truck and slid over to her. She put her head on his shoulder. He wrapped his arms around her and held on, his nose buried in her fragrant hair. He rocked a little, as if they were in a rocking chair.

"Oh Joseph, grandma has bone cancer! There is no medicine to treat it anymore."

"Cathy, I'm so sorry. I knew she wasn't feeling well, but nobody ever said anything about cancer." He held her tighter.

After more sobs, she sat up, sniffling. He let go and sat back.

Gently he asked, "How long has this been going on?"

"Years. Several years before the announcement of The Noah Option and folks forming up into ARK communities. We still lived on our ranch in Oregon. They, they ..." She closed her eyes again as fresh tears rolled down.

"They?"

"Those government creeps! Excuse my French, but they are slimy pond scum!"

"What happened?"

"I'll tell you, but start the truck. We better be getting back with what I have."

Joseph slid back behind the wheel and started the truck. He put it in gear and drove.

"When grandma was first diagnosed with bone cancer, she was sent to a specialist. They wouldn't give her chemotherapy or anything for the pain. They made her suffer. They made her suffer on purpose!"

"Why?"

"In those years, in the final stages of that Obamacare, all private health insurance companies had shut down. All doctors, nurses and hospital people had to work for the government. Everyone's medical treatment had to be approved by a 'navigator' working for the government."

Joseph's grandfather had died quickly from a heart attack, so he had no experience with long illnesses. He was puzzled.

Cathy continued. "The navigator found out that grandma had been active with one of those 'Tea Parties' years before. She told grandma that the government was kind to its friends, but turned its back on its enemies. She said that because of her past work with a Tea Party, grandma could not have chemotherapy."

"What!?" Joseph could not believe what he was hearing.

"She might have beat the cancer if she had gotten chemotherapy early on. They wouldn't give it to her." Another tear rolled down Cathy's face.

"Grandma begged the navigator to at least let her have some medicine for the pain. The navigator would not approve the doctor's prescription for medicine to kill the pain. When Grandma asked why, the woman told her, 'You people have a saying: Live with your answers. Time for you to live with yours.'"

"I can't believe someone would be so cruel!" Joseph shook his head.

"Joseph, there is such a thing as evil, and it is loose in this land. Believe it. When that happened, that's when Dad and Mom decided to find an ARK to live in."

"So this place is an ARK?" He looked puzzled.

"Well, yeah! Why do you think so many white and black families are living on Tribal Lands? They made a deal with your Tribal Elders to lease land here."

"Oh. I never asked. Thought that if the Elders wanted me to know why, they'd tell me. I was brought up to mind my own business."

"That's a good attitude to have. I wish more people felt that way."

Joseph's mouth set into a frown. "How do you deal with your Grandmother's pain now?"

"You'll have to ask Mom and Dad. That's family business, and you aren't family."

She lowered her head a little and looked at him from under her eyebrows. "Yet."

He wanted to smile but kept a straight face. Wouldn't be right, what with Cathy's grandma and all.

When they pulled up at the Peterson farmhouse, Joseph helped carry in the groceries and supplies. Cathy went into her grandmother's bedroom and shut the door. After five minutes, Cathy's mother came out. Her eyes were red.

"Mrs. Peterson, Cathy told me about her grandmother. I'm real sorry." Joseph held his hat in his hand and spoke softly.

"Joseph, would you like to see her? Sometimes a new face cheers her up. I'll warn you though, so you won't be shocked. She's down to about 85 pounds, like a 12 year old."

"Yes ma'am. I'll see her if it's OK." He followed Mrs. Peterson into the dimly lit bedroom. A small frail body lay under the sheets. Her head was propped up on pillows, her thin grey hair plastered to her head by pain-sweat. Cathy sat beside the bed, spreading a wet washcloth across her grandmother's forehead.

"Cathy, is that your young man?" Grandmother's voice was weak and squeaky.

Cathy smiled at her. "Well, Grandma, he's a young man, but I don't rightly know if he's mine or not."

"What's your name, young man?"

"Joseph Wakini, ma'am."

"That's a Shoshone name. A strong name, if I remember my Shoshone stories rightly."

"Yes ma'am. Wakini the black bear defended what was his against the grizzly Wakinu. Wakini the black bear won the fight. Wakini was strong."

"Do you have all your teeth?"

Joseph was startled by this question. "Why … yes." He blushed.

"Cathy, he's young, strong, and has all his teeth. Better stake out your brand before some other young filly canters by. Besides, he's good looking."

"Grandma!" Now Cathy blushed.

"I may be weak and sick, but my eyes work just fine, thank you very much!" She winked at Cathy. "You better pay attention to what I'm telling you. Some of it might be true!" Turning her head, she inhaled sharply and cried out.

Mrs. Peterson stepped up to the bed and poured a tablespoon of some homemade pain remedy from a corked bottle. "Take this, mother." She put the spoon to the old lady's lips. With an effort, she swallowed it.

CHAPTER TWENTY

Assistant Deputy Undersecretary for FDA Nutrition Enforcement Cal Reeves walked into the grocery store on his way home from work. There were no shopping carts. The check-out lines were jammed with people pushing shopping carts stacked high with groceries. He was shocked to see the shelves bare of everything except pet food, magazines, and plastic children's toys.

He walked the aisles in a daze, looking helplessly at empty shelves stretching as far as the eye could see. Finally, he grabbed a thirty pound bag of dog food and waddled to a check-out aisle.

When he got home, his wife met him at the door, looking scared. "Cal, I only have enough food in the pantry to get us through the weekend. What will we do?" His children looked eagerly at the bag he was carrying. Their faces fell when they saw the picture of the dog.

"Daddy, we're out of my favorite cereal, Sugar Crunchies. When can you get more for me?" His six-year-old daughter Angela looked at him with her practiced "puppy-dog" eyes from under her brown bangs. His heart sank.

*   *   *   *   *   *

By Thursday of the next week, they were eating the dry dog food. He swallowed his pride and called some of the food companies that he regulated.

"Fred? Cal Reeves here with the FDA Nutrition Enforcement Agency. Listen, there is no food at any grocery store in a thirty mile radius of my home. My family was caught short. Can you spare me anything from your warehouse? I'll take anything you've got."

"Sorry Cal. When the IRS rationed food and gasoline, they forgot that grocery distribution center trucks use more fuel than private citizens. We got the same rationed amount as any citizen. My delivery trucks used up their fuel allotment in the first week of the month. Since last Friday, nothing has come in and nothing has gone out. I let my employees take home whatever food they could carry on Tuesday. A hundred or more looters broke in on Wednesday and pistol-whipped me. They cleaned us out. There's not even a can of cat food or a bag of bird seed in the place. I can't help you."

Hanging up, Cal looked bleakly at his wife. "Nothing. Looters cleaned him out."

"Cal, you're the Assistant Deputy Undersecretary for FDA Nutrition Enforcement. Surely you have clout somewhere?" Her face hardened into her patented frown of disapproval.

He remembered that their neighbor had a garden behind a high wooden fence. He went to the back yard. Seeing no one, he brought out a step stool and climbed over the chain link fence into the neighbor's back yard. He froze when he heard barking. A Doberman Pincer ran around the corner of the house and bit his shin. The dog didn't let go. He yelled in pain.

His neighbor, a small grey-haired woman in a gingham dress, white socks and tennis shoes opened the back door and peered out behind the security chain. A shotgun barrel slid out under the chain. Seeing him, she came out and down the steps, pointing the shotgun at him. She approached him.

"Mabel! Call off your dog for the love of God."

"Cruncher! Back." The dog released him and sat by her side. The dog kept looking at him. She kept the shotgun trained on his chest. "Don't recall you ever saying anything about the love of God before. Told me just last month I was a fool for donating to a church charity when the government did it so much better."

"Mabel, I have children. We don't have any more food. I just wanted something from your garden." He winced from the pain in his leg.

"You could have asked."

"I … I never thought of that."

"You and your other government cronies stopped thinking about *asking* about twenty five years ago. You just started *taking*. I guess you never got in the habit of asking, when you discovered you could just *take* from other folks."

"Mabel, I'm sorry. We're just so *hungry*."

"So are a lot of other folks, thanks to your government foolishness. Well, time to start living with your answers. Eat regulations. That's what you make, isn't it? Regulations? While you were busy making regulations, I was busy planting tomatoes and raising Dobermans."

She shoved the barrel of the shotgun at him. "Now git!"

He climbed back over the fence without another word.

Back in the house, he dialed 911. "I want to report a neighbor threatening me with a gun."

"Sir, I'm the last dispatcher still on duty. All of the policemen and firemen are home defending their own families and children. Looters are breaking in and setting fires everywhere. I've got one ambulance driver left and two nurses at the emergency room. I'm only taking calls for life-threatening wounds."

"But I'm Cal P. Reeves, Assistant Deputy Undersecretary for the FDA Nutrition Enforcement Agency. I have Federal Priority over ordinary citizens. I demand that you send a police car over to deal with this crazy neighbor with a shotgun!"

"Mister, there are no police cars to send. I have another call to take." *Click.*

Next he dialed the FDA Nutrition Enforcement SWAT Team where he worked. They had heavy weapons and body armor. They would be more than a match for Mabel's shotgun.

"*Beep.* All of our FDA Nutrition Enforcement SWAT Team members are on a raid to protect unsuspecting citizens from illegal, unsafe, unauthorized, un-inspected and un-regulated goat's milk. Please leave a message and we will assist you in making the nation's food authorized, safe, controlled and regulated."

"But there is no food to regulate," he shouted into the phone. Suddenly it hit him.

He sank to the floor, his eyes wide in horror. *We regulated the food away.* He curled into a fetal position on the floor and unconsciously put his fist to his open mouth.

* * * * * *

Ten days later his children had distended bellies from lack of protein. Cal thought, *they looked like the photos of starving children in Somalia. But this is America, land of plenty! Where is the plenty?*

His daughter looked at him with sunken eyes. His son, nine years old, had every one of his ribs visible. Cal was so weak he could hardly move. His wife stayed in the bed, her breathing shallow.

"Children, listen to me. Go next door and knock on Mrs. Fulle's door. Ask her for something to eat for yourselves. Say *please.* Go now."

The children went and knocked as they were told. They heard furious barking and backed up a step. The door opened on the chain and Mabel Fulle looked at them from behind her shotgun. She lowered it.

"Mrs. Fulle, we are so hungry. May we please have something to eat?"

"Well now, since you *ask* so politely, yes you may. Come in." Mrs. Fulle prepared some oatmeal for the children and warned them to eat it slowly. She added water to dehydrated milk and served it to them.

"How are your mother and father?"

The boy Cal Jr. moved his lips. "They're barely able to move. I'm scared."

"Well, let's take them some oatmeal. I'll go with you."

Carefully locking the door behind her, she looked both ways, cradling her shotgun. The door of the Reeves house was unlocked. The children took her to their mother first. Mrs. Fulle cradled her head and spoon-fed the oatmeal to her. The mother fell asleep.

Mrs. Fulle found Cal Reeves in his recliner chair, semi-conscious. She kneeled beside him and began spoon feeding oatmeal to him. When she was finished, she brought a damp washcloth and wiped his face with it. He roused and looked at her.

"So? You remembered who I am? Good. I'll see that you are pardoned for that unauthorized firearm. Bring me more food. Now!" His eyes flashed with his old bravado.

She stood. "Still think you can bend reality to your wishes with arrogance and a command, eh? Tell you what. I'll allow you to re-take your *Course in Reality*."

She looked out of their back window. "You'll feel stronger in the morning. If I see you and your wife spading up your backyard by 9 a.m. tomorrow, I'll bring over some seeds for you to plant. If not, then I won't. Your choice."

"You can't talk to me that way! I'm the Assistant Deputy Undersecretary for FDA Nutrition Enforcement. I don't 'spade' anything. I hire gardeners. I regulate gardeners."

"Then regulate yourself some food. I'll be watching. 9 a.m. Bye." She picked up her shotgun and marched out.

*   *   *   *   *   *

At 9 a.m. the following morning, Cal Reeves hobbled out to his back yard, leaning on his wife. Then he stood with his arms crossed. He looked defiantly at Mrs. Fulle's windows. His wife took a step toward the tool shed they kept for their Mexican gardener.

"No! I forbid it," He glared at her. She stopped.

The children came out of the house and went to the shed. "Children, stop!"

Cal Jr. kept going. His sister looked back at her father, and then followed her brother. They both emerged with hoes and went to the fenced plot. They began feebly chopping at the ground with the hoes.

Mrs. Fulle emerged from her back door with her Doberman and her shotgun. She went to the fence between their yards and called to the children. She took seed packets from her apron and gave one to each child. Then she told them how to plant the seeds. They went to the plot and began planting.

"No! I tell you I forbid this! You are the children of a Federal employee. We regulate, we do not do manual labor. That is for the ordinary people like Mrs. Fulle!"

He was too weak to go after the children. Red-faced, he hobbled back into his house.

They kept planting. Afterwards, they knocked on Mrs. Fulle's door and asked for food. *Please.* She fed them. This repeated day after day.

* * * * * *

Six days later the children told Mrs. Fulle, "Mom and Dad are dead. Can we live with you?"

"Oh my dears. I am so sorry. Of course you can live with me. But you must help with the chores and working in the garden beside me."

"We will." They both were expressionless. She hugged them and fed them. After dark, she took the dog for protection and went next door. She dragged the bodies to the far side of the yard and buried them in shallow graves. The next day she took the children to the graves and led them in a prayer service for their parents.

"What's prayer?" asked Angela.

"It's talking to God, our heavenly Father," said Mrs. Fulle.

"Who's God?" asked Cal Jr.

"I'll introduce you to Him tonight. He left some messages for us in a book called the Bible. I'll read you one of his messages tonight."

* * * * * *

The next day, a van pulled up in front of Mrs. Fulle's house. It had the logo of a painting company on the side. The Doberman began barking inside the house. Isaiah Mercury sat in the passenger seat. He dialed a number. It rang inside the house.

"Hello. This is Mabel Fulle."

Isaiah said, "A nation of laws,"

Mabel replied, "And not of men."

"Thomas and I are outside in the van. May we come in?"

"Give me a minute to put Cruncher in the back room. It takes him a while to get used to strangers."

Five minutes later Isaiah and Thomas sat drinking coffee with Mabel Fulle at her kitchen table. She had sent the children out to work in the garden, with the dog for protection.

"Mabel," said Isaiah, "We got your message about taking in these two children. We agree that you and Cruncher alone are not enough to guarantee their safety. For most individual looters and burglars, a dog is more than enough, but they are forming armed gangs now. Eleven families near here have been shot for their food. Even the children."

"Isaiah, I'm not sure what you can do, but I thought I'd at least ask for any help and ideas you can give me." Mabel looked worried.

"Mabel, Thomas and I think it is time for you and the children to relocate to an ARK community for safety. We are too few to be able to protect so many of our sympathizers spread out over such a wide area."

Mrs. Fulle glanced out her back window at the open gate to her garden. The dog sat at the gate, and she could see the children hoeing.

"I hate to give up my garden. I've worked so hard on it."

Isaiah smiled. "I know. Tell you what. I'll stake you to a starter set of Carver's Legacy super seeds. Your new garden at your ARK will yield quickly. I happen to have an inside source for the seeds."

Mabel laughed. "That's right, your wife is Dr. Grace Washington, inventor of the seeds. It must be right handy to have a Nobel Prize winning botanist in the family. Won back when Nobel Prizes meant something. OK, it's a deal. When can we move?"

"You can only take what we can fit in the van," said Thomas. "How soon can you be packed up?"

"Two hours." She walked to the back door and called out, "Children! Pick whatever is ripe and put it into the basket. Remember how I showed you? Bring up what you've picked in 20 minutes."

She turned back to Thomas and Isaiah. "I better get Cruncher used to the two of you. I'm not leaving without him."

Thomas looked at Isaiah. "I figured. Now you know why I put those dog biscuits in your jacket pocket before we left. When Cruncher's hungry, he'll start with you!"

Isaiah laughed. "Not to worry. With a big dog like Cruncher, I'll just be the appetizer. You'll be the main course!"

Chapter Twenty-One

A HOMELAND SECURITY DRONE FLYING OVER A WESTERN STATE detected green fields surrounded by dry devastation. *What is this?* thought the Homeland Security drone operator. Most of the western farms and ranches were dry husks, he knew. Even the farms collectivized as "American Prosperity Camps" by the Department of Labor were mostly dry dustbowls.

He tapped out a command for greater magnification from the drone telephoto lenses. He saw healthy cattle, horses, and pigs. He saw farm workers on tractors harvesting farm fields. *This can't be a collectivized farm,* he realized. *Collectivized farms don't use tractors. They use teams of horses or oxen.*

Under the motto 'Everybody is entitled to a job,' no mechanized equipment was allowed on the state-run farms/labor camps. All picking, harvesting and processing of crops was done by hand. Interned citizens worked twelve hours a day. Thirty year old women and men looked sixty after two years in the camps.

Checking his map coordinates, he saw that the location spotted by the drone was in the middle of an Indian Reservation. He picked up his phone and dialed his supervisor.

"Ma'am? We have detected an unauthorized agricultural endeavor." He paused, listening. "Understood. But there is a potential problem. It's located within a Shoshone Indian Reservation. Yes. A sovereign nation."

*　*　*　*　*　*

Two military Humvees in camo paint pulled up to the newly gated entry to the Wind River Shoshone Reservation. Low dry hills surrounded the area. A Homeland Security Agent in tactical garb got out of the passenger side of the lead vehicle and swaggered up to the guard shack.

A uniformed police officer of the Shoshone Tribal Police greeted him with a polite smile. He was tall. His long black hair was braided and hung over the collar of his shirt. "Hello. You are on the sovereign soil of the Shoshone Nation. Please identify yourself."

The agent smirked and barked, "Cut the crap. You know who we are. Homeland Security. There was never a gate here before. Who authorized this gate? This has to come down."

The Shoshone police officer continued his serene smile. "Sir, you are on the sovereign soil of the Shoshone Nation. Please identify yourself and state your business."

"We don't have to identify ourselves! Our uniforms and vehicle icons speak for themselves. Now answer my question! Who authorized this gate house across a public highway?" He moved his hand to the butt of his pistol.

Suddenly a hand covered his weapon hand, holding it down against the holster. A split second later a head butt shattered his nose and blood spurted out. "Aagh!" he yelled, clutching at his nose. His weapon hand was grasped and twisted to hyper-extend the arm. Simultaneously the tall Shoshone ducked under the arm, then straightened up and jerked the arm down. "Aagh!" the agent yelled again as his arm snapped in two over the shoulder of the policeman.

Agents spilled out of the Humvees, crouching behind the opened doors with their pistols raised and aimed at the guard house. Shoving the moaning agent out the door, the Shoshone policeman crouched behind his metal desk and keyed a microphone for the public address system on top of the guard house.

"Attention federal agents! You are on the sovereign soil of the Shoshone Nation, where you have no jurisdiction. A video feed is capturing this scene and it is now being shown live on C-Span, FACTS News, ZNN, dot-ARK and the United Nations International Human Rights Television Channel. The Director of the US Civil Rights

Enforcement Division of the Department of Justice has already issued a ruling that uninvited intrusion on Tribal Lands is a violation of our civil rights. We are streaming this feed directly to him. In addition, the United Native-American Nations of the US have petitioned the UN for protected status as independent nations under the UN Charter. Pending a vote of the UN General Assembly, all Indian Reservations in the US are under the protection of UN Peacekeeping forces."

One of the Agents had pips on her collar. She spoke into a bullhorn. "Shoshone officer! This is Deputy Director Maudire VanJones. This is B.S. and you know it! Homeland Security has the higher jurisdiction here. Stand down! We outnumber you. You can't hold all of us off."

The Shoshone officer replied on his P.A. speaker. "Federal agents! Train your binoculars to the north. A full platoon of the Shoshone Self-Defense Forces is deployed along that ridge. They are armed."

She looked through her binoculars. Troops lined the ridge. Several rifles were aimed at them. *Blast*, she thought in panic. *We are outnumbered.*

The policeman spoke again. "This is bullet-proof glass, but I ask you to hold your fire. We have a UN representative here who will show himself. This is Russian Brigadier Major Atka Naqui of the UN Peace Keeping Mission to the Native American Nations of the U.S."

A squat man in a Russian Army uniform and the Blue Helmet of the UN peace-keeping forces stepped into view from the back of the guard shack. The Shoshone policeman handed him the microphone.

In a thick Russian accent, he rasped, "I am Brigadier Major Atka Naqui, of the Russian Army, now detailed to the UN Peace Keeping Mission to the Native American Nations of the U.S. This nation is under UN protection. Any incursions by U.S. forces may result in additional reinforcements from the UN. My ethnicity is Siberian Yupiks, from the coast of the Chukchi Peninsula, which gives me further protected status under your laws as a person of aboriginal origin."

A cell phone began ringing in the lead HumVee. The blue helmeted Major spoke again. "That call is from your Justice Department. Pick it up. I will wait."

Red faced, the Deputy Director stomped back to the vehicle and jerked her cell phone from its cradle.

"Deputy Director VanJones? This is the Director of the Civil

Rights Enforcement Division of the Justice Department, authorization code *Marx1848*. We have just received calls from three senators, five congressmen, the UN Human Rights Commissioner, and the Bureau of Indian Affairs alleging a violation of the protected class status of Native Americans. I don't have to tell you how that will play with our progressive allies. Stand down. You will undergo an administrative disciplinary hearing for your infringement of the rights of a protected class of minority citizens. Return to your base at once. That is an order. This conversation has been recorded and will be used against you. Do you understand? Respond!"

Looking down and turning away from the agents she commanded, she stuttered, "But sir, I was ordered here by my superior in the Department of Homeland Security! I was only following orders!"

"Deputy Director VanJones, you and your agents are ordered to stand down! Do you acknowledge? Respond!"

"I understand. I acknowledge. I will stand down and return to base." She touched the call closed. Instantly the phone rang again.

"Deputy Director VanJones?"

"Yes? This is VanJones."

"This is Deputy Director Prochinski of the State Department. Office of UN liaison relating to Newly Independent Nations. VanJones, the Shoshone Indian Nation has appealed to the UN for emergency diplomatic recognition and protection as a sovereign nation. Since their original treaty with the U.S. Government called them and the 566 other Indian Nations on Reservations 'sovereign,' we have to defer to the authority and jurisdiction of the UN on this one."

"What?" she shouted into the phone. "Has everyone gone mad? This is an Indian Reservation in the middle of the United States of America! Crimes on reservations are investigated by the FBI, for pity's sake! The Feds have always had jurisdiction, and WE ARE THE FEDS!"

"Deputy Director VanJones, you are hereby ordered to stand down. Any further action by you may constitute a war crime, punishable by an international tribunal composed of judges from Iran, Yemen, and the Chechen Republic. My authority trumps the chain of command within Homeland Security. Charges of insubordination to a superior officer will be added to the charges against you if you do not comply."

Holy international bureaucracy, she thought. She gritted her teeth and turned back toward her agents. "Agents! Stand down. Holster your weapons. We are ordered back to base."

She got back into the lead HumVee. The PA from the guard shack crackled again. "Your point man needs medical attention. Please retrieve him."

Two agents cautiously advanced. They lifted the fallen agent, who howled in pain. Between them they helped him back to the lead HumVee. Both vehicles left.

In the guard shack, two more people stepped out from the back. One was Sarah Young. The other was Chief Quishindemi of the Shoshone Tribal Council.

The brown wrinkled face of the Shoshone leader radiated dignity. "I thank you, my brother Atka Naqui from across the Pacific. You have helped us this day."

Major Naqui bowed slightly. "I am glad to be of service. Although I wear the uniform of the Russian Army, I feel a kinship with your people. Please accept this gift from my tribe, the Yupiks of the Chukchi Peninsula."

From a cloth bag, Atka removed a walrus tusk with carvings on it. The Shoshone Chief cradled it reverently in both of his hands and studied it.

"It is a work of great beauty and soul. I will display it in the Hall of the Tribal Council. We will look on it often and remember the friendship of Atka Naqui of the Yupiks from across the western ocean." He bowed slightly to Atka.

"I will now return to my post." Major Naqui bowed in turn, then stepped out of the building and drove off in a blue SUV with UN markings.

The Chief gazed at the dust of the departing vehicle thoughtfully. "So, even a Major in the Russian Army in the service of the United Nations still manages to feel some loyalty to a family group, a tribe. Maybe there is hope for humankind after all."

"Chief Quishindemi, I thank you on behalf of the Ark families," said Sarah.

"Sarah Young, our Tribal Council made a treaty with you and the other Ark people. You have honored your side of the treaty. You have lived here in peace on the land you have leased from us. You have obeyed our laws and accepted our sovereignty. In these trying times, this has been good for both our peoples. Your lease payments of food crops and cattle have helped my people eat during these times of famine."

Sarah smiled. "You are welcome. We thank you for the protection of your Shoshone Defense Forces."

"In these times of chaos, we will do what we can to defend ourselves and our treaty brothers and sisters." The Chief's eyes twinkled over a small smile.

He added, "Your suggestion of invoking the Civil Rights Division and the United Nations was brilliant. I have no love for the United Nations. They are yet another collective of power-grabbing politicians who only want to rule others. But this move pits the UN against the U.S. Civil Rights Division who claims to support UN 'human rights' initiatives. They will be tied up in politically correct turf-wars and in-fighting for months, if not years. This is the time for us to re-assert our rights as sovereign nations. The Ark people have inspired us to re-learn independence. My people are responding to the challenge of survival, unburdened by the heavy hand of federal handouts pressing our shoulders down. We are beginning to grow our own crops and do for ourselves."

"Chief Quishindemi, I am glad to hear it. We want to trade with you as equals."

"Sarah Young, in the Bible story of the Ark, there is a Rainbow, is there not? Do you think you will ever see a rainbow signaling the end of this flood of abuse and power-lust?"

"Maybe not in my lifetime, Chief. We will hope, we will work, and we will pray. The event is in the hand of God."

"Wakinu, the grey grizzly defeated by the black bear Wakini, left a trail of scattered snow when he ascended to the Eternal Hunting Grounds. You call it the Milky Way. If there is redemption for that old thief Wakinu, maybe there is hope for this world. I will pray for our world when I see the trail of snow Wakinu left behind in the night-sky. Maybe the rainbow trail of hope in the day-sky will come to us all one day. I will pray for that."

Sarah held out her hand to the chief. He held it between both of his hands. Looking into his eyes, she whispered, "In prayer there is much hope. Go with God, Chief Quishindemi."

Lowering his own voice, he replied, "Go with God, Sarah Young."

 **Chapter Twenty-Two**

The collectivized farms, rechristened 'American Prosperity Camps,' served as forced labor camps for the unemployed. They were also the food production units for the subsistence rations handed out by the Department of Agriculture.

When the president was questioned about these camps at one of his frequent press conferences, he replied, "We don't call them labor camps; we call them American Prosperity Camps, where our motto is 'Work together for national prosperity. Be happy in your work, for work will make you free.' The Americans working there are patriotic volunteers who wanted to do their part to help with our economic recovery."

The FACTS news reporter followed up: "If these workers are there voluntarily, then why are the camps surrounded by barbed wire fences and armed guards? We have pictures of the fences and the guards on our website and televised on our nightly news."

President Fletcher shifted uncomfortably. *These reporters and questions were supposed to be screened!* "Hal, the fences and guards are there to keep the volunteers safe. Counter-transformation terrorists and saboteurs have been targeting these camps. They want to stop the dynamic projects of these collectives which produce food in abundance and all manner of consumer goods. Not luxuries, mind you, like washing machines which waste water and pollute the earth with phosphates, but tin wash tubs and corrugated tin washboards. Good old hand-operated tools that don't consume climate-poisoning electricity and provide healthy exercise at the same time."

"So anyone at these camps is free to leave any time they want to?"

The president paused, thinking hard. *Were there any radios or televisions in the camps? Would they hear about my answer?* No, he decided. Labor Secretary Tianin had emphasized to him that no communication with the outside world was allowed at the camps.

"Yes, Hal. These are free American citizens who freely volunteered to contribute their skill sets. I must point out, however, that technically these skill sets belong to the American State which provided the education to develop them. They didn't build their own skills! But volunteers are free to enter and leave."

"Then there is no objection to me entering a camp and interviewing some of these volunteers?"

"None whatsoever. This is a free country." He looked over at Labor Secretary Tianin standing in the back. He nodded and she nodded back. She would coordinate with Homeland Security to have Mr. Hal Enry detained and investigated by the FBI on suspicion of digging up secrets vital to American security. He would never reach any of the American Prosperity Camps.

When President Fletcher looked back at Hal Enry's face, he saw no deference or fear. That enraged him. He gripped the sides of the presidential podium tightly to control himself.

Scowling, he thought, *I think it is high time to issue Presidential Executive Order 10-291: The Press Registration and Supervision Headquarters (PRESH). My handlers won't approve, but I'm going to surprise them and do it right now. I've had about enough of these impertinent questions that challenge my executive power as President. Ninety percent of the media is in our pocket, but it's about time we brought the other ten percent to heel. I don't care what the my handlers think. I'll do it now. After all, I __am__ the President, and I __do__ have a pen.*

Clearing his throat, he began: "Ladies and Gentlemen, my fellow Americans, We are now going to make an unscheduled announcement. This was planned for a few weeks from now, but We judge this to be the right time."

While his press secretary looked panicked, he droned on "We hereby announce Presidential Executive Order 10-291: The Press Registration and Supervision Headquarters (PRESH). I, We, will today sign this

Presidential Executive Order, and you are all invited to the signing ceremony in the Oval Office."

Looking over at his Chief of Staff Sim Smythe, he said "Sim, clear my calendar for today at 5 p.m. Signing ceremony. Oval Office." Smythe nodded obediently, thinking, *So, he can think for himself and pull off a surprise or two. We better watch him more carefully.*

"This Presidential Executive Order establishes oversight authority over the press. We've had far too many of these leaks which threaten our national security. We know reporters only want to cover the facts, but sometimes they go too far. This has got to stop.

"The new Press Registration and Supervision Headquarters will certify, vet, and register all journalists for any media whatsoever, television, print, or internet. This agency will issue official Federal Press Credentials. Without this credential, no journalist will be permitted to practice journalism in any way shape or form anywhere in the nation. This agency will revoke press credentials whenever it is determined that a journalist has abused his or her press privileges and endangered national security or the national interest. To obtain this Federal Press Credential, all journalists must take mandatory training in sensitivity to federally protected groups, hate speech protocols, the Responsibilities Owed to World Citizenship, Politically Correct Interpretation of the Constitution, and the journalism course entitled Cultural Respect Supercedes Facts-Based Reporting, offered through the well-respected non-profit group, Disrespected Cultures of the World."

Without waiting to be recognized, Hal Enry spoke: "Mr. President, who decides whether or not a journalist has abused anything? You refer to 'press privileges' but doesn't the first amendment make free speech and a free press a right? No one in the USA that I know grants me that right. I am endowed by my Creator with rights, not the government."

Shaking his briefing papers into a neat stack, President Fletcher drew down his brows severely and replied in a stern tone, "Hal, that's the kind of thinking that got us into this flurry of leaks that endanger our country. We can't afford it anymore. In order to protect the freedoms we all enjoy, the government has to control freedom of the press. We know this requires trust. As We said in our first presidential election campaign, 'Trust in Me, for I am the Change you have been waiting for.' Things have *changed*, Mr. Enry. You would do well to remember that. No further questions."

He strode off, nose held high, leaving the White House Press Corps buzzing among themselves. The Press Secretary had recovered his composure and stepped to the podium. He smirked at Hal Enry.

"In one hour, we'll be accepting your applications for the certification process whereby we will determine whether you'll get the required PRESH Credentials. Dismissed."

Chapter Twenty-Three

John Young passed the coffee pot. Representatives of thirty-five families in Ark-Shoshone had gathered in his barn. He and Joseph had set up a makeshift table and benches from saw horses, hay bales and planks. The gathered men and women had grave looks on their faces. They wore weather-faded work shirts, jeans, and bib overalls. Each had left behind a husband or a wife to protect families and farms.

Jacob Pierce sipped from his coffee cup. "Mighty good coffee, Sarah."

John Young snorted. "That's my coffee, not that nasty stuff Sarah and Joseph make. Sarah's a good cook and a good shot, but coffee is the one thing I'm good at."

"Sor-ree!" said Jacob. He laughed and so did several others who knew John and Sarah.

"I just want points for the one thing I can cook well," said John. "Even if it's only coffee."

"Ten thousand points to you!" smiled Jacob. "Sarah, we appreciate your report on what happened when the Homeland Security folks came to call. When you first proposed the strategy of calling on the Civil Rights Division and the UN, I thought we were inviting the foxes into the hen house. I'm glad the Shoshone Tribal Council agreed to it. Now I see the wisdom of pitting our enemies against each other."

Sarah looked pleased. "Since 'cultural sensitivity to minorities and the UN' is a prime virtue for these otherwise totalitarian government control types, I thought we could hoist them on their own petard. And sure enough, it worked!"

"How did they find out about us? The Shoshone have pretty much cut off the outside world due to looters and gangs. They patrol the major roads in and out. We have our own little oil well and micro-refinery for fuel and lubrication of tractors, so we don't go to town for that. We have our own electricity from our own lake-fed hydro-power plant, so we are off the grid. We don't drive vehicles in the line of sight of the outside world and we don't visit the outside world. So how did they find out about us?"

"Drones, that's how." Everyone turned to see who spoke. Joseph Wakini blushed and took off his straw cowboy hat.

"Joseph, how do you know this?" asked Jacob. He looked perplexed.

Joseph remained seated. "I've been listening to some short wave radio broadcasts from other Ark locations and from scattered CRM (Constitutional Resistance Movement) cells. Several of them say that the same type of drones the government used in the Mideast are now patrolling our skies, looking for pockets of resistance: ARKs, CRM cells, and Prepper settlements."

John Young spoke up. "It's true. Joseph and I tinkered with an old short wave set we found and got it to working. He listens more than I do, but I heard the same thing from another ARK on another reservation."

"But what's to see with our ARK? We have the same old buildings as any other ranch. Nothing new and shiny about us. How would they know we're an ARK?" Jacob scratched his head.

"Easy," said Joseph. "Our fields are green. Everything else is brown and abandoned by farmers unwilling to work as slaves of the collective on their own land. Even the collectivized farms with plenty of slave manpower are mostly brown, because the people running them are government types who know nothing about how to farm them properly. Plus, the environmental groups have cut off irrigation water to," here Joseph made air quotes with his fingers, " 'save the planet.'"

"Oh," said Jacob. "That makes sense."

"And another thing," said Joseph. "The drones see us working with tractors and combines. Nobody else has the fuel for that. The prosperity camps ban the use of motorized equipment in the name of global warming and political correctness. Any moving machine stands out like a sore thumb in this lunar landscape of 12th century peasant farming."

"So, unless we let the land go fallow and do everything by hand, they will find us," mused Sarah. "If we do that, we'll be at their starvation levels within three years, living mostly off our stored food. That's not a long-term solution."

Joseph stood up. "There is another way."

All eyes were on the eighteen-year-old, but he didn't seem self-conscious. "Joseph, we're all listening. Tell us," John Young said. *Didn't know the boy had it in him to speak up like this. I'm proud of him.*

"Well," he began slowly, "I've been capturing cell tower signals and GPS satellite signals with a cell phone that I modified to passively receive only, not transmit. They can't know its location, because it never transmits."

The crowd murmured, impressed.

"Go on," said John Young.

"Well," he slowly began again, "I've analyzed the digital code they use, and I believe that I can program a cell phone as a transmitter that will send out a false location code. I believe that I can trick the drone into thinking it's getting a GPS fix from the satellite, when in fact it is getting a GPS location code from me. It will relay false coordinates to the drone drivers."

"So what you're saying is," John Young haltingly said, "is that we can send them …"

"On a snipe hunt!" said Joseph triumphantly. "They'll think we're someplace else!" His face shone with anticipation. He had created something the grown-ups would admire. He had pulled his own weight. Pulling your own weight got you a lot of respect in the ARKs.

The group cheered. Men began slapping him on the back. Women hugged him.

Cathy Peterson rushed up and gave him a big kiss on the lips in front of everybody.

"Joseph! You did it! I'm so proud of you!" He turned red and looked around to see what people would say. They kept patting him on the back and smiling at him. He exhaled in relief, but then worried, *What will Cathy's father say?*

Just then he heard Cathy's father talking in his ear and slapping his back. "Well done, lad!" He hugged Joseph and pitched his voice low, "Mrs. Peterson and I would be proud for you to court Cathy, in case you were wondering."

Then he stepped back, holding Joseph by his shoulders and smiling insanely. Joseph was dazed. *Wow! So it's OK if I date Cathy. I was afraid to ask, and now he just up and told me it's OK. Thank you, Lord. Sometimes you send the answer before I even ask the question.*

* * * * * *

After the meeting broke up, a small group stayed behind. Six of the more technically inclined men, women, and teenagers wanted to work with Joseph on Operation Snipe. They talked tech talk for another hour.

"Joseph, can you talk to the other ARKs on your short-wave radio about this?" asked John Young.

"Yes, but we don't have a code worked out. If I use short wave, the Feds will be listening and learn our plan."

"A long time ago there was a movie, Windtalkers, about Navaho Marines who used the Navaho language as a code the Japanese could not break. The Navaho words are now known and even published on the internet. But, what about Shoshone?"

Joseph stared at John. "That's brilliantly simple! Just a few old linguistics professors ever bothered to learn Shoshone, so now the only ones who understand it are Shoshone living on the three remaining Shoshone reservations. And all three have ARKs on their reservations!"

John smiled big. "I've estimated that there are sixty or more ARK locations on western reservations, all shielded from the Feds by the renewed sovereignty claims of each band or tribe of Native Americans. If we can get sixty Shoshone willing to travel secretly to these other ARK locations, we will have an unbreakable code: Shoshone."

"That's so random and crazy, it just might work," said Joseph. I'll ask Chief Quishindemi for permission to speak to some of the younger Shoshone. Many of them are eager to emulate the ARK people or join an ARK. They've seen up close how they can prosper if they don't take the Man's compassion crack cocaine. I'll bet that the CRM units will help smuggle them to other ARK locations. The CRM already runs coyote routes into Mexico."

"Done! I know how to contact one of the CRM units. Just tell me when you're ready." John's eyes shone. "Joseph, would you do me a favor?"

Joseph looked puzzled.

"When you have Shoshone speakers in place in some of the other ARKs and are ready to test the network, would you have them use these phrases for the test, if they can be said in Shoshone? It's just a sentimental thing for me, for the symbolism."

"Sure. What do you want them to say?"

"Two phrases. First, 'the chair is against the wall.' Second, 'John has a long moustache."

"May I ask, what is the significance of those two particular phrases?" asked Joseph.

"'John has a long moustache' was the code phrase transmitted to the French Resistance just before the D-Day invasion of Normandy. It signaled them to begin blowing up railway lines and other things to slow down the Germans."

"And the other?"

"'The chair is against the wall,' was a code phrase used in the movie *Red Dawn*, sent to resistance fighters behind enemy lines, in the zone of America occupied by the Russian and Cuban Armies. I've always liked that movie. Now we are pretty much living out that movie."

"O.K. John, you got it."

"Thanks Joseph." He turned, hesitated, then turned back. Joseph?"

"Yes?"

"You work for me, on my farm, but today ..." he hesitated again, then looked straight into Joseph's eyes. "Today, you became a leader. A leader for this ARK. Soon, you may be leading many ARKS." His eyes misted. "Joseph, I'm proud of you."

John stood up straighter. "Just so we're clear, I'm still the boss of the farm. But, I want to offer you a five year plan to buy half of the farm, not with money, but with work. You interested?"

"That's a big yes! Mr. Peterson just gave me permission to court Cathy. I have to plan for my future."

"Son, that's great! I'm happy for you and Cathy." He hesitated again. "Just so we're clear, when it comes to ARK business, you are my leader. Where you lead, I'll follow."

John held out his hand.

Dazed again, Joseph shook his hand. *What just happened? Mr. Young said he would follow me? Me? How did I possibly earn that privilege?*

"Uh, Mr. Young?" He turned back to Joseph. "Mr. Young, how could I possibly earn the right to lead much older men and women like you and Mrs. Young and the others? You were the ones who built a producing farm. You created a job for me."

"On the farm, I'm the boss," repeated John Young. "For the ARK, you were the man with a plan. That counts for something. It's not age, it's ideas and initiative. You showed both. If you believe in your plan, don't back down. Take charge and make it happen. Everyone in this ARK is ready to follow you, and they want you to succeed."

Stunned all over again, Joseph stood there as John Young walked back to the farm house. *Well then, I guess I'm a leader. Let's see, when can I get the next GPS download? Thursday. Yep, I can be ready by Thursday.* He began walking to the farmhouse where a hot supper waited for him.

CHAPTER TWENTY-FOUR

GRACE WAS DRESSED IN AFRICAN ROBES AND HEAD GARB. HER PLANE was on approach to the international airport in Hawaii. She was traveling on a Botswanan passport under an assumed name in order to escape detection. *It's risky to change planes in Hawaii, but it saves 18 hours of travel time to the United States. What was left of them,* she thought.

When the passengers deplaned, they saw that the terminal was patrolled by Chinese soldiers carrying AK-47 military rifles. *What in the world?* thought Grace. She turned to one of the television monitors in the terminal as Al-Jazeera News came on. Soledad O'Brien, covered in a burka, was speaking. Only her eyes showed.

"Today Al-Jazeera is proud to announce that our anti-imperialist allies in China have reclaimed the Hawaiian Islands. Long known to be part of the ancient territory of mainland China, Hawaii has now been liberated by the People's Army of China. The cabal of corporate capitalists who rule America are learning that their evil and illegal rule over this ancient province of China has ended. Long live the Chinese province of Hawaii!"

Oh my dear God, thought Grace. *It's begun. The vulture nations have gathered to pick the bones of a weak and dissolving United States.* She wiped a tear from her eye.

The passengers were formed into five lines to pass through Chinese passport control. Grace looked at the line to her right and gasped. She saw Diana Nomenski staring at her.

Nomenski strode across to Grace, ignoring the shouts of the Chinese guards.

135

"You!" Nomenski glared at her. "You and those who think like you are a blight on the planet! Now we have you!" Two Chinese soldiers grabbed Nomenski by her arms.

"What are you doing?" She screamed. "This woman is an enemy of the planet! Arrest her! There are arrest warrants for her in the United States. She is on the FBI Most Wanted list, I tell you! Let me go and arrest her!" Nomenski struggled but could not free herself.

A Chinese Army lieutenant swaggered up. "What is the meaning of this?" He demanded.

"You have to arrest that woman!" screamed Nomenski. "She's Grace Washington! She's wanted by the police in the United States!"

The lieutenant backhanded Diana without warning. "It is I who give the orders here!" he shouted. "This is Chinese soil now. I do not have to do anything. And you will not give orders to soldiers of the Red Army of China! Give me your passport!"

The line Grace was in had moved, and she was next to have her passport stamped.

Dazed, Diana reached into her inside jacket pocket for her passport. The lieutenant grabbed her wrist and jerked her hand out. He twisted the passport from her grasp. "Do you think you can reach for a weapon? Search her!" The two soldiers slung their rifles over their shoulders and began forcibly groping over every inch of her body.

"What are you doing?" she screamed and squirmed. "You have no right!"

Again the lieutenant backhanded her. A thin line of blood trickled from the corner of her mouth. "It is YOU who have no right!" he shouted. "You are no more than a dog here! You will cower when I raise my voice!" He raised his hand as if to backhand her again. She flinched involuntarily. "WHO is in charge here?"

"I ..." she began. His hand lashed out in a savage slap. She cried out this time.

"WHO is in charge here?"

"Y...You are." She looked down and away.

"Good! Even old dogs can learn new tricks, if they are shown who is the master." He looked down at her passport. Then he scanned the bar code into his phone. He studied the screen for a minute.

"So. You are the Director of PRIS! You and your organization have been useful to us in the past, and you will be useful to us in the future. But first, you will have to be re-educated to the proper degree of subservience. Corporal Chien!"

"Yes sir?" The man on Diana's right came to attention.

"Make arrangements for Ms. Nomenski to fly out on the next transport. Book her into the political reeducation camp for high level progressives run by our partners in North Korea! A twelve-month stay at least. Maybe more for someone of her lofty aspirations."

"What! You cannot just send me ..." Diana's loud objection was cut off by a rifle butt to her ribs. She sank to the ground, clutching her side.

"Once again, WHO is in charge here?" shouted the lieutenant. The corporal poised the rifle butt for another jab at her ribs.

"Y... You are ..." mumbled Diana, moaning in pain from a fractured rib.

"Corporal Chien!" shouted the lieutenant.

"Yes sir!"

"Make that eighteen months in the North Korean camp. This old dog is stubborn and used to being the top dog. She will need more re-education. But when she comes back, she will lick my boots." He stared down at her, then allowed himself a thin smile of satisfaction. "Take her away!"

Grace watched Diana being marched away. She had moved through the Chinese passport control with her Botswanan passport. She had witnessed the little drama between Diana and the lieutenant while waiting for her bag to be searched.

You forced a socialist 'paradise' on the rest of us, thought Grace. *Now you'll be on the wrong end of a socialist paradise, the receiving end. Your will be done. To yourself. Time to live with your answers.*

Chapter Twenty-Five

Grace Washington put her elbow on the open window of the pick-up truck door and touched the top of the window frame with her fingers. It was an old 1996 GMC pick-up with an extended cab. The paint had lost its shine long ago. Now it was a rusty-tan variegated hue that blended with the dry landscape they were traveling through. Brown hills and tan vegetation stretched as far as the eye could see. No human habitation in sight.

She glanced over at the driver, a young man with coppery skin and a straw cowboy hat pulled low on his forehead. Ray-ban aviator sunglasses hid his eyes.

"You might want to close your window. We're about to hit a dusty patch up ahead."

She reached down and worked the manual crank to roll up her window. The air immediately felt stuffier. She rolled up the cuffs of her faded plaid work shirt.

"My name is Grace Washington. What's yours?" There had been no time for introductions when she transferred from the CRM operative's jeep to his truck.

"Joseph. Joseph Wakini." He did not offer a hand to shake. His work-gloved hands twisted the wheel, dodging potholes and rocks in the dirt road. He was a bit shy in the presence of this woman. She was almost a legend in the ARK communities.

"That name stands for working for what is yours and protecting what is yours. It's in one of the traditional Shoshone folktales. Wakini the black bear."

"You are well informed."

"I decided to do some homework when I learned where the CRM was sending me."

"I'm proud of the name Wakini. Like the traditions of many tribal cultures around the world, it's a name I am expected to live up to."

She smiled at his impassive young face. "I have a feeling that you will." Her dimple showed.

Clearing his throat, he asked, "Is it true that you invented the idea of The Noah Option, building self-sufficient communities to survive the collapse?" It was common to refer to what was happening in the United States as 'the collapse.'

She laughed. "Well, it's true that I invented the name 'Noah Option' as a code word to alert everyone that it was time to get out of Dodge. But many people had come to the same conclusion on their own. Many had begun preparing to protect their families and survive the collapse. Some of them had the nickname 'Preppers.' When those folks began to network and help each other they adopted my code words. They called their communities ARKS, and the code word to leave and go to the ARKS was The Noah Option. My husband Isaiah and I devised methods to spread information to help people prepare. Isaiah set up the internet domain .ARK on offshore servers."

She looked to her right at the lonely landscape. "As for the rest, people did it themselves. Americans are the original do-it-yourselfers. All we ask is 'laissez nous faire' – leave us alone to do it."

He nodded. "I've seen parts of the Noah Option speech some people recorded on their DVRs. You and Isaiah were awesome." She smiled as she looked at the horizon.

Farm buildings were visible in the distance. As they got closer, Grace could see a cluster of pick-up trucks, tractors, and horse-drawn buggies and wagons near the barn.

"Everybody heard you were coming. They all wanted to meet you. You are legend to them. I know it's a security risk, but its been a tough couple of years. Everybody needed a morale boost. You are the boost."

As he got out of the truck, he shouted, "Clem, Frederick! Round up a crew and start spreading that camo netting over these vehicles! Drones may be over us any minute."

Two men waved at some others, who ran up. They lifted 2" x 4" x 10 foot studs attached to the camo netting and began walking the netting above and over the vehicles.

Joseph took Grace by the arm and quick-stepped her into the barn. Men, women, and children lined three sides. Grace heard a murmur of voices that muted when she entered. They all looked expectantly at her.

Joseph took off his straw hat and his Ray-bans and gestured to Grace. "Everyone, this is Dr. Grace Washington. Dr. Washington, meet ARK-Shoshone."

They all applauded. Grace looked over at Joseph and did a little curtsy in her jeans and hiking boots. Somebody in the back shouted, "We all love you Grace! We pray for you and Isaiah every night."

Grace's eyes misted. She looked at the faces hungry for hope. "Thank you. Thank you especially for your prayers. Isaiah and I pray for you too. We all need prayers in these trying times."

Joseph looked over at her with full eye contact for the first time. "You are taking a big risk coming back. Everybody in America knows your face and name. You are on the FBI's most wanted list. Your picture is posted in every post office and supermarket. There's a $500,000 reward for your capture. Why did you come?"

"I didn't want to, at first. Isaiah and I were safe in New Zealand. But we saw the news reports about the food riots in the cities, mob violence and innocent families getting beaten and herded into these so-called 'prosperity camps.' Isaiah couldn't stand it. He had to help. After praying about it, I saw that it was the right thing to do."

She began twisting a strand of her hair. "Here's a story they probably don't teach in history classes anymore. When the United States entered World War I, the American Expeditionary Force marched into Paris. The American General Pershing laid a wreath at the grave of Lafayette in France. American lieutenant colonel Charles Stanton said, 'Lafayette, we are here.'"

She looked at Joseph. She reached out and laid her hand on his arm. She turned and looked at the faces. "ARK America, we are here."

The group moved in with extended hands. They began shaking her hand. Children reached out to touch her. Grace squatted down to one little redheaded girl and said, "How old are you?"

The toddler grinned and held up one finger. "One."

Her mother said, "Fourteen months."

"What's your name?"

"Grace."

Grace looked up at the girl's mother standing behind the child. Her face was shining. "We wanted to be reminded that there is hope and help and goodness and decency somewhere in this world. We named her after you."

Grace's face began twisting. The tears came. She reached out and picked up the little girl. Smiling through her tears, she said, "Grace is a gift from God, and this girl is a gift from God. The grace of God gives us the confidence and the courage to do the right thing."

Glancing at Joseph, she said, "I have a name to live up to. Let's get to work."

* * * * * *

"How often have the drones been flying over your ARK?" She looked around at the seven people who comprised the leadership council for ARK-Shoshone. Three women and four men, including Joseph. They sat around the kitchen table in John and Sarah Young's house.

John Young spoke up. "They started about five months ago. About once a week. Six weeks ago, Homeland Security tried to enter the reservation. They were turned back by the Shoshone Self Defense Force, plus some political judo involving the United Nations. After that the drone flights increased to about twice a week."

"From what I've been told, the drones detect your green farm fields in the middle of brown desolation. The drone drivers then realize that these must be independent farmers who use their own judgment and experience to plan their farming methods. Which of course works. That's why your fields are green. Therefore, they deduce that you are operating outside of government's incompetent control."

One of the women said, "Brown for bureaucrats. Green for genius."

Grace looked at her. "How right you are. The fields on the collective farms are brown to pale green because they are run by social engineering types appointed by Progressives. They are full of theories about how to run society with central planning, but they don't know a thing about farming."

John Young shook his head. "Busybodies with power – forcing everybody else to live under their pet theories. Just like Pol-Pot in Cambodia. He and his fellow revolutionaries from the universities forced urban people into the country at gunpoint to be peasant farmers. Pol-Pot and his crowd didn't know anything about farming, and the crops failed. The country went into starvation, just like the U.S. today. Paul Johnson laid it out in his history book *Modern Times.* But these fools can't be bothered to learn from history. They think history begins and ends with them."

Joseph wrinkled his nose as if he smelled something bad. "The point is, they can't stand knowing that anyone is operating outside of their omnipotent incompetence. They know that once word gets around that free and uncontrolled people are growing plenty of food, their slave citizen populations might realize there is a better way. Even starving slaves have been known to revolt."

John looked around the table. "They'll be back for us. And they won't let UN diplomacy stop them the next time. They'll slaughter the Shoshone Tribal Self Defense Force and round us all up. Or liquidate us."

"That's why I'm here." Grace pulled out a small bag of seeds. "These are my latest hybrid super seeds. In addition to needing less water, fertilizer, and insecticide, the yield is 70 percent more than what you use now. And you'll get four harvests per season instead of two. There are sixty sacks of various seeds in the back of the pick-up truck Joseph drove in. Enough for all the families in ARK-Shoshone, courtesy of Nutritional Abundance Industries and my boss, Minerva Stone."

Grace passed around the open seed bag. "Here is the really important thing: these seeds need less sunlight. You can plant them under small irregular patches of dusty brown camo cloth and they will produce like crazy. Even though you cultivate less ground, you'll get a bigger yield. More than enough to feed your own families and put aside enough for two more years of survival."

"Next week, the CRM will begin smuggling in truckloads of camo cloth to you. They may airlift it and parachute pallets down to you at night. You'll be able to farm and garden small patches under the brown camo cloth. The drones won't be able to detect you."

One of the men asked with a frown, "How will we get seeds for the next year's planting? The CRM may not be able to smuggle seeds in to us. And Minerva Stone may not be so generous next year. The crops we grow from these hybrid seeds won't produce viable seeds able to sprout the next season."

"I've been working on that. I've managed to develop a new strain of hybrid seeds that can germinate. You have them in your hands. You won't need to buy or obtain your next supply of seed stock from Nutritional Abundance Industries. You will simply set aside ten percent of your harvest for your next season's seed corn. You won't have to buy seeds from us for each new planting."

"But you're giving us these seeds for free now. Why?" The man wasn't hostile, only curious.

"Because we have decided it's in our best interest to give free seeds to ARK communities. If the ARKs survive this collapse and rebuild civilization, we'll have free and independent customers to buy from us in the future."

John Young spoke again. "But we will be restricted to what we can grow under small patches of camo cloth."

Grace took a deep breath. "Isaiah is working on a software bug to throw them off, but it isn't ready yet. It won't be ready in time for this planting season. So you'll need to use the camo cloth for now."

"One more thing," John frowned. "They've been here once. They know where we are. Regardless of drones seeing green or not, they'll be back to capture or kill us. Make an example of us."

"That is a real danger. That's a job for my husband Isaiah's software skills. Can we access .ARK from here?" Grace looked around at the faces.

Joseph said, "Yes. I've devised an invisible hack into the nearest cell phone tower."

"Then Joseph, you should alert him to our danger. Don't mention that I'm here. We're trying to keep our locations on a need-to-know basis, even from each other."

Grace stood up from the table. "So, shall we plant some seeds?"

The frown faded from the man's face. He stood and held out his hand to Grace. "It's a deal, partner." Grace shook his hand vigorously. She smiled so big her dimple showed.

Joseph stood up. "Let's get to work before Wakinu sticks his paw in where it doesn't belong. I have sixty sacks of seed that need to be offloaded onto other trucks and buggies." He pulled on his work gloves, put on his hat, and started for the door.

Grace looked after him as the door closed behind him. "That's the kind of bear I like to deal with. Grab it and growl." She started pulling on her own gloves.

"Grrrr!" said John Young. "Caleb, you grab it, and I'll growl!" The others laughed as they headed for the door.

CHAPTER TWENTY-SIX

AFTER HIS *COURSE IN REALITY* WAS OVER, THOMAS AND BARRY BLOCK brought Alexander back to Thomas's house in a suburb of San Francisco.

"You can stay here a few days until you decide what you want to do next," Thomas told him.

Judge Block was disappointed that Alexander had not immediately offered to join the CRM as he had done. *Well, he's young and unsure of himself. Maybe he'll come around*, the Judge thought.

"Alexander, I've got to go to work. Make yourself comfortable. Solomon, can I drop you off somewhere?" Solomon was the Judge's CRM code name. Thomas loaded some drop cloths into his van and got behind the wheel. The Judge got in beside him. The van backed out, then went down the street.

Alexander looked in the refrigerator. No beer or wine. No frozen pizzas. Oh well, I can call for take-out. He unconsciously reached for his wallet. His pocket was empty. Then he remembered. His fellow Occupiers had taken it. *Ungrateful creeps! I marched with them! I lived in tents with them! I partied with them! I was one of them! I did my part for the Occupy Movement. I earned some street cred, but all they could think of was my father. It's not fair! I can't help who my father is... my father...*

Just then his stomach growled. There were plenty of groceries, and Thomas had shown him where the cookbook was. But nothing to just nuke in the microwave and eat immediately. It required some preparation. And he was hungry! ... *My father...*

He picked up the land-line phone and dialed his father's office number on Wall Street. His father's assistant answered. "Chairman Sorosander's office."

"Mrs. Crump? It's Alexander. I need to speak to my father right away."

"Alexander! Your father has been worried sick about you. Are you OK?"

"Yes, I'm fine. I can explain everything, but I need to speak to my father. It's urgent!"

She connected him. "Alexander! Are you safe? Where are you?"

"Dad, I'm safe. I'm somewhere near San Francisco. Everything is OK."

"Thank God! Your Occupy friends were all over the news claiming that you were a spy and that they wanted millions in ransom for your safe return. I gave them the money, but then they did not return you. I had private security firms searching for you. After so many weeks went by I thought that the Occupy people had murdered you."

"No Dad. They wanted to, but some people rescued me."

"Rescued you? Who?"

"Dad, I'll tell you everything but right now I need money and credit cards. The Occupy people stole mine."

"I know. I saw the ridiculous charges they ran up after you disappeared. Ten cases of Dom Perignon. For 99 percenters they certainly like to live like the 1%." He paused.

"Dad, I'm hungry *right now* and I can't even pay for a pizza delivery!"

"What?"

"I want to order a pizza and I don't have any money or credit cards. Do something!"

Sorosander Senior gritted his teeth. *Just like his mother, helpless.* "OK, write this down. Here's the address of the nearest American Express Office. They will give you a new card and some cash. It will be ready in one hour."

"Dad, I'll need cab fare to get there. I can't walk that far! I've been through an ordeal!"

"OK, I'll send a limo to pick you up. What's the address?"

"Dad, I don't know! They kept me blindfolded until I was in the house."

"I thought you said you were safe! Are you a hostage?"

"No! But I don't know where I am. It's complicated. Can't you do something?"

"Oh for Pete's sake! Alright. I have a friend in Homeland Security. Stay on the line. I'll have him trace this number and send some agents out to pick you up."

Within the hour, a black government SUV pulled in front of the small bungalow and two armed agents got out. They were wearing brown military style uniforms. Alexander met them at the front door.

"Alexander, you are to follow our instructions exactly. This is now a matter of national security. Leave a note here saying you'll be back tomorrow evening." He did so. The agents hid surveillance devices in Thomas's bungalow.

One hour later he was showering at an airport hotel suite with a fresh change of clothes. The Homeland Security Agents interrogated him. Five and a half hours later his father walked into the suite. He hugged Alexander briefly, then sat down heavily at the dining table. His two personal body guards remained standing. The Homeland Security Agents remained seated at the table.

Sorosander Senior looked over Alexander carefully. He could see that the boy had muscled out quite a bit. His cheeks were sun-tanned. He looked healthy.

"Have you eaten?"

"Yes. Twice, from room service." Alexander III sat down across from his father.

"You look healthy enough."

"Yes. I had a workout every day. Chopping firewood."

"My friend at Homeland Security emailed a transcript of your statement. I read it on the plane. So, you've been in the company of the Constitutional Resistance Movement? Just associating with them is treason. That's a minimum of thirty years in a federal penitentiary. It could even be the death penalty. Did you know that?"

"Dad! I was kidnapped! I didn't choose to go with them! I had no choice!"

"But you didn't try to escape."

"I didn't know where I was! Somewhere in some mountains. I had no car and there was no road. What was I supposed to do? They told me there were guards posted in all directions to catch me if I tried to escape. These were serious dudes! They wouldn't even give me a sleeping bag or a camping stove. I didn't even have a video game to pass the time! Just books. I had to chop firewood to keep warm and cook. Do you realize how much carbon is released by a wood fire?"

Sorosander II looked at the senior officer from Homeland Security. "Deputy Director?

Maudire VanJones stood up and looked down at Alexander. "Associating with seditious groups is punishable by death or a 30 year prison term, by executive order of the People's President. There are no exceptions and no extenuating circumstances. There won't be a trial because you've already admitted to this in your signed statement. We'll take you straight to jail. Or to the chair."

"What! But that's not fair! I did nothing wrong! I was just in the wrong place at the wrong time and got scooped up by the wrong people! I'm innocent! Dad! You've got to do something!" Alexander began to sound panicked.

His father leaned over the table and took Junior's hand in both of his.

"Alexander, I've spoken to my lawyers and I've spoken to my friend in Homeland Security. There is a way you could come out of this OK. Better than OK, actually. You could become one of the People's Heroes of the People's Democracy, a national hero and a role model for young people everywhere. Far more important than any of your Occupy friends will ever be. A month from now you could be in the White House, on television, accepting the Medallion of the Order of People's Heroes from the People's President himself. You could be offered an important executive job in Homeland Security, helping to hunt down traitors."

Alexander exhaled, a long slow breath. He looked out the window, then back at his father. "Would I get to wear a uniform and carry a gun?" His father nodded. "And be the boss of some agents?"

His father smiled and looked up at the Deputy Director, who nodded. *We have him.*

Chapter Twenty-Seven

Deputy Director Maudire VanJones now commanded a five state Region of the Search and Destroy Division of Homeland Security. She sat across from Alexander and began the briefing. Sorosander senior sat and listened.

"You are now a secret agent of the Search and Destroy Division. Your mission is to infiltrate the Constitutional Resistance Movement and their ARK hideouts. You will ask to join their movement. You will ask to be sent to one of the ARK locations. You will pretend to be one of them."

Alexander listened intently. "That is so cool! Do I get a badge?"

Sorosander senior groaned. "No! You idiot! You are a *secret* agent. If you had a badge they would know who you really are!"

Alexander looked blank, then said "Oh! I get it."

The Deputy Director continued. "You will have nothing to link you to us. You have to talk like them and agree with their opinions. Remember, you are pretending to be one of them."

"Pretending. Got it." Alexander nodded.

"You will take this small backpack with you. Tell them that you went back to the Occupy tent city to try to get your stuff. Tell them that you couldn't sneak in, so you took this backpack left on a bench by one of them. Tell them that you stole some money from one of the girl's purses. Tell them you bought these new clothes with some of the money. Here's $800 in cash."

Alexander folded the bills and stuffed them into his jeans pocket.

"Now this next part is very important, so pay close attention. In the left-hand padded strap of this small day-pack, we have sewn in ten of these packets." She held up a plastic packet about the size of the sugar packets in restaurants.

"Each packet mixes with five gallons of water. When you are at one of the Ark locations, volunteer to spray liquid plant food on the vegetable gardens that they are eating from. Then spray this instead. This is concentrated, so you should be able to spray the gardens feeding over 100 people from one five gallon solution. When they eat these vegetables, they will get sick with the virus and die within 26 days max. Questions so far?"

"Is corn a vegetable?"

The Deputy Director raised her eyebrows at Sorosander senior, who avoided her gaze. "Yes, corn is a vegetable. Spray it if you can."

"O.K. ... Oh! Wait. What about me? I have to eat too! I'll get the virus and die." Alexander gave his father his panicked look again.

"No. Pay attention." She pushed forward the right hand strap of the day pack. "In the right-hand padded strap of the day pack, we have sewn in 12 capsules of an antidote to the virus. Each capsule will protect you from the virus for ten days. Take one right after you first feel nausea and a headache together. That means you have the virus. Then take one capsule every ten days after that. You'll be safe as long as you take one every ten days."

Alexander was thinking. He took a pencil and did some math on a napkin. "But, that means I'll run out of the pills and die after only 120 days!"

"That's right. You have 120 days to complete this mission and get back to us. We'll give you more pills when you get back. Your mission is to infect as many ARK locations as you can in 120 days."

Alexander looked worried. His father said, "Relax Alexander. This is a piece of cake. You just have to con these people into sending you to an ARK, and then another and another. Then get back before 120 days are up. You managed to con your professors at Harvard into giving you passing grades for four years, and professors are smart people. How hard can it be to con these CRM people? Most of them never even went to college, let alone became professors! You can do this in your sleep."

Alexander took a deep breath. "Well ... O.K. I'll do it. When I'm a Special Agent in Charge, will I have my own office?"

Maudire nodded. "Yes, you'll have your own office. With a window. Not even my office has a window."

Alexander stood, grabbed the backpack and slung it over his right shoulder. "When do we start?"

"This evening, when your note said you'd return. We'll drop you off about three blocks from the house. You can tell them that you hitch-hiked to town and back."

Alexander stepped up to the Deputy Director and touched her badge. "My own badge ... let's do it."

His father shook his hand. "Son, you'll be an important man."

"Thanks Dad." This was the first time his father had treated Alexander like he might be doing something important. *Finally, I get some respect*, thought Alexander. *Finally, I'll be important!*

* * * * * *

The judge returned to Thomas's house that night. Alexander smiled when he saw him. "Judge, I've decided what I want to do next. I want to join the Constitutional Resistance Movement and help people in the ARKs to survive."

Judge Block grinned. "Welcome aboard! Has Thomas told you about our 'no busybodies' rule?"

Thomas spoke up. "Yep. And the 'self-defense only' rules of engagement."

"And Alexander," the Judge looked him straight in the eye, "do you agree to all of this? Without reservation?"

"Yes." Alexander returned his gaze unflinchingly.

The Judge turned to Thomas. "Would you administer the oath?"

"I'd be delighted." Thomas raised his right hand. Alexander raised his. "Repeat after me. I do solemnly swear..."

Afterwards, Judge Block sat at the kitchen table. "Sit down, Alexander. The CRM has a mission for you. We need a young man to take more cell phones to an ARK location. You will have to hike and backpack for several days on your journey. Since you camped with the

Occupy San Francisco crowd, I assume you are familiar with sleeping bags, tents, and freeze-dried food?"

Alexander twisted in his seat. "Well, I slept in sleeping bags and tents alright, but we never actually cooked meals. We usually ordered pizza for delivery."

"Well," said the Judge, "you learned some basic cooking during your *Course in Reality*. Freeze-dried food is simple. You'll do O.K."

Alexander twisted a little again. "Well … I guess so."

The Judge spread out a map. "You won't leave for a week. We'll provide transportation from here to Lander, Wyoming or as close as we can get. From near Lander, head north. At noon each day, build a campfire with damp wood to send up a lot of smoke. After two days, somebody from the ARK should show up and guide you the rest of the way."

Alexander stared at the map. "What's out there in Wyoming?"

The Judge smiled. "Nothing for miles and miles, except more miles and miles."

Chapter Twenty-Eight

Joseph Wakini kept watch from the hay loft of the barn. The night sky was brilliant with stars. He had a goose down sleeping bag pulled up above his waist. Propped against a hay bale, he faced out the open door of the loft.

He sipped the last of his hot coffee from a thermos. Then he again scanned down the twin rows of solar LED lights. They extended for half a mile at fifty foot intervals. His home-made landing lights. Faint, but effective.

The thrum of a small plane engine faintly sounded in the distance. Joseph pushed the sleeping bag down and stood up. He scanned the western sky with binoculars. Suddenly a light appeared, brighter than a star. Joseph climbed down the ladder. His horse was saddled and ready in the closest stall. The Appaloosa snorted white breath into the frosty air.

After opening the barn door, Joseph swung into the saddle. He cantered in the direction of the twin lines of glowing LED lights. The light in the sky grew brighter and the engine noise grew louder.

The plane had touched down by the time Joseph pulled up his horse at the near end of the row of lights. He pulled out an orange safety vest and put it on over his parka.

The bright landing lights of the taxiing plane lit him up as he sat his horse. He held up his left hand to shield his eyes. Then he turned his horse away from the advancing plane. Large white letters on the orange vest read FOLLOW ME in the light of the aircraft. He trotted toward the barn, the plane following.

He led the plane to the left of the barn, next to rolls of hay piled under tarps. Turning to face the plane, he raised both arms up to form an X. The pilot killed his engine and his lights.

Joseph dismounted and tied up his horse. Clicking on his tactical flashlight, he shone it on the ground to light the way as the pilot approached.

"Help me with this camo-cloth. It's stapled to ten foot poles so we can lift it over the plane." Joseph held up one pole and shone his light on the other. The pilot picked it up.

Together they walked the camo-cloth over the single engine plane. Joseph produced some peg hooks and a mallet. They pegged down the edges of the cloth around the plane.

"Follow me," Joseph said in a low voice. He led the pilot back to the farmhouse. Inside the kitchen, he turned on an LED lantern and placed it on the table.

"Have a seat." Joseph lit the burner and put on a kettle. When he turned back, the pilot had unzipped his parka and removed his ball cap. The lantern shone on his face.

Joseph stopped short. "You!"

"Yep, it's me," said Isaiah, now rubbing his hands together for warmth. "Mr. You."

Joseph's mouth was hanging open. "But … it's you!"

"I'm considering changing my name to 'You,' since that's what everybody seems to call me nowadays." Isaiah smiled mischievously.

"Mr. Mercury," Joseph flustered, "I just wasn't expecting … you!"

The tea kettle whistled and Joseph jumped. Looking around wildly, his eyes finally focused on the kettle. He took it off the burner.

Suddenly shy, Joseph said, "You want hot chocolate?"

The door opened and Sarah Young stepped into the room, clad in a woolen robe. She saw Isaiah and stopped. "You!"

Isaiah looked at Joseph. "See what I mean? Yes, I'd love hot chocolate."

Sarah stammered again, still staring, "You!"

Joseph abruptly grinned, then laughed. Isaiah joined in. Sarah shook herself, as if awakening from a dream. "What's so funny?" she asked wonderingly. She sat down.

Joseph and Isaiah just laughed harder. Wiping tears of laughter from his eyes, Joseph poured the hot water and mixed in the chocolate mix. He set down one mug in front of Isaiah and the other in front of Sarah.

Isaiah extended his hand to Sarah. "Hello, I'm Isaiah Mercury. But you can call me 'you'."

Sarah shook his hand gravely. "Well I declare! I never expected to meet … you!"

Isaiah looked at Joseph and winked. Joseph put on his hat and gloves. "I've got to go collect those landing lights and put away the horse. Mr. Mercury, I'll see you in the morning."

Sarah was still staring. Joseph added, "Miz Young will give you a place to sleep." Sarah continued her hypnotic stare at Isaiah. "When she wakes up." Joseph shook his head and went out the door into the cold Wyoming night.

* * * * * *

Joseph returned to the kitchen at 5:30 a.m. to build a fire in the woodstove. Sarah Young was already up, mixing pancake batter.

"Pancakes?" said Joseph. "You only make pancakes on Sunday mornings. He glanced at the clock. "At eight."

Sarah vigorously stirred the batter, making a rapping noise against the side of the ceramic bowl. She was dressed in one of her better dresses and aprons.

"Couldn't sleep. Imagine! Isaiah Mercury, practically the Noah of the ARK movement, here in this house! Who would have imagined?" She looked around, distracted. "Where is my best syrup pitcher? I can't serve him maple syrup out of a *bottle*."

Joseph stood up. He had just put the match to the kindling in the stove. It was crackling nicely. He stepped up to the cupboard and reached up.

"Here it is." He handed her the ceramic pitcher.

"Oh." She stopped and looked at it. "Thank you."

John Young came down at six-thirty and said, "O boy, you have breakfast ready! Let's eat."

Sarah acquiesced, and the three of them ate a breakfast of pancakes, scrambled eggs and bacon. With lots of coffee.

At seven-thirty Isaiah entered, looking sleepy. "Is that bacon I smell?"

Full of nervous energy, Sarah jumped up and poured the batter for fresh pancakes. Isaiah sat down and poured himself a cup of coffee. Then he extended his hand to John Young.

"I'm Isaiah Mercury. Thank you for your hospitality, Mr. ... ?"

"Young. John Young. Sarah's husband. Well, I've got chickens to feed." He stood up.

"I'll feed 'em," put in Joseph. He stood and put on his parka. "You've got to catch up on Mr. Mercury's news."

Isaiah poured more coffee into John's cup. "Well," John said slowly, "in that case ..." He sat down and sipped his coffee. Joseph went out.

Isaiah leaned toward John. "You and I have to plan how to best develop young Joseph's software talent."

Leaning back in his chair, Isaiah sipped his own coffee. "With a little help, that boy can do some serious mischief to the government's surveillance capabilities."

John nodded. "Yes. And I've got some ideas for some of the most fun mischief since blivits at Halloween."

"Blivits? You mean two pounds of crap ..."

"... in a one pound bag!" John shook with laughter.

Laughing hard himself, Isaiah wheezed, "and you put the bag on the neighbor's porch ..."

John slapped the table with the palm of his hand. "... and light the bag on fire and ring the doorbell, and then ... and then ..." He choked on more laughter.

"... the neighbor comes out and stomps out the fire." Sarah put a platter of pancakes in front of Isaiah.

"Yes," she said drily, "you two eight-year-olds aren't the only ones who know that old joke." She broke into a chuckle. "Especially if the crap in the bag is dog crap."

"Sarah!" John looked shocked. Then all three of them broke into laughter again.

Chapter Twenty-Nine

Later, Sarah said, "It feels like Sunday. Let's have a short service. I know you're a Christian, Mr. Mercury, from your broadcasts. John and I are Mormons."

The four of them each said a prayer. Isaiah read the 23rd Psalm. "The Lord is my Shepherd, I shall not want ..." They ended with a hymn.

"My, Mr. Mercury, you do have a fine singing voice," said Sarah.

"Please, call me Isaiah. As for singing, you should hear my wife Grace."

Sarah smiled. "We have."

It was Isaiah's turn to be shocked. "You have? When? Where? How?"

"Right here in this kitchen. Six weeks ago." Sarah put her hand on Isaiah's shoulder. "Didn't you know?"

"No. I didn't know. Grace and I thought it best to maintain a communication silence between us when we are behind enemy lines. In case the Feds, or Reds, I should say, had broken our encryption. Communicating with each other might make it easier for them to find us."

Sarah smiled. "That pancake batter was made from some of her fast-growing wheat. She showed us how to plant and cultivate it. So, you see, you are being nourished by her love today."

Isaiah's eyes misted over. "Can I have pancakes for lunch?"

*　*　*　*　*　*

After lunch, Joseph and Isaiah talked software and wrote code together. John and Sarah watched and listened. John had said, "If we only understand five percent of what you two talk about, that's still more than we know now. And any knowledge is potential power."

Forty-eight hours later, Joseph and Isaiah both collapsed into bed and slept for ten hours straight. John had covered all of Joseph's farm chores. "That boy can do us more good by learning from Isaiah and writing code than he can milking cows," John told Sarah.

When they came out of their hibernation, Sarah had hot coffee and breakfast ready for them. "Oh … bless you," said Isaiah. He drank deeply. "My cup runneth over …"

Sarah put scrambled eggs in front of them. "Thou preparest a table before me …" Joseph said. He dug into the eggs.

"I'll say a blessing for us," said Sarah, "seeing as how you two can't wait. Lord, thank you for this food. Bless Joseph and Isaiah and bless the work of their hands. May their work be like thy rod and thy staff to comfort us and protect us, so that we will fear no evil. Amen."

"Amen," mumbled Isaiah and Joseph with full mouths.

John and Sarah tucked in themselves. "So," asked John as he passed the biscuits, "what digital stones have you two concocted?"

Sarah raised her eyebrows quizzically. "Something we can throw at them with your David's Sling app?"

Isaiah and Joseph looked at each other and started giggling.

"Even better," Joseph managed to choke out.

Isaiah looked at John. "You remember how we were talking about Halloween pranks?"

John nodded, taking another bite of his biscuit.

"Well," said Isaiah, "Joseph and I have created … drum roll please?"

Joseph drummed his fingers on the kitchen table, then stopped and blurted, "The digital Blivit!" He sat back, shaking with laughter.

"What on earth?" said Sarah. She shook her head. "Boys and their potty humor …" She buttered another biscuit for herself, smiling.

* * * * * *

Before lunch, Isaiah retrieved a satellite transmission device from the plane. He and Joseph set it up in the loft of the barn and worked to aim it at the southern sky.

"I used to use the HughesNet satellite, but now I have my own geo-synchronous satellites," Isaiah explained as they aimed and calibrated the dish.

"Your own? How?" demanded Joseph eagerly.

"Through a series of shell companies, I contracted with the Russians to put my satellites in orbit. We are about to lock onto ARK ONE."

"That is so cool," breathed Joseph.

"Upload ready? Go!" Isaiah tapped in more code sequences on his keyboard.

"One Blivit, about to be deposited on Uncle Fascist's front porch." Joseph smiled as he tapped in his own code sequences.

*   *   *   *   *   *

After bouncing through several dozen servers around the world (to make it untraceable) the "Blivit" was delivered to the digital doorstep of tens of thousands of federal agencies, including the Socialist Security Agency (formerly the NSA). The SSA was charged with spying on all Americans everywhere "for the security of the People's Socialist State."

As soon as it was within the computer networks, the Blivit "set itself on fire" – sending out the precise signals that would alert the automatic anti-malware protection programs of its presence. The protection programs went into "stomp and delete" mode. They "stomped," – killed, the malware, and deleted it from the network.

Every "stomp" smeared and scattered digital "ARK-bots" throughout the network. The protection programs were programmed with a list of digital locations to stop the mal-ware from infecting. It was precisely that list of locations that got smeared with little ARK-bots.

Every "delete" action automatically sent back to Isaiah's hackers a digital copy of the government's protection program. They would reverse-engineer it and learn how to slip past it undetected the next time.

The Feds had "stomped" on the Blivit, and then tracked digital dog dung back into their own digital houses.

Watching the first "stomp" on his monitor screen, Isaiah said "Gotcha!" He and Joseph whooped and exchanged high fives. Isaiah shouted "The digital Blivit has done 'dung' its doo-ty!" They both collapsed laughing.

Chapter Thirty

Isaiah was helping Joseph stack hay bales in the barn. John Young used an old fashioned hay baler on his farm. Joseph had lifted up a pallet of hay bales with one of the tractors pulled inside the barn. It was a warm day, and he and Isaiah had stripped to the waist. Sweat trickled over their broad chests and muscular arms. They formed a bucket brigade – with Joseph grabbing and swinging a hay bale over to Isaiah, who swung it up and over to make a stack of the bales.

They paused and leaned against hundred year old wooden barn beams. "Whew!" wheezed Isaiah. "Gets the oxygen pumping to your brain!" He walked over to the open loft door and looked out, breathing hard. Wisps of hay stuck to his chest and hair.

"And the sweat pumping everywhere else!" laughed Joseph.

"I get some of my best ideas when I'm jogging or exercising, so I don't mind the sweat so much." Isaiah straightened up. A sharp whistle came from the direction of the farmhouse.

"Get back!" warned Joseph. "That's the warning that a drone is coming over. We don't want them to see any signs of human activity."

Isaiah stepped back from the open door. They heard a faint jet engine noise. Joseph lowered his voice. "We heard that a drone fired a missile at some ARK farmers in the Sierra Nevada valley. Killed one and crippled the other. They were driving their tractors, out plowing."

Joseph looked away. "I know it's stupid to lower my voice. No way a drone at ten thousand feet can hear me talking. It's just instinct, somehow."

"A good instinct," said Isaiah. "It made me pay attention to you and listen to your warning quicker." He got a blank look on his face, then muttered "Wavelengths."

Joseph looked puzzled. "What?"

Isaiah looked up at him. "Wavelengths. I was thinking about wavelengths of the sound waves of the human voice. Didn't you say that the drones were keying in on the green fields of the ARK communities, when most of the collective farms were brown?"

"Yes. From what one CRM mole inside the Search and Destroy Division of Homeland Security tells us."

"Now that our Blivit has shown us how to get past their cyber-security, we can hack into the drone transmissions and decode which part of the transmission signals the color wavelengths that the drone is seeing with its cameras."

Joseph danced completely around in excitement and smacked the barn beam with the flat of this hand. "And selectively recode optical transmissions at certain ARK coordinates to read as brown instead of green! Like putting digital sunglasses over the drone eye! Yes!"

Isaiah grinned. "When do you want to start?"

"Tonight!" Then he frowned. "I forgot. Cathy's coming over for supper with us. Say! She's getting pretty good with writing code herself. Can she help?"

"Sure. We need to train as many people as we can on this stuff. For redundancy. Besides, she might be better at it than you are!"

Joseph blushed. "No way! She is better at calf-roping though. But that's only because she's owned a horse since she was nine. I can code rings around her!"

"Sounds like I'd better set up a drone roping contest. See which one of y'all can write digital lariat code the fastest!" Isaiah chuckled.

The whistle sounded again. "All clear," said Joseph. "You're on for that digital lariat thing! Race you back to the house for supper!" He grabbed onto the ladder and slid down, his boots gripping the sides. "Last one in does the dishes!" he whooped as he ran for the house.

Spluttering, Isaiah managed to yell "Cheater!" after him, then climbed down the ladder and put on his shirt before trudging up to the house. *Hope he saves some for me. That boy must have a hollow leg, the way he puts away the groceries!*

*   *   *   *   *   *

After three days of intensive coding, Isaiah and Joseph were ready to put sunglasses on the drones. Using his satellite uplink, Isaiah coached Joseph through the steps of entering the Federal network with passwords supplied by the digital blivit. Then Joseph added the "drone sunglasses" reprogramming to the optics interpretation sub-routine. The file name was the prefix for upgrade patches, so that it would not arouse the suspicion of federal anti-virus scans.

"Bam!" said Joseph. "To a drone, our land now looks just as brown as anywhere else. We just hung out a sign: nothing to see here, move along, move along! I put it into the master file for all drones patrolling the western states. That should add protection for other ARK locations that are islands of green in a sea of brown." He turned from the console and executed a fist bump with Isaiah.

Isaiah laughed. "That'll teach them not to mess with Joseph Wakini!"

Joseph took a deep breath and looked thoughtfully at Isaiah. "Now there is the problem of Homeland Security making a return visit to ARK Shoshone. They won't let UN diplomacy stop them this time."

"Joseph, I have an idea for that problem. I've got my software team at my company working on it. Did you ever have that dream about needing to take one last final exam in order to graduate from college or high school? But you can't find the room where the final exam is administered?"

Joseph looked blank. "Nope. I was home schooled."

Isaiah laughed. "So that's why you're so good at math and science! Well, let's just say that dream gave me an approach to our problem with Homeland Security. I'll let you know what we develop."

"If you say so." Joseph looked mystified.

"Joseph, there's not much more I can teach you about coding and out-foxing the Federal network. As Sergeant Preston of the Mounties used to say to his dog, 'I think our work here is done, Yukon King.'"

"What?" Joseph looked blank again.

"If you ever get bored of a winter's night, watch some of the old TV Westerns from the 1950s that I brought. On DVDs."

"Oh. So you're leaving?"

"Yep. I'll fly out tonight. I've got several other ARK stops to make, and then I'll eventually wind up in Laramie. I'm hoping to catch up with Grace there. I found out that was her next stop with the CRM. Help me get the plane ready?"

"You bet. Say, how did you learn how to fly?"

"I left you some flight simulator DVDs. You get through those, and someday when it's safe for private planes to fly again, I'll teach you."

"Really? I'll hold you to that."

Isaiah reached over and tousled Joseph's hair. "I'm counting on it. Before I go, we are going to celebrate! I'm cooking some ribs with my award-winning barbeque sauce. I persuaded Mrs. Young to let me do the cooking just this once. You, young man, are in for a treat!"

"Cool! Can I invite Cathy?"

"Absolutely. But I warn you, once you have eaten my cooking, and tasted my secret sauce, you and Cathy will never be satisfied with any other barbeque cooking or barbeque sauce for the rest of your life!"

"Then I'll just have to hack into your recipe database and steal your secret recipe!"

"Just try! It's all protected by my proprietary firewall software."

"You forget that I am now a master hacker, taught by my master Obi-wan Isaiah!"

"If you practice your cooking as well as you practiced your coding, someday you will become a Jedi barbeque cook, and then I'll share the secret recipe with you. My secret sauce is a powerful weapon, like the light saber. It gives shy people the strength to do what must be done!"

"And the Jedi mouth trick of major bragging and exaggerating!"

"Just for that, no seconds for you!"

* * * * * *

Alexander was on his second day out from his drop off in Lander. It was cold at night. He was glad of his goose down sleeping bag. Outside of his *Course in Reality*, he had never really gone backpacking. His time with Occupy San Francisco was more like camping out in your parents' back yard. They took turns going to motels every other night with their parents' credit cards.

He watched the dark smoke rise from his noonday campfire. *I sure hope they find me soon. I'm tired of this. I want a hot bath.*

Just then he heard a horse nicker. He stood up and looked north. A horse's head and someone in a straw cowboy hat was visible over a stand of sagebrush about sixty yards away. He waved his ball cap and yelled "A nation of laws ..."

The rider came forward to within twenty feet. A pleasant contralto voice said "and not of men." He saw blond curls under the hat. White teeth grinned out from above a bandana pulled up to her chin.

"Are you a mirage? Or have I died and gone to heaven?" If there was one thing Alexander liked to do, it was flirt. Of course, he wasn't very good at it. He didn't have to be, once girls found out who his daddy was. But he didn't know that.

He took three steps toward her, when suddenly a dog was between them, snarling and showing *large* teeth. He jumped back. "Whoa! What's that? A coyote?"

"Kemosabe! Sit!" The dog immediately sat. "Sorry about that. He doesn't like strangers getting too near me." She swung out of the saddle and removed one glove. "My name is Cathy Peterson." She held out her hand.

Alexander kept his eye on the dog and slowly stepped forward and took her hand. "My name is Alexander. Boy, am I glad to see you. I was getting tired of trying to keep warm in a sleeping bag out here by myself. Of course, if I had someone as pretty as you to share a bag with, it wouldn't be so bad." He winked at her.

She wrinkled her nose. "Nobody but a skunk would want to share a sleeping bag with you! Whew! When was the last time you took a bath?"

Flustered, he tried to charm his way out. "Don't remember. I've been on the road all the way from San Francisco, sleeping in truck beds and barns. *Lonely* barns." The girls of Occupy thought it was egalitarian to sleep with as many men as expressed an interest. Alexander was unfamiliar with the custom of wooing a girl.

He took a step toward her. She took a step back. The dog came between them again with a snarl. His nose was pointed right at Alexander's crotch.

"Mister, where I come from, men don't start hinting about sex to a woman they've just met. It's disrespectful." She glanced down at the dog, still snarling. "And dangerous."

He stepped back. "Sorry. I was just trying to be friendly."

She frowned. "Those comments were anything but friendly. Keep your distance and mind your manners. I'm bound to help you since you were sent by the CRM, but I don't appreciate your leering looks and suggestive comments."

She turned and whistled. Another horse trotted up, saddled and bridled. "Pack up your stuff and lash it across the saddle bags. We have to set a pace to make it in before dark."

Keeping his eye on the dog, he backed away and began packing up. After tying down his backpack behind the saddle, he struggled to mount the horse. Cathy finally moved up on her horse and held his horse's head still while he climbed up.

"Ride much?" She looked critically at him.

"Actually, this is my first time," he admitted.

"Well then," she said. She shook out a length of her lariat and tied his bridle to it, then looped it around her saddle horn. "Now you won't wander off. Just hold on to the saddle horn and try to keep your boots in the stirrups. I'll do the rest."

She whistled, a different note this time. The dog trotted up and looked at her inquiringly. "Kemosabe. Make sure he keeps up." She turned her reins and headed north. The dog trotted back and nipped at the heels of Alexander's horse. The horse jerked forward abruptly, nearly unseating him. He bounced behind uncomfortably.

Chapter Thirty-One

At supper that night at the Young farm, Alexander started to eat as soon as a plate was put before him. Mrs. Young spoke, "Alexander? We generally don't begin until everyone is served and we say grace. Would you say grace for us?"

Wiping his lips hurriedly with his napkin, Alexander bowed his head and mumbled "Lord, we thank you for this food. Amen."

"Thank you, Alexander. What is your last name? You know we are the Youngs and of course Joseph Wakini. And you already know Cathy." Mrs. Young passed the platter of biscuits. Alexander took two.

"Ma'am, when they swore me in, they told me to use first name only, for, like, security reasons, you know?" He bit into a biscuit. "These biscuits are mighty good, ma'am." He was still shy about his surname after his bad experience with the Occupy people. His father was not likely to be popular with the ARK people either.

"Thank you, Alexander. So, what did you bring us?" She passed the gravy.

"Cell phones, ma'am. The latest models, with the latest CRM apps loaded. With the latest encryption so we can communicate freely. They sent enough that we can distribute some to the other ARKS too, if we have a way to send them."

After supper, Alexander kept looking admiringly at Cathy. Mrs. Young intervened deftly. "Alexander, we share chores here. Would you do the dishes? Cathy, I imagine you best be heading for home. Joseph, would you help her get saddled up?"

Alexander shuffled sullenly over to the sink while Cathy and Joseph walked to the barn. *I'm a secret agent! Secret agents don't do dishes! This sucks.*

As soon as they got to the barn, Cathy giggled and hugged Joseph. "May I have a kiss, Mr. ARK leader?" She puckered up. Joseph looked over his shoulder to see if anybody was looking. Then he obliged her. Thoroughly.

He began saddling her pony. "What do you think of Alexander?"

She frowned. "Not much. He made suggestive comments to me when I first found him." She giggled again. "Kemosabe taught him some manners, though."

Joseph grunted, tightening the girth cinch. "Good."

"Hey." She held his cheeks with her hands. "Look at me." He did. "I love YOU." She released him. "Besides, Daddy taught me how to take care of myself."

She put her thumb under his nose and pushed. "Oww!" He pulled back and rubbed his upper lip. "O.K., O.K. Between your thumb and Kemosabe, you are well protected. I think I'd rather face Kemosabe than your thumb!"

"And don't you forget it, mister!" She threw her arms around his neck and kissed him again. *I won't,* he thought. *I sure won't.*

* * * * * *

The next morning after breakfast, Alexander leaned back in his chair. "Ma'am, that was a very good breakfast. Thank you. I want to volunteer for chores. I learned a few things about gardening when I was in my *Course in Reality* in the woods. Could I help take care of the garden? I also brought a concentrated mix of a new plant food that the lab in New Zealand sent over for the ARKS. I could mix some up and spray it on the vegetables. It's good for corn, too."

Mrs. Young looked pleased. "Well. I like a man who steps up to carry his own weight. Meet me in the garden right after you finish the dishes and I'll show you our spray equipment. And the business end of a hoe. Then we'll visit other families and spray their gardens too."

Alexander's face fell. *What! Dishes again! I must be the only secret agent in the world that has to wash dishes to keep from blowing his cover.*

* * * * * *

Two days later, Joseph spoke to John Young. "I've got nine young Shoshone braves who are willing to travel to other ARKS to form a network of Shoshone Wind Talkers. We plan to leave tomorrow. The elders have agreed to give us two horses each, so that we can pack provisions for the journey. Will you be OK without me? Is this guy Alexander any help at all?"

John grunted. "I'll be OK. You should take Alexander with you. He can help you teach people how to use the new encryption apps and spray the new plant food. He's not much use here. City boy."

Joseph made a face. "I can teach people these apps without him."

John put his hand on Joseph's shoulder. "I know, and this is your call as ARK leader. But, as a back-up, doesn't it make sense to have two people along who can teach the apps? In case something happens to one of you?"

Joseph frowned. "I guess you're right. Besides, I don't want to leave him behind where he'll be bird-dogging Cathy. He does have a certain amount of big city charm."

John laughed. "More likely Cathy will kick him and his charm into the next county. And then he'll get chewed up and gnawed to little pieces by Kemosabe if he tries to come back."

Joseph allowed himself a small smile. "O.K., I'm convinced. Can we get two horses and a saddle for him?"

"I'll contribute one, and I believe Cathy's father will contribute the other."

* * * * * *

Cathy was at the corral to see Joseph off. She took off her bandana and tied it around his neck. Then she leaned her forehead against his chest. "Dear Lord, this man is precious to me. Please bring this man home safely to me. Amen." *Amen*, thought Joseph. "Cathy," he whispered in her ear. "Cathy, I love you."

She looked up at him. "I love you too. Kiss me?" He glanced nervously at the other Shoshone boys and Alexander. He knew he would be in for teasing on the trail. He kissed her anyway. Thoroughly.

* * * * * *

At ARK Ute, Joseph and Alexander were able to train four people in the use of the cell phone apps. ARK Ute elders also agreed to take in two of the Shoshone boys as their Wind Talkers. Alexander sprayed their garden crops with the plant food formula he had brought. Some ARK farmers had large horse trailers to drive them and their mounts most of the way to their next ARK location in one night. After leaving the trailers, they slept for the rest of the day and traveled during that first night. Their ponies were mountain-bred and sure-footed in the dark. It was the seventh day since they had left ARK Shoshone.

* * * * * *

In ARK Shoshone, Cathy Peterson's father was the first to show symptoms. Dr. Dreen was puzzled. This was no flu he had ever seen. Soon six other people in the ARK showed the symptoms. Then realization dawned on him. *Dear merciful Lord, it's Diana Nomenski's EarthPurge Virus!* He had some of the data relating to its development, but nothing about the antidote. He hurried over to John Young's farm.,

"John, we're in danger. Remember that deadly virus I told you about? Being developed by PRIS in Chicago? This is it. ARK Shoshone is infected with it. It is spread by means of the food supply. I have some data about the virus in this flash drive that I want to transmit to Grace Washington via New Zealand, if I can use your uplink? She might be able to help us, if it's not too late."

John walked Dr. Dreen to the hidden communications closet and fired up the computer and the satellite dish for upload to the ARK ONE orbiting satellite. While he waited for it all to boot up, he asked "Doctor, remind me how this virus is spread?"

"It's designed to be sprayed on food crops and vegetable gardens. The virus is hosted on the food until it can enter humans and multiply."

"And how long after exposure were symptoms supposed to appear?"

"Seven to eight days. Let's see, what was going on here seven days ago?"

They both looked at each other in horror. "Alexander sprayed our gardens! It was him!" they shouted simultaneously.

John frantically tried to align the dish on the satellite signal. "And now we've sent him to five other ARK locations to do the same thing! We've got to warn them! We've got to warn Joseph! But how? He's already left ARK Ute. He'll keep radio silence until he reaches the next ARK location. Some of these ARKS don't have satellite uplink communications. By the time we get word to Joseph that assassin will have infected a third ARK, and maybe be moving on to a fourth. Joseph wasn't sure he'd go to all six ARKS himself."

Finally the dish locked on to the satellite. Dr. Dreen began uploading his data about the virus and composing an urgent SOS message for the Nutritional Abundance Industries scientists in ARK Pacific. And he prayed. Prayers of desperation.

*   *   *   *   *   *

With his knowledge of how the virus worked, Dr. Dreen was able to slow the progress of the virus with the medicines he had on hand. *But I'm fighting a delaying action. If we can't get an antidote, everyone will die.*

Six had died already, including his own youngest child and Sonia Hughes-McLauren's baby. He remembered a scripture reading from his childhood – one of the Sundays after Christmas – "A voice was heard in Ramah, ... Rachel weeping for her children ... because they are no more." He sobbed for his child.

Like King Herod destroying the baby boys of Judea, he thought bitterly, *that evil Diana Nomenski has reached out and killed our children after all. We were complicit in her evil virus, and it has followed us here. God forgive me.*

Chapter Thirty-Two

John Young and Cathy went in to talk to her mother. "June, I know you are hard pressed with Paul being sick, but this is life and death. Cathy's the best rider in ARK Shoshone. If we don't get word to Joseph about this fellow Alexander infecting all the food, Joseph may take him to all six of the ARKs we planned on visiting. Thousands more could die from this thing. I think I can use your horse trailer to drive Cathy and her pony just over the Utah – Nevada border on Interstate 80. We could make it tonight by chancing the highway checkpoints and driving all night. Then she could ride south and overtake Joseph and his Shoshones and warn them about Alexander and the virus.

"If she's successful, the next night I could run the highway checkpoints again and get them all back home for Dr. Dreen to try to treat with the medicines he has. It may not work, but it's all we've got. June, this is asking you to put your only daughter at risk, but many others will be put at risk if we do nothing. As far as I can tell, Cathy ate from your stored food, so she's not infected with the virus. Will you let her go?"

June Peterson was weak herself from the first stages of the virus. "John, we have to help others when we can." She looked at Cathy. "Baby, you can't cure us or save us by staying here. But you can save other people by going. Go with my blessings."

Cathy hugged her mother, then got up and faced John. She had tears in her eyes. She looked at her sick mother, then back at John. "Let's go."

*   *   *   *   *   *

At five the following morning, John was leading Cathy's pony out of the trailer, just over the Nevada line from Utah. They had managed to avoid all roadblocks but one, far west of Salt Late City, in the middle of nowhere. There was only one police car and it was 3 a.m. John decided to gamble that the lone policeman was asleep in his car. He did not slow down. He smashed through the wooden barricades. A half mile further, he stopped and jumped out of his truck cab. He pulled out a police issue set of tire spikes and spread them across the two lanes behind him. Then he sped on. He never saw a police car, so he imagined the spikes had done their job on all four tires when the police cruiser rolled over them at high speed. Nobody carried four spare tires.

He quickly got Cathy saddled up, then opened the back door of his crew cab. Kemosabe jumped out, barking. He petted the mutt. "Good boy. You take good care of Cathy."

He turned back to Cathy. She swung into the saddle. He reached up and took her gloved hand and kissed it. "Cathy, the sun will be up in another 30 minutes. Ride at a canter, but don't hesitate to rein in if the ground looks uneven. A horse with a broken leg will not help anybody. Go with God!"

She pulled her reins towards the South. "God, be with me."

Three hours later she thought she saw them on the horizon. A dark clump that kicked up a little dust. She pulled up and took out her binoculars. It was them!

She kicked her pony into a gallop and raced across the prairie after them. Kemosabe was falling behind, but she knew he would catch up to her later. She kicked up a lot of dust. Too much dust.

One hundred twenty three miles away in Salt Lake City, a drone driver in Search and Destroy Division Drone Control picked up an optical on a linear moving dust trail. Vectoring his drone closer, he saw that the dust trail was a straight line across the desert. Too straight to be a natural phenomenon like a dust devil. He flew closer and lower. He increased his magnification. A girl on a horse, galloping as fast as she could. *Probably in training for a horse race*, he thought. Not a CRM subversives target.

The nineteen year old corporal glanced over his shoulder at his commanding officer, a second lieutenant. He was occupied, not paying attention. The corporal thought: *this has been the most boring duty assignment ever. Nothing ever happens. Well, I think I'll make something happen.* He centered his targeting cross hairs on the horse and rider. Then he armed and fired his weapon – an air-to-ground missile.

He watched the screen with the horse at the center. The center of the screen suddenly blossomed into a flare of light. He averted his eyes. When he looked back, there was a crater in the desert floor. *Cool! This is better than video killing games. This is real. She must be splattered all over that crater. I wonder if I can see any blood!*

"What's going on corporal? I heard the tone signaling a launch." The lieutenant had walked rapidly to the corporal's flight station.

"Sir, I thought I saw some insurgents following a girl on a horse. Now I'm not so sure. But I got the girl anyway. But maybe she wasn't an insurgent?"

"Well even if she wasn't, it will send a message to the population – *get permission for all travel not pre-authorized by the Citizen Travel Control Authority, or run the risk of a drone strike.* Well, corporal. Your first kill. A commendation will go into your file."

"Thank you, sir."

"Resume normal patrol pattern." The lieutenant walked back to his desk.

*   *   *   *   *   *

Three miles away, Joseph and his group of Shoshones heard the explosion, then felt the pressure wave. When they looked back, they saw a plume of smoke. Joseph immediately knew what it was.

"Dear God, that was a drone strike! Right where we passed thirty minutes ago. Could someone have been following us? No. It had to be a friendly who knew where to look. We've got to go look for survivors. Richard Littlehawk and James Swiftwalker, come with me. The rest of you proceed on toward Ark Ute 2."

Joseph and the other two cantered in the direction of the smoke plume. Thirty minutes later, they arrived at the crater. There wasn't much left, but they could tell it had been a horse and rider. One severed leg of the pony had been blown to the edge of the crater.

Then Joseph saw something move out of the corner of his eye. He turned and saw Kemosabe trotting up with something in his mouth. Cathy's straw cowboy hat. It was shredded. He suddenly could not see. He gripped the saddle horn and swayed. When he steadied himself and looked again, Richard had dismounted and was kneeling beside the dog. He was holding the hat. He looked up at Joseph.

"It's Cathy's hat, Joseph." He held out the hat toward Joseph.

Joseph passed out and fell out of the saddle. When he woke up, Richard was dribbling some water over his lips from a canteen. He heard a truck engine. A door slammed. A shadow fell over him. He looked up. John Young was standing there.

"Joseph!" he cried out, then kneeled. "Richard, is he OK?"

Richard shook his head. "He's in shock." He reached out and pulled over Cathy's hat and handed it to John. John looked at it and then fell to his knees.

"No! No! Dear God, no!" He clutched the straw hat and rocked it from side to side like a baby. Kemosabe came up and licked his hand and whined.

Joseph sat up. He took the canteen and poured water on his face. He stood. He swayed for a moment, then steadied himself.

John sat up, then turned to one side and pushed himself up. He walked over to Joseph. "She was coming to warn you."

"Warn me of what?"

"There's a virus in ARK Shoshone. Remember the one Dr. Dreen told us about? The deadly genetically-modified virus? It's there. Six people have died already, including Dr. Dreen's youngest child."

John reached out and gripped Joseph by the elbow. "Joseph, the virus is spread by spraying it on food crops."

Looking down, Joseph murmured, "Spraying … " He looked up sharply. "Alexander!"

"Yes! Alexander sprayed our crops and infected us. I drove Cathy through the blockade to catch up to you and warn you. Before you took Alexander to more ARKS."

John looked at the crater again. "But I forgot about the drones. I forgot to warn Cathy about kicking up dust in a straight line. I told her to canter to catch up to you." John looked up at the sky. "God in heaven,

I caused her death! I forgot to warn her about the drones!" He slumped against Joseph, sobbing.

Joseph helped John slide down to a sitting position. Then he looked at Richard with a terrible calm on his face. "Richard. We have work to do."

Richard nodded, then caught up his horse and mounted.

Joseph looked at James. "James, you stay here with John. You have your walkie-talkie?" James nodded. "You'll hear from me or Richard within two hours. If not, go home with John."

Joseph caught his own pony, then took another look at the crater. He mounted. Looking around, he whistled. The dog came running. "Kemosabe. Come." The dog looked back at the crater and whined. "I know. Come."

Horse, dog and rider trotted off together, towards the South. Richard Littlehawk trotted beside him. They did not speak.

Chapter Thirty-Three

Joseph and Richard cantered up to the Shoshone group. Joseph reined in and said to Richard, "I'll take care of this." Richard nodded. He turned and with a gesture signaled the others not to interfere.

Walking his horse up to face Alexander on his mount, Joseph reached out with his left hand and grabbed him by the throat. "Where is it?" His voice was low and hard.

Gagging, Alexander spluttered out "Where is what? What are you talking about?" He used both of his hands to try to pry away Joseph's grip. Suddenly releasing his grip, Joseph leaned over and slid his arm around Alexander's neck. Then he flicked his reins and walked his horse back. Alexander was pulled off his horse and kicked his feet out helplessly, held off the ground in a choke hold. He clutched at Joseph's arm around his neck, to no avail.

When he sagged and stopped kicking, Joseph dropped him to the ground. He lay there, coughing and retching with his hands on his throat. Joseph dismounted. He took a knee beside Alexander, looking down at him.

"I'm only going to ask you one more time. Where is it?"

"I ..." he coughed, " ... don't know what you are talking about."

Joseph stood up and whistled. Kemosabe trotted up. "Kemosabe! Bite!" Snarling, the dog bit into Alexander's forearm and worried it with jerks of his head.

"Aahh! Call him off! Call him off! I'll talk! I'll talk!"

"Kemosabe. Sit." The dog backed off two feet and sat, keeping his eyes on Alexander. Alexander sat up, clutching at his left arm with his right hand. The other Shoshone had dismounted and gathered in a circle around them.

"I'm bleeding! I need first aid! I need a bandage!"

"Kemosabe." The dog rose off its haunches. Alexander's eyes widened. Then he looked at Joseph.

"The backpack! It's in the backpack!"

Joseph looked over at Richard, who retrieved the backpack from Alexander's pack horse. Richard dumped out the contents and rifled through them. "I don't see anything."

Joseph looked back at Alexander, then at the dog. Kemosabe growled.

"The padded straps!" Alexander screamed. "It's in the padded straps!"

Richard found the slit in the stitching and pulled out eight plastic packets. Then he pulled out eleven capsules from the other strap. "What are these?" Richard asked.

Alexander was holding his torn arm to his body and rocking back and forth, whimpering. Joseph looked at the dog. "Bite." Kemosabe seized the arm again and gave a vicious jerk.

"Aahh! No! It's the virus! The packets are the virus!" The dog kept tugging at the arm.

"Kemosabe. Sit." Again the dog backed off and sat.

"Tell us everything." Joseph's voice was flat and drained of emotion.

"The packets are a virus. You mix it with water and spray it on the vegetables. People get sick 7 or 8 days later. They made me do it. You have to understand … they made me do it!" Alexander was sobbing.

Richard held up a capsule. "And the capsules?"

"They … they are an antidote, a temporary antidote. There is no cure for this thing. Each capsule protects you for ten days. Then you have to take another one for another ten days. They only gave me twelve capsules."

"Why only twelve?" Joseph spoke in the same low voice.

"They wanted to make sure I came back to them. I have to go back before the capsules run out, or I die too!"

"What did they promise you?"

"That I'd be famous and important. That I'd have an important job with the Search and Destroy Division of Homeland Security. That I'd have an office with a window! They said if I didn't do it they'd put me in jail or execute me! For just knowing someone in the CRM! It wasn't fair! What could I do? I had to do what they said! I had to!" He rocked himself, cradling his torn arm.

"How long until you die from the virus?"

"Twenty six days."

"Richard, we all ate spaghetti before we left Wind River, for the carb loading. Did anybody eat anything from the vegetable gardens in ARK Shoshone?" They all shook their heads.

Joseph looked around the circle of seven Shoshone youths. His brow furrowed as he calculated. "We ate vegetables from the ARK Ute gardens two days ago, after Alexander had sprayed them. That means we all have twenty four days to live. We have five days before we start feeling sick."

Joseph prodded Alexander with his boot. "How about you? When did you eat sprayed vegetables?"

Alexander looked scared. "Same as you. Two days ago. But I took a capsule. That gave me ten extra days. So, I've got thirty-four days to live, unless ..."

Joseph kicked him. "Unless what?"

"Unless we get more antidote pills. As long as we keep taking them every ten days, we're OK. They were supposed to send a huge supply to all of the Homeland Security Bases, just in case they got accidentally infected. Maybe if we turn ourselves in at the Homeland Security base in Salt Lake City, they'll give us more pills!"

He looked imploringly with his puppy dog eyes at the youths circling him. "It's worth a try! They are fair people! Let me bring you in. They'll owe me a favor for capturing you guys. I'll call in a favor and they'll give me plenty of pills for all of us!"

The circle of faces looked stony. Joseph walked outside the circle, staring into the North, where some smoke was still drifting away from the crater. He stared a long time. Then he turned back and walked inside the circle.

"There are eleven capsules left and ten of us, counting me and James. We will all take one now. We'll give the eleventh pill to John Young.

That gives us thirty-four days to live, and fifteen days before we start to feel sick. Isaiah was going to meet his wife Dr. Grace Washington in Laramie. She's brilliant, and her specialty is genetically modified biological organisms. She's our only hope. If I can contact Isaiah, maybe he and Dr. Washington can help us."

He turned to Richard Littlehawk. "Richard, we will break radio silence. Use the walkie-talkie to speak to James back at the crater. Speak Shoshone. Ask him if John brought his satellite telephone with him, and if John can take us back to Ark Ute? We'll all try to get back home from there."

He turned and looked down at Alexander. "Get up and get on your horse."

"But I'm bleeding!"

"Then bleed."

An hour later they were all back at the crater. John had spread camo netting over his truck to avoid notice from drones. James got two shovels from John's truck and formed a burial detail. He found two pieces of wood and made a rough cross with baling wire. They gathered around the grave and took off their hats.

Joseph started to speak, but then his face twisted up.

John stepped up. "I'll do it." He had pulled a new testament out of his glove box. "Jesus said, there is no greater love than this: that a man lay down his life for his friends. This girl was full of life and love. She helped everyone she met, even those," here he turned and looked at Alexander, who had fashioned a sling for his arm, "who showed her disrespect."

John wiped his eyes. "She lost her life trying to warn all of you about the deadly virus. She knew she was taking a risk, but she did it anyway." John looked over at Joseph. "For those she loved." John's voice quavered. "No greater love."

Joseph took the bandanna from around his neck and tied it around the crosspiece of the rough wooden cross. It was the bandana Cathy had given him. As he bent over, he whispered, "I love you, Cathy. I'll never forget."

He walked away toward John's four-wheel drive truck.

He opened the passenger door of the truck and leaned against it. When John walked up, he asked, "Can we contact whoever sent Alexander to us with your satellite phone? We need to warn them of the security leak."

"I think so." John got out the unit and punched in code numbers. Then he texted *ARK Shoshone for CRM-SF Code Name Solomon. Urgent security breach call soonest.* He looked at Joseph. "Now we wait."

Twenty minutes later the phone beeped. John answered. "Hello, Solomon? ARK Shoshone Contact One here. We have a security breach. I'm putting you on speaker."

Joseph and John did not know it was Judge Block. He spoke. "ARK Shoshone Contact Two here. Solomon, be advised, the man Alexander you sent to us was an agent of Homeland Security Search and Destroy Division. He has infected two ARKS with a genetically modified virus that kills in 26 days. Your cell may be compromised as well."

The voice crackled with static. "We are compromised. Someone here has been arrested and executed. We have been tracing it down. Let me speak to Alexander, if he's still alive?"

Joseph was stony faced. "So far. Just a minute. Richard! Bring Alexander over here please." Richard brought him, with the dog following closely.

The judge spoke. "Alexander? Thomas the painter is dead. Executed by the Search and Destroy people. Why, Alexander? Why did you betray him? He was a friend to you."

"It's not my fault!" Alexander whined. "They threatened me with prison and execution, just because I was around you people. I told them you kidnapped me, that I was taken against my will! But they wouldn't listen."

"Thomas and I saved you from a literal crucifixion by your Occupy friends, as I recall. It wasn't against your will then. Thomas was good to you."

"I know, I know! He even gave me extra cans of food when I was in the woods on your stupid *Course in Reality*. He said he felt sorry for me. He was compassionate! More than you!"

"Oh!" the Judge said. There was sadness in his voice. "That explains it. The tragedy of too much compassion. The tragedy of the compassion that caters and coddles without requiring people do something to help themselves. The compassion that becomes enabling. Too much compassion has killed again. Thomas' over-compassion sabotaged your *Course in Reality.*

"You learned nothing. I should have noticed the clues. You didn't have to work to eat, so you didn't learn to take care of yourself. Thomas took care of you. Too much compassion killed Thomas, who offered you compassion, and now it has killed you, who received his compassion even after you were capable of helping yourself. You got something for nothing, and it made you good for nothing. Predictably, you did not feel grateful. Instead you resented Thomas and turned him in to the authorities. You would have turned me in too, if you knew where to find me."

Alexander was silent. He began to cry.

"Alexander, you called your father, didn't you? Why?"

"I was hungry, and I had no money for a pizza. I knew Dad would get me some money."

"Alexander, there was food in Thomas's refrigerator."

"Yes, but it had to be cooked. I wanted something to eat *right away!*" He sniffled and hung his head.

"Solomon? I'm dying of this virus. I need the antidote pills! Can't you help me?"

"No Alexander. Unneeded compassion has killed enough people already. You'll get no compassion from me. I recall telling you that your *Course in Reality* is not optional. Only when you take it is optional. Time to take the course for real this time. No cheating. Live with your answers, Alexander. Good bye." Joseph motioned with his head, and Richard led Alexander away.

The Judge paused. "ARK Shoshone Contact Two? Those deaths are on me too. I liked that young man and thought I could save him from the Dark Side. I was wrong. I missed the clues after he came back from his *Course in Reality.* How can I help?"

"Our only hope is Dr. Grace Washington. She passed through here weeks ago. She was supposed to meet her husband Isaiah Mercury in Laramie. Can you track them down and tell them to contact us via this uplink unit? Isaiah knows which unit."

"I think we can do it. Turn your unit on each night at eight and leave it on for an hour. Just one more thing. Did they promise Alexander any rewards?"

Joseph frowned. "Yes. An important job. And an office with a window."

Joseph could hear the sigh through the static. "So he wanted to be important. Sold his birthright for an office with a window. Jesus wept. Cheaper than thirty pieces of silver. Solomon out."

Joseph conferred with John. "Can you get us out of here in your truck and horse trailer? We can't take all the ponies, so we'll set the rest free. They'll make their way to the pastures in the next ARK nearby."

John nodded. "Yes. We may run into patrols on the Interstate, so we'll have to pull the United Nations sovereign nation bluff again. Luckily, I printed up Diplomatic UN Credentials for all of you before," he paused and swallowed, "… before Cathy and I left. What about him?" John nodded toward Alexander.

"You heard Solomon. Time for him to live with his answers. He had the opportunity to learn wilderness survival skills during his *Course in Reality*. Time for the final exam."

Joseph strode toward the staked out horses. "OK, everybody! We are leaving with John. We can take two horses. Cache the saddles and supplies beneath a camo tarp below that thicket of sagebrush and mark the coordinates on your cell phone navigation app. We may need them for another operation. Let the rest of the horses loose. They'll drift toward the springs and green grass at the next ARK. Richard will notify the people at the next ARK to be looking for them. When you're done, jump into the back of John's truck."

Alexander looked pitiful. "What about me?"

"You?" Joseph looked right through him. "Seven people have died because of you, including my fiancé. You're lucky I don't kill you where you stand. Instead, you're getting a chance you did not give to others. We're leaving you here. Your best chance is to walk north until you reach Interstate 80. Then you can hitch-hike to Salt Lake City. Or, you can wait here and hope somebody will rescue you. Except nobody knows you're here. There is plenty of food in the cache. But there is no firewood here and it gets below freezing at night. If you walk out it will keep you warm."

Joseph got into the truck with the others. He called out, "I won't say good luck. I will say, Live with Your Answers." The truck bumped away across the uneven terrain.

Alexander yelled after them, "Ha! I'll have the last laugh! My father is rich and powerful! He'll send people to find me and give me antidote pills. I'll live and you'll die! Besides, I'm a secret agent for the most powerful government agency there is! More powerful than the military, even. The Department of Homeland Security, that's what! Keeping this nation secure from creeps like you! So there! They'll find me!"

I'm not walking, I'm waiting. Walking is boring. There was enough food for eleven of us in that cache. I'll live. I'll wait right here, and they'll find me. They'll take care of me. The DHS and my Dad. It takes a village, and they are my village.

The next spring coyotes found the carcass, thawing out. Alexander had died because he wouldn't help himself. He died with his answers.

Chapter Thirty-Four

Grace woke up, disoriented. It was dark. She lay on her back, fully clothed in jeans, boots, flannel shirt and puffy parka. Reaching out, she felt coarse polyester fabric on both sides of her, stretched tight over something. The place where she lay swayed and then bounced a little.

She sat up, remembering. *I'm in the bed of a military type transport truck.* She looked at the luminous dial of her watch. 4:30 a.m. She reached into a pocket and brought out an LED flashlight. Shining it around her, she recognized the sacks of seeds she had been lying on. Her seeds. Quick growing super-seeds for people holed up in ARK locations. The seeds that would enable the ARK people to feed themselves, store enough surplus for two years, and still have enough left over to feed ten times their number.

The Constitutional Resistance Movement was smuggling her through Laramie, Wyoming on her way to the next ARK location. She would analyze their soil conditions and show them the best methods to cultivate her seeds.

The canvas cover of the truck bed was stenciled "FEMA EMERGENCY MEDICAL SUPPLIES." The local CRM resistance fighters believed that masquerading as a government agency would allow them to travel the public highways without fear of being stopped. They had gotten through two traffic checkpoints on the interstate highway so far with counterfeit credentials. Grace stayed hidden underneath seed sacks stenciled "ORGANIC ANTISEPTIC SEEDS. INEDIBLE. GRIND AND APPLY TO WOUNDS."

Crawling over the seed sacks, she pushed up the canvas cover and looked out. She saw city buildings in the faint pre-dawn glow. There were no streetlights. No lights at all.

In the collapsed local economy, electricity was turned on for two two-hour time periods per day, one in the morning and one in the evening. Nobody kept refrigerated foods like milk and butter anymore. The duration of electricity was not enough to keep those foods from spoiling. People ate out of cans and gardens and used the brief periods of electricity to cook food, turn on their lights, watch television, use computers, use the internet and charge cell phones.

The truck took an exit from the interstate onto surface roads. They planned to refuel at the FEMA depot in Laramie. Next they would get fresh drivers from a CRM Safe House. She pulled the canvas down and got ready to hide under some of the lighter sacks again.

Suddenly, she heard gunfire. The truck stopped. Reaching into her other pocket, she thumbed on a walkie-talkie. "Grace? Stay hidden. This looks like a gang roadblock. We'll try to talk our way through." She whispered "Roger that." She burrowed under the sacks.

Armed men in ski masks surrounded the truck. The driver wound down his window. "FEMA! We are taking emergency medical supplies to Fort Collins. Let us through."

The man closest to the driver pointed an AK-47 at him. "Progressive America Brigade. This is our territory and we give the orders here. What's in the truck?"

"Like I said, emergency medical supplies."

"We'll see for ourselves. Stay in the truck."

With guns drawn, they began rummaging through the contents of the truck. They tossed aside sacks and found Grace. They pulled her out of the truck and zip-tied her hands behind her back.

They shined a flashlight in her face. "Who are you?"

Don't they know? she thought. My face is on FBI most-wanted posters in every grocery store in America. She blinked, "They said I could hitch a ride. I'm trying to get to my mother in Fort Collins."

The one who seemed to be the boss said, "Some of this stuff might be food." He pointed his gun at the driver. "You! Drive the truck where you're told." Motioning to the two holding Grace, "Put the woman in the cab with the other two." Two masked men got on the running boards and pointed pistols at the driver and passengers. The truck moved off slowly.

* * * * * *

The masked men zip-tied the hands of the two CRM operatives, then locked them and Grace in a tool shed in the parking lot of a warehouse. They drove the truck inside the building and closed the loading door behind it.

Within fifteen minutes, the tin door of the tool shed opened. "The profs want to talk to you." They pulled all three of them up. Then they pushed and shoved them into the warehouse.

"Who are the profs?" asked Grace. "You'll see," was the short answer. They were pushed onto seats in an old break room. They looked around. An old calendar on the wall carried a business logo that read *Jason's Vending. Fine beverages and tasty snacks. Ready when you want them!* The masked men bound their ankles to the chair legs with duct tape.

A goateed man with a ponytail entered the room. His army surplus field jacket was open, revealing a faded red "Che Guevara" t-shirt. He had an automatic pistol in a shoulder holster and an ammo belt slung across the other shoulder. He wore a "Che" style beret.

His eyes were gaunt. His clothes hung loosely on him. Two more entered. One was a thin man, similarly dressed in "revolutionary chic" clothing. The other was a woman, a Laura Croft wannabe, with two ammo belts criss-crossing her torso and a gun on both hips. The belts were festooned with ammunition. Her tank top revealed skinny arms.

Grace recognized the symptoms of malnutrition. She had witnessed enough cases from her work in Africa to notice the signs quickly. She also sized up the situation easily. Pol-Pot strutting dictator wannabes, with Pol-Pot results: starvation. They've recreated Pol-Pot's Cambodia here in America.

The three of them walked around Grace and her two companions. The ponytailed one circled a second time. He paused in front of the two CRM resistance fighters. "You two I do not know." He moved in front of Grace and seized her chin in one of his dirty hands. "You I know."

He walked behind a table and sat down facing them. His two acolytes sat on either side of him. "You," he said pointing his finger at Grace, "are an enemy of the people. You're on the FBI most-wanted list. You refused to turn over the secret of your miracle seeds, which belong to everybody."

Grace's mouth was set in a tight line. "That's odd. I don't remember seeing everybody working alongside me in my lab when I developed them."

Ponytail slammed his fist on the table. "Enough! The state fed you, clothed you, educated you and provided the infrastructure of a modern society for you to live in! The state created you, so what you create belongs to the state. Which is everybody. Those seeds? You didn't build them! The state made you who you are, so the state owns those seeds. When you withhold the secret of those seeds, you are stealing from the state, which is everybody! You stole from all of the rest of us! You are a common thief!"

Grace answered from under lowered brows, "My mama fed me. My daddy clothed me. I worked my way through school. I paid taxes, too much in taxes, for your so-called infrastructure. My mother and father created me biologically and spiritually. I created the rest of me through my own study, self-discipline and prayer. I did invent those seeds. I worked hard to develop those seeds. It is you and your followers who are the thieves! We are the makers and you are the takers. And I notice that after I and the other makers left this country to the takers like you, the infrastructure crumbled pretty quickly."

She sniffed the air. "Bathe much?"

The woman leaped from her chair and slapped Grace hard. "Capitalist scum! We gladly sacrifice the bourgeois vice of hot water and daily bathing to the people's revolution!"

"You mean the people with the will to work and the technical know-how to generate electricity 24 hours a day? Those people? They decided to stop being your slaves. I've heard your short wave radio broadcasts promising rewards for any electrical engineers who will come back to work at the power plants. But there are several problems with that plan."

The woman had raised her hand for another back-handed slap. "What's that, pig?"

"You will also need mining engineers to mine the coal, and railroad engineers to run the coal trains to the generating plant. Oh, wait. I forgot, you decided to shut down the coal-fired generating plants. And you forgot about that thing called weather. Not enough sunny days to keep the solar panels going? Not enough windy days to keep the windmills turning? Oh wait, I forgot. You decided to ignore that little thing called reality. Now you are living with your answers. How's that working out for you?"

The woman slapped her again, harder. Grace tasted blood from a split lip. The two CRM men struggled against their bonds in a fury.

Ponytail leaned forward. "What we want from you right now is food. Is it safe to eat the seeds labeled ORGANIC ANTISEPTIC SEEDS?"

"Hungry? Why isn't everybody feeding you?"

The woman raised her hand for another slap and Grace flinched. In a lower voice, Grace asked, "Who are you? Why do the others call you 'profs'? Who am I talking to?"

Ponytail sat back, curled his lips and crossed his arms. "I'm Dr. Melton Clifton, Professor of 19th century Romantic Literature at Wyoming State University. This (he nodded at the man on his left) is Dr. Fitzwater, Professor of Scientific Sociology and Socialism, and your sparring partner is Dr. Speward, Professor of Feminist Studies of Gender Inequality. Until last September, we were co-directors of the Eugene Debs Prosperity Camp and Collective Farm."

"What happened last September?"

"Counter-revolutionary traitors on the farm waited too long to harvest. We lost 80% of the crop. Counter-revolutionary thieves from the city stole the rest. These young men, our security detail, were once our students at the university. Our heroic cadre is barely surviving on what's left of the vending machine food in this warehouse."

Grace frowned. "So, like Pol-Pot, you make-believe revolutionaries tried out the role of make-believe farmers. When you didn't know when to harvest, you lost the crop. You blamed it on your slave labor on the farm in order to avoid being blamed yourselves. You've managed to recreate the starvation of Pol-Pot's Cambodia. I assume you recreated the Killing Fields too?"

The woman snarled, "We executed the traitors who sabotaged the harvest!" She seized Grace roughly by the chin. "Every one." She licked the blood from the corner of Grace's mouth. "Like we'll execute you," she purred. Grace jerked her head away.

"Looks like you enjoy your work." Grace looked sick.

"I do," leered the Croft wannabe.

"Enough!" shouted Ponytail. "Traitor Washington! Can we eat the seeds or not?"

"Can you trust the word of a traitor?" Grace growled.

"We'll decide whom to trust! The seeds! Safe? Or not?" He leaned over the table with menace in his eyes.

"They might be safe," said Grace quietly. She raised her head. "Or they might not. What does Scientific Sociology tell you about this subject?"

"We can make you talk! We won't hesitate to torture traitors!" thundered Ponytail.

"And I'll tell you whatever you want me to say. I'll even save you the trouble of torture. Do you want me to say it's safe? OK, it's safe." She smiled.

"We can't trust what she says!" screeched the woman.

"Wait." Ponytail sat back and exhaled. "OK, look. We're reasonable people. We can offer you a job with power. You can be in charge of all agriculture in the People's Progressive Wyoming. You will be the Agriculture Czar. You can run all of the farms. Power. Prestige. Thousands of people obeying your orders."

"And I'll obey your orders. Tell me how to run the farms and I'll tell your farm slaves to do it the way you told me to do it. I'll play ball with you. Just give me your orders."

"No, no!" screamed Ponytail. "You're missing the point! You have expertise in agriculture. We want you to tell us what YOU want us to do to make a good harvest."

"OK. First, let me and my friends go."

"What? No! We can't let you go! We need you so you'll tell us what to do."

"So I'm not free to go? A prisoner? Then you're in control. Tell me what to do."

Ponytail looked at the woman. "Very well. Dr. Speward, do what you have to do."

Speward pulled out several bamboo slivers and a lighter. She burned the bamboo in the flame until it glowed red at the tip. "I'm old school," she said pleasantly. "No waterboarding for me. Jamming burning bamboo into sensitive places works just fine. I noticed your beautiful fingernails."

"Hold up her hands." One of the masked young men twisted Grace's hands up behind her, still bound with zip ties. Speward walked behind her with an obscene grin on her face. Grace screamed and then fainted.

Just then the door was kicked open and several men entered with peculiar hand guns. They quickly shot tranquilizer darts into all three professors and their masked students.

Ponytail grasped at the dart in his shoulder, then relaxed and slumped to the floor. The others followed.

More people poured into the room. They wore the CRM insignia. One cut Grace and the others free. A flask of brandy was put to Grace's mouth. She drank and then choked and pushed it away. Someone gently rubbed antibiotic cream on her split lip. Then she examined her finger.

"Grace, I have to pull it out in order to treat it. This will hurt. A lot." Grace nodded dumbly, then held her hand up. She abruptly jerked the bamboo out. Grace screamed again, then feebly reached for the brandy flask. The woman gently rubbed antibiotic cream on her finger, then bandaged it.

"What's your name?" Grace's voice was weak.

"Audrey Barnes, field medic with CRM." She continued kneeling by Grace's chair. "Dr. Washington, I'm sorry it took us so long to get here. When your truck didn't arrive at our safe house, it took some time to track down which gang had taken you and where they had taken you."

The CRM man who had driven the truck was given back his sidearm. He looked at the three professors with hatred. Chambering a round, he said softly, "Grace, we can save the taxpayers the expense of a war crimes trial in a few years. They deserve to die."

Another CRM soldier entered the room and addressed the commander. "Sir, we've done a quick search of the warehouse." He dumped out a sack on the table. "There are only twelve packets of very stale candy left in the place. Not worth the risk of eating it."

Grace looked up at the driver. "Commander? Let them live. Let them live with their answers and twelve moldy packages of candy. Let them starve with their answers. I noticed that none of them had any calluses on their hands. They haven't been doing any manual labor. Let them live out their dream: not lifting a finger to help themselves or anyone else. Strutting around giving orders to the last."

She picked up a package of the moldy candy and tossed it onto the slumped body of the woman. "Live with your answers."

Chapter Thirty-Five

AN ENCRYPTED MESSAGE WENT TO ALL CRM UNITS LOCATED WITHIN a radius of ARK locations in the continental US: *begin Operation Misdirection*. A CRM unit operating along the I-80 corridor in Wyoming swung into action at midnight.

Breaking into a state highway department garage, a nine-man CRM squad took three trucks. One truck had a hoist. The other had a hydraulic auger and pile driver. The third had a bucket lift.

At eight rural exits west of Rawlins, Wyoming, the squad switched the highway signage from the north side of the exits to the south side and vice-versa. They returned the trucks before the DOT crews arrived the next morning. Five of them actually worked for the DOT. Local people noticed the switch the next morning, but said nothing to the authorities. They were all sympathizers to the CRM cause. Many had received smuggled emergency food rations from the ARKS.

CRM sympathizers and agents within county road crews turned county road signs in the wrong directions. Like the French Resistance during WWII, they intended to make it hard for the Homeland Security forces to find their way around the countryside.

One week later, a second message to CRM units instructed: *begin Operation Wild Goose Chase*.

The week after that, a Homeland Security HumVee pulled up in front of the local Wal-Mart in Rock Springs, Wyoming before the opening hour. A sergeant and three agents entered the store and demanded to see the store manager. A woman came out of the back.

"I'm Roweena Clark, the store manager. How can I help you?"

"I'm Sergeant Jenkins of Homeland Security. We have orders to confiscate and destroy all paper maps and road atlases. Tell your people to bring them to us at the back of the store."

Unbeknownst to the Sergeant, this order was actually generated by CRM saboteurs and inserted into the Homeland Security routine email traffic. CRM had spread the word to its sympathizers to hide, hoard and preserve paper copies of road maps, road atlases, and topo maps. Most maps had sold out at retail locations the week before, but each store kept a dozen or more copies to hand over to Homeland Security.

"Are maps now outlawed, Sergeant?" Roweena Clark raised one eyebrow.

"Presidential Executive Order 8593 makes it illegal for citizens to travel more than thirty miles from their homes or place of work without internal passport permission from Homeland Security. Destroying maps makes it more difficult for citizens to violate this new regulation. Your maps, please?"

"Of course." She went to a cash register and used the public address system. "Attention all employees. Bring all maps, road atlases or topographic maps to the loading dock in the back."

The agents took quick-light charcoal bags from the garden section and started a fire in a trash barrel in the rear parking lot. About six employees filed to the back with maps in their arms.

"Dump them in the fire!" instructed the sergeant. They complied.

"Sergeant? I have a question." Roweena stood to his right as he watched the fire consume the maps. He turned to her.

"If someone does get internal passport permission to travel, how will they be able to find their way without maps?"

The sergeant's mouth twisted into a sardonic smile. "Anyone with travel permission will be given a map freshly printed from our Homeland Security Google satellite maps. They will be required to turn in the map to Homeland Security when they reach their destination. We control the maps, so we control anyone's ability to navigate. We also control internet access to Google maps and MapQuest, in case you are wondering."

"I see. Thank you." Roweena turned away and smiled a little Mona

Lisa smile of her own. As a member of the Constitutional Resistance Movement, she knew something the sergeant didn't know.

*   *   *   *   *   *

A convoy of eight HumVees and four armored personnel carriers headed out on a Search and Destroy mission under the personal command of Homeland Security Deputy Director Maudire VanJones. They headed east on I-80 from Salt Lake City. She rode in the command vehicle.

East of Rock Springs, they took an exit for one of the small state roads that would lead them north to the Wind River Shoshone Reservation. Deputy Director VanJones intended to keep the element of surprise by avoiding the more heavily traveled and populous highways as much as possible.

There'll be no UN force to protect them this time, she thought. She rubbed the scar on the web of her right hand. It ached when she rubbed it. She grimaced. *This is a small taste of the pain I'm about to inflict on these degenerate traitors who resist our rule and my commands.*

The highway signs matched what their vehicle GPS systems were telling them. They drove for four more hours, following their GPS instructions.

We should be there by now, thought VanJones. "Sergeant," she barked at her driver. "Why haven't we reached the reservation? Don't you know how to follow simple GPS instructions? Tell the convoy to pull over!"

The lieutenant from the lead vehicle walked back to VanJones' command vehicle. "Sir, I don't understand it. We have followed our GPS navigation instructions exactly. I could have sworn we passed that same barn over there two hours ago."

VanJones blushed scarlet as she realized the GPS systems were compromised. She had been made to look foolish in front of her men. Isaiah's virus, code named Operation Misdirection, was causing both the GPS and their Google maps to send them in circles.

"Doesn't anyone know how to navigate by the sun or a compass or something!" She screamed in impotent rage. "Lieutenant, if you can't get us to our target coordinates, I'll bust you and promote someone else who can!"

The lieutenant's face took on a bewildered look. They didn't teach formal geography or map reading in public schools anymore. The seventh grade class was called Social Geography of Capitalist Oppression. The maps were pictograms illustrating the location of oppressed peoples and oppressor peoples. Longitude, latitude or how to read map coordinates was no longer taught. He grew up with GPS and GooHoo maps on smart phones and pads. The computer voice known as "Comrade Carla" always told him where to turn. Homeland Security and military officer candidate schools only reviewed how to use GPS and Google maps. Few people under the age of thirty knew how to use a paper map. 'Comrade Carla' told them where to go. Big Brother Government told them they didn't need to know how to read maps.

The lieutenant stammered out, "Sir, I don't know what else to do! I don't know if it's even possible to navigate by the sun. Nobody here has a compass other than the one on our phones and GPS pads." He quivered a little in fear. He knew what Deputy Director VanJones was capable of.

"Everybody out! Out of the vehicles! Form up here!" she screamed again. She didn't know how to read a map either, so she covered for her ignorance and embarrassment by screaming. All the agents exited the vehicles, weighed down by tactical gear and weaponry. They formed a cluster before her.

"Can't ANYONE in this incompetent unit of bumblers figure out how to get us to Lander?" She glared at them and let loose a string of expletives that would blister the paint on the truck.

Murmuring to each other, they all looked around at the horizons. Several pointed in one direction, several in another. They began arguing. They were all city recruits. No one spoke up to Deputy Director Maudire VanJones. They shuffled their feet and looked down. Nobody knew what to do, but nobody would say so.

"Lieutenant! In my command vehicle! Now!" VanJones slid into the back seat. He followed. "Close the door!" He did.

She grabbed him by his shirt lapels and shook him. "Lieutenant, listen carefully and you might keep your rank. This is what we're going to do …"

Five minutes later, the Lieutenant emerged from VanJones' vehicle. "Alright, everybody, form up on me! Now!" The ragged group of agents moved in closer to the Lieutenant.

"From this moment, this mission is classified! You will speak of this to no one unless specifically asked. This is what happened: we found the ARK nest of traitors and we killed them all and burned their farm buildings. There were no prisoners and no survivors. They were all killed resisting arrest, even the children. Sergeant! You will write up the Search and Destroy mission report which will say this. Smith! You will alter the satellite photos on today's date to show heat signatures consistent with burning buildings."

He glared at the assembled agents. "This mission was a success. Do you understand? What was this mission?"

"A success, sir!" They all repeated in unison.

"I can't hear you!"

"A SUCCESS, SIR!" They all stood at attention.

"Anyone who doesn't remember this mission as a success will find themselves guarding Eskimo traitors at a Prosperity Camp in Nome Alaska! Do you get me?"

"WE GET YOU SIR!"

"Alright! Get to work creating the evidence of a successful mission. Fire your weapons into that hillside! Bury excess ammo to simulate 90% ammo expenditure on the mission. Conduct simulated self-defense drills in pairs! I want to see bruised cheeks, eyes, hands, and arms. Tear your clothing and rub it in the dirt! Fill out injury reports for at least twelve agents. At the base bars tonight, you WILL brag to your buddies about how many traitors you killed. NOW GO!"

Deputy Director Maudire VanJones never showed her face for the remainder of the trip.

And so the Search and Destroy tactical unit returned to Salt Lake City triumphant. Another positive action report on another mission led by Deputy Director Maudire VanJones. Bar bragging backed up the story.

All over the Western States, similar Homeland Security Search and Destroy missions in rural areas met similar "goose chase" results: driving around and around and never finding their target destination.

Fearful of reporting failure, the mission commanders heard through the grapevine about a certain Wyoming mission and how to ensure their mission was reported as a success. Amazingly, the Western Region of Homeland Security tallied a 100% mission success rate.

Deputy Director Maudire VanJones was promoted to command of the entire Western Region.

Chapter Thirty-Six

Isaiah piloted his single engine Cessna into Laramie Regional Airport on the west side of Laramie. He had his credentials prepared to show as the Chief Inspector for the Federal Department of Minority Equal Results in All Aspects of Society (FDMERAAS). This was a small airport that only operated during daylight hours. He expected to easily intimidate any local official questioning his lack of a flight plan.

After the Fixed Base Operator's line man had tied down his aircraft, Isaiah rode with him back to the office. The man behind the counter asked him, "How many days will you be parking your aircraft here? Our rates are fifty dollars a day. Fuel and maintenance extra, of course."

Isaiah laid his Federal ID Card on the counter. Summoning up his most arrogant voice, he said "Indeterminate. My agency requires that we pay one hundred dollars a day for aircraft parking." The man's face brightened considerably. "Here are the vendor forms for the charge-back of thirty-eight fifty for the Federal Government Vendor Privilege Fee, the eighty three dollars sustainable sustenance fee for all government transactions, and the set-up fee for first time transactions for the FDMERAAS Department. That fee is Fifty-one dollars eighty cents."

The man's face fell considerably. Isaiah continued, "Fill out these forms in triplicate and sign here, here, and here. And initial here and here. I'll pick up the forms when I'm ready to leave." Isaiah was enjoying this immensely. Especially since he had just invented those fees and forms the day before and printed them from his laptop computer. Outside, a car driven by CRM people was waiting for him.

They were taking him to a CRM safe house near the University, where he would meet Grace. It would be the first time they had been together in nearly five months. He noticed the burned out buildings and cars littering the streets. Just like Detroit years ago, he thought. Detroit had been like a 'nature preserve' for socialism. See the socialists in their native habitat: their buildings and neighborhoods crumbling back into forest lands, taxed into poverty, left unprotected from lawless human predators, but all equal in their misery. He shivered. Now all America is Detroit.

At the safe house, high fences topped with barbed wire surrounded the place. He opened a metal door and walked in. There was Grace!

He rushed up and engulfed her in a big hug, swinging her off the floor. "Oh Grace! Oh Baby! I'm so glad to see you! Dear Lord, thank you for keeping my Grace safe for me." He covered her in kisses. When he set her down and stopped to take a breath, she nearly stopped his heart with her big dazzling white smile.

He started to hug her again, but she put a hand on his chest. "Easy, tiger. I'm eager to see you too, but have you seen the message from Solomon in San Francisco? It's red alert. Thousands of lives are in danger. PRIS has concocted a deadly genetically modified virus that kills in 26 days. They've given it to the government. Homeland Insecurity has infected two ARK locations so far. I've been searching for a lab to work in. The University here is nearly deserted because of the food shortage. Their labs have most of the equipment I'll need. I'll need your help in creating bio-chemical computer simulations and testing DNA and RNA code sequences."

He slumped. "Just when I thought we were getting ahead of the curve. Anybody we know?"

Grace's face was sad. "Isaiah, it's ARK Shoshone. They have 18 days left. Remember Joseph Wakini? He and a small band of Shoshones have 34 days, due to a temporary antidote they took. I know we haven't seen each other in nearly five months, but we have to get to work immediately. Their lives are ticking away."

He looked at her longingly, then sighed. "Lead the way."

* * * * * *

The CRM provided security for the University building where they worked. CRM also provided fuel for the emergency generators which supplied power, since the city grid averaged four hours per day and voltage fluctuated minute by minute. Grace shared work remotely with her team in the Nutritional Abundance Industry labs in New Zealand. They had the data Dr. Dreen had provided about the development of the virus.

Isaiah also worked remotely with his team in New Zealand at Promethean Software International. They programmed complex DNA and RNA resequencing simulations. Since lab tests with actual virus cultures took time, the fast computer simulations were invaluable to Grace and her team. They ruled out all but the most promising recombinations to use for the valuable lab testing time.

Joseph and his band of Shoshones reached ARK Ute by donning ceremonial Shoshone garb and claiming diplomatic immunity under the UN Charter for the Sovereign Nationhood of Indigenous Peoples. John's clever ID cards overawed the low-level Homeland Security Travel Restriction Enforcement Agents. Ordinary Americans needed permits for their daily travel to work and the food ration distribution depots. Nobody called them supermarkets after the government took them all over. Joseph's group asserted diplomatic priority for the Shoshone Nation.

Another CRM operative managed to use Isaiah's plane to fly to ARK Ute to pick up the virus packets for Grace to study. Also, a human blood sample: Joseph Wakini in the flesh.

Grace was slumped over her lab countertop sleeping when Joseph walked in with the packets. Isaiah was in a corner, his hands flying over the keyboard. When he heard footsteps, he didn't look back. "Is that the beef stew? Just put it on the countertop."

Joseph said, "Isn't one blivit enough?"

Isaiah jumped out of his seat and enveloped Joseph in a hug that nearly cracked his ribs. "Joseph! I'm go glad to see you! How are you feeling? Any symptoms?"

Isaiah stepped back with both hands on Joseph's shoulders. He studied Joseph's eyes and saw the deep sorrow there. Joseph's eyes seemed to be looking at a far horizon, scanning plains and rivers and far snow-covered peaks. Looking for a rider who wasn't there.

"Joseph. I heard about Cathy. I'm so sorry."

He hugged Joseph again, more gently. He murmured, "God of Abraham, Isaac, and Joseph, send comfort and healing to this boy. You've given him a heavy cross to bear." He stepped back, and searched Joseph's impassive face again.

Then Isaiah stood tall and placed his hands on Joseph's shoulders again. "Lord, this day this boy has become a man. Fill him with strength like unto Michael the Archangel, a mighty warrior, for he wrestles not just against flesh and blood, but against principalities, against powers, against the rulers of darkness of this world. Amen."

Joseph's gaze came back from the far places. He looked steadily at Isaiah. "Amen. Ephesians, if I remember rightly. Thank you. I need all the help I can get, spiritual and otherwise."

"Joseph, I am here." Isaiah searched his face. "Just ask."

By the time Grace woke up, Isaiah had already taken a blood sample from Joseph and was preparing a slide for Grace to study. "Joseph! You're here! God bless you for coming. Your blood will be a big help. I'll be able to study how it's resisting the virus, and hopefully reverse engineer that antidote. I'm sorry about Cathy. Do you want to talk about it?"

"Dr. Washington," he began.

"Grace, please."

"Grace, I don't have time or the patience for emotional support right now. We're on a short deadline. We have a job to do."

She saw the steady gaze of a man on a mission. "Yes. Of course." She turned back to her counter covered with notes. "Tell me about these packets of virus."

Chapter Thirty-Seven

For the next three hours Grace was on Skype conference call with Sonia Hughes-McLauren, Dr. Dreen, and her own research scientists in Christchurch. Finally she shut it down and sent Joseph off to bed.

She went to Isaiah, still typing in the corner of the lab. "Isaiah?" she said softly.

"Umm?" he said, distracted.

"Isaiah, we need to talk," she said sadly.

Recognizing her serious tone, he stopped typing, turned, and faced her.

"Baby, what is it? Bad news?"

"In a way, yes." She looked deeply into his eyes. "Isaiah, I can't create a cure in time to save these people. Even with your fast computer simulations, there isn't enough time. Unless ..."

His heart felt like it was squeezed. "Unless?"

"Unless I open one of those packets and put the contents under the electron microscope to get a good look at the actual virus. Then I can work faster." She took a deep breath.

"But Grace, this lab doesn't have air locks and we don't have bio-hazard suits here. There would be no sure way to isolate you from the virus."

"Exactly." She took another deep breath. "And there is no guarantee of success in finding a cure."

"So you're saying ... No! You can't do that! You are the most brilliant mind in bio-engineering today. You won the Nobel prize for bio-engineering. There may be more threats! Deadlier threats! If you die from this virus, the whole world would be left defenseless against the next virus. And selfishly, I don't know that I could carry on without you."

She hugged him and laid her head against his chest. "All of that is true. And I'm afraid. But ... thousands will die if I don't try. Joseph will die if I don't try. Isaiah, remember, this is why we came back. We have to help. We have to try. We're running out of time."

"Grace, Grace I don't know if I could bear it, losing you."

She pulled back and held his face in her hands. "And I would be torn up if I lost you. But look at Joseph; Joseph is somehow putting one foot in front of the other. And you were there. You saw how he looked at that girl Cathy. I don't know how he does it."

Isaiah's eyes melted. "I do. We always seem to forget that we can get help."

He slid down to his knees. She sank down to her knees. They touched their foreheads together and closed their eyes. Isaiah spoke. "Dear heavenly Father, we know all things are in Your hands. Not a sparrow falls without Your notice. Give us Your courage. Send us Your comfort. Fill us with Your wisdom. Strengthen us with Your endurance. We can't do this without You. Help us to succeed and save lives. Yet not our will, but Yours be done. Amen."

They both rose from the floor. Isaiah said, "I'll send Joseph to stock food in the break room for you. I'll get some duct tape so we can seal off the doors." He started walking.

Grace called after him, "Tell Joseph to include toilet paper with those supplies."

* * * * * *

"Isaiah, I'm ready to seal it up." Grace looked tired and frail from her long hours.

"Grace!" his voice was urgent. "Are you sure about this?"

"Isaiah, I need to be alone in here."

"I'll go with you." Isaiah stepped to her side of the door and began taping the door seams with duct tape.

"Isaiah! This is dangerous!"

"Then I'll stand by you. Remember our song? By Ben E. King? *Stand by me?* You stood by me, and I'll always stand by you. Grace, I can work my programs just as fast from within here. Maybe faster if I can see exactly what you are doing."

"Isaiah, this won't work. There is not enough toilet paper for the two of us."

"Then we better work fast, before it runs out."

*   *   *   *   *   *

For the next 48 hours Grace and Isaiah worked around the clock, with brief naps at their desks. Joseph and the CRM agents watched them through the glass of an adjoining conference room. They communicated with them through walkie-talkies. Simulation after simulation on Isaiah's computer. Trial after trial on Grace's lab equipment.

Hour forty-eight. Grace straightened up from her electron microscope. "Ha!"

Isaiah had dozed off with his head on his keyboard. He woke up and rubbed his eyes. "Whaa …?"

Grace had her game face on. "HA! I've got you now, you little booger! You think you can come into my house and tell MY enzymes what to do? WRONG! Now MY big bad RNA sequence is going to elbow its way into your wimpy little genetic chain and tell your bossy little RNA sequences to SWITCH OFF!"

Isaiah stood up. "Grace? Grace, are you trash talking to … a virus?"

"You bet I am!" She walked down to the mass spectrometer. "Just let me verify these organic molecules and BAM! I own you!"

Isaiah rubbed his eyes again. "Grace, does this mean … ?"

The mass spectrometer blinked out a spiky pattern. "I GOT YOU NOW!" she shouted. She ran back to the electron microscope and began manipulating controls.

"You think you can get past my zone defense! WRONG! You are messing with the GOLDEN TIGERS OF TUSKEGEE, and you are messing with the wrong team! Your scrawny little RNA sequences are hereby SLAM DUNK SWITCHED OFF! BAM!"

Grace began dancing around the room in a victory dance. "We are the T, IG, the T-I-G-E-R-S TIGERS! That's right! We are the T, IG, the T-I-G-E-R-S, and we are G, are G, are G-O-L-D-E-N, GOLDEN! And we kicked your little virusy BUTTS! Whooo!"

The walkie-talkie on the table crackled. Isaiah picked it up. Joseph was staring through the glass. "What's going on in there?"

Isaiah grinned. "You, my man, have never been to a Tuskegee University Golden Tigers basketball game! What you just saw was a vintage championship victory dance. Grace has a vaccine that both cures and prevents! She can shut down the genetic instructions that allow a virus to give orders to your body's enzymes. I believe that if you give us another thirty-six hours, we will have neutralized all the virus particles in this room and can begin producing vaccine for export to all the ARKS. Then it will be time to kick some virus butt!"

"Well, what can I say? Go Tigers!" Joseph managed a smile.

*   *   *   *   *   *

Joseph and Isaiah leaned over a table studying a large multi-state map.

"O.K. Isaiah, here's the game plan. You and Grace fly back to ARK Shoshone with a vaccine supply and vaccinate everyone there. I'll travel with a CRM unit back to ARK Ute and vaccinate everyone there. Then my eight Shoshone Wind Talkers and I will smuggle the vaccine onward for preventive treatment at the other four ARKS. Grace says she's working with her lab in New Zealand to start manufacture of enough vaccine to inoculate or cure all CRM units and ARK dwellers in America within three weeks. They'll keep producing until we have enough for all Americans. She's already trained some CRM folks here to produce vaccine at this lab, but this is not a very secure location. We're loading trucks with some lab equipment that Grace can use at ARK Shoshone to produce vaccine on a small scale."

Isaiah looked at Joseph with new respect. "When John told me you were elected leader for ARK Shoshone, I was skeptical. Now I see why they chose you. This is a good plan. Just one question. Why not come back to ARK Shoshone with us?"

Joseph looked down. In a low voice, he said "There's nothing there for me now. I can do more good out here in the field. I can help more than just one ARK. I can help resist this flood of vile tyranny. Now that I'm outside the ARK, I've seen firsthand the petty cruelties of this regime."

He looked up. His eyes burned with intensity. "Isaiah?"

"Yes?"

"While you and Grace were locked in the lab, I worked on some more code and inserted it into the federal network." He paused. "I can not only falsify what a drone is seeing, I can reprogram the drone's mission. I can even take control of a drone in real time."

Isaiah felt a chill. "Joseph." He saw a dry desert country behind Joseph's eyes. He almost whispered, "Joseph, I know I don't have to remind you that we are pledged not to attack, only defend ourselves. Those who argue that the ends justify the means forget that after a while the means become the ends. That's how these government types began to love cruelty for its own sake. If you walk down that path you become just like your enemies. You don't want to be like them."

"Isaiah!" Joseph gripped the edge of the table until his knuckles turned white. He cried out, "Isaiah, help me! I'm wrestling with dark thoughts. I do want revenge! They killed Cathy! They killed six people in my community, including small children. I hate them!"

"I'm here Joseph. Lord, give him comfort and wisdom and strength. Give him the strength to turn away from vengeance. 'Vengeance is mine, saith the Lord.' Only God has enough power to grasp vengeance and not be corrupted by it. Vengeance is deadly like that virus. It invades you and takes you over and begins to control you. It consumes you like a cancer, and soon nothing is left of you. Only vengeance remains, walking around in your body. Vengeance is a strong demon, Joseph. But you can overcome it, with God's help."

"God, please help me!" Joseph cried. "Help me let go of vengeance. Help me to trust that You will work things out in Your own way. Help me?" He bent over the table and rested his head on the surface, sobbing. "Oh Cathy! I miss you so much! Lord, I miss Cathy." His first tears since her death crossed his face.

Isaiah gently placed his hand on Joseph's shoulder and stood for a few minutes. Then he quietly walked away. Fifteen minutes later Joseph pushed up from the table. He wiped his face with his bandana. He whispered, "Thank You, Lord." Standing tall, he walked off in search of Isaiah.

Chapter Thirty-Eight

The delivery van lumbered down Highway 191 toward ARK Ute. The logo on the side of the truck was for a popular convenience store. By bribing a certain government official, the store had been allowed to keep operating, even though the shelves were mostly bare. Joseph sat in the front passenger seat. His eight Shoshone comrades were sitting on the floor in the back, along with four CRM commandoes.

Suddenly his phone beeped. He checked the screen.

"A drone! Pull over while I activate stealth mode." His thumbs rapidly moved over the screen. "It's not working! Why isn't it working?" His brow furrowed, then went smooth as realization dawned on him. "This is the version of the David's Sling app that Alexander brought us. It's been compromised. So, how can I fight back …? Aha!"

His thumbs flew faster than before.

"There! Now the drone can't detect us." A warbling tone interrupted him. "Missile lock! Everyone out! Run!" The driver jumped down from the cab and ran to open the doors in the back. Joseph never lost his intensity, manipulating screens on his phone. He glanced at the side mirror once, to see his comrades running over a low bluff beside the road, seeking cover from an impending explosion.

"If I can just …" he talked to himself. "There! I've paused the missile launch sequence. But it kept the lock on our original coordinates even though I changed what the search programs were seeing. The weapons lock and fire are on a separate sub-system, so changing what it saw did not stop the missile targeting and firing sequence. I only have thirty seconds before they override the pause function! What else? What else can I do ... ?!"

Using his own "drone control" program, Joseph took control of the drone and vectored it away from his position. At the same time, the screens of the drone drivers in Salt Lake City showed the original trajectory and terrain. He sent the drone back to its base. Then, as a safeguard, he changed the targeting coordinates of the missile to those of its home base. This was in case the missile was launched anyway, since the drone drivers were ready to launch at the van.

At the drone base, the drone driver saw a message appear on his screen. Joseph texted: "WARNING! Drone drivers, stop your attack! Your drone missiles are now reprogrammed to hit your own location. An attack against us will strike you instead. This is your only warning."

The driver exclaimed "What the ...! Lieutenant! Sir! Come look at this! Our systems have been breached." The lieutenant rushed over and read the screen. Then he pulled out his secure phone and called the Director for the Western Region of Homeland Security.

After the lieutenant had explained the situation, Maudire VanJones laughed. "I'm sitting upstairs monitoring the situation. That rag-tag bunch doesn't have one percent of one percent of our technology resources! They're bluffing! Put me on their frequency. I want to talk to them."

"Director, you are now on their voice frequency."

"Attention, rebel scum! This is Western Region Director Maudire VanJones of Homeland Security Search and Destroy Division. Resistance is futile. I'll give you one chance. If you lay down your arms and stand with your hands up until we reach your location, I'll spare your lives. You have three seconds. Comply or die!"

Joseph spoke into his phone. "You saw our warning. We will defend ourselves. If you want our arms, Xerxes, come and get them. Molon Labe."

"I don't know who Xerxes is, scumbag, but you just forfeited your only chance to live. We're launching a Hellfire missile directly at you."

Remembering C.S. Lewis' definition of hell, Joseph responded, "Your will be done."

"You better believe my will be done. Lieutenant, fire at will. Those who resist must die."

Her eyes narrowed. *These are the ones who thwarted my EarthPurge virus attack! These are the ones who stubbornly resist our control of their miserable little lives! As if they had the right to control their own lives! Soon they and their kind will be wiped from the earth. Those of us who are meant to rule will achieve total control. My will WILL be done!*

She rubbed the scar on the web of her right hand and scowled, muttering to herself, "... kill them, like the vermin they are."

The lieutenant relayed the order. The drone driver put his cursor over the launch button on his screen. He clicked on the button.

Four minutes later hell came home. The Hellfire missile struck the roof of the drone control facility first, blasting a forest of antennae and satellite dishes over the edge of the roof. The office of the base commander was in the center of the top floor. He and his aides were vaporized in the heat of the explosion. In the high-ceilinged drone operations room below, the ceiling caved in, showering debris on the heads of the drone drivers and smashing their consoles. A fireball followed, killing everyone still alive and melting down the circuit boards and most of the plastic in the consoles. The stench of burning plastic filled the room. The only sound was the crackling of the flames.

In the corner office of the top floor Deputy Director Maudire VanJones lay burned and semi-conscious. As her eyes glazed over in death, she remembered Captain Ahab's dying curse against the white whale. *From hell's heart I stab at thee; for hate's sake I spit my last breath at thee.* She murmured, "My will be done ... for hate's sake."

Joseph was able to monitor the internal 911 calls and the roll-out of the fire trucks and EMT vehicles on the base. He found a traffic cam near the base and took a look. Dense black smoke, heavy with toxic fumes from burning plastic, rose high into the air.

Dear God, was this vengeance? No. No, I warned them first. This was self-defense. Joseph opened his door and called out "All clear! The drone is gone. Load up and let's go." The men trotted over the crest of the bluff and climbed back into the truck.

Did I do right? Joseph wondered. *The drone would have killed us. We would not have delivered the vaccine that will save thousands of lives in*

ARK Ute. It was self-defense. Joseph didn't know it yet, but his own self questioning was his spiritual armor against pride and vengeance.

*   *   *   *   *   *

Grace and Isaiah occupied a guest bedroom in the farmhouse of John and Sarah Young. They had decided to stay in ARK Shoshone for a while and work on vaccine production and software tools to defend against the government oppressors. Grace had recruited some of the brightest young people to work with her in manufacturing the vaccine against the EarthPurge virus. John Young cleaned out one of his tool sheds and they set up the equipment from Laramie there.

Isaiah worked in the Young's secret closet housing the satellite uplink dish and other communication equipment. After dispatching a warning to all CRM and ARK people about the security breach in his David's Sling App suite, he set about correcting the problem. He even added a new function. Within a day he had the patch and posted it on a secure page of .ARK for downloading. Then he sent out the "encryption breached – reload" code they had previously agreed on: "Enigma." That told everyone to delete their copy of David's Sling and reload it from the pre-arranged web page on .ARK.

*   *   *   *   *   *

President Fletcher was frustrated. He knew that the Constitutional Resistance Movement was still out there, because they had just sabotaged one of the Drone Operations Command buildings in Salt Lake City. The head of the Search and Destroy Division of Homeland Security told him that the Utah sector would be unable to conduct drone surveillance for seven months or more, until a temporary Operations Center could be set up and more drones manufactured.

All of the drones controlled by Salt Lake City had self-destructed when the center had been blown up and severed their links. They followed their programming protocol to avoid technology capture by the resistance commandos. The time to manufacture a drone had gone from four months to sixteen months, due to the number of engineers disappearing or "gone ARK." Drones would have to be diverted from other sectors to provide coverage for the Salt Lake City sector.

The President had summoned his Secretary of Homeland Security to the Oval Office. "Madame Secretary," he began, "we want you to step up arrests of questionable citizens. We have got to root out these CRM and ARK people. Since the drones have been hacked and sabotaged, they are less useful in finding these so-called ARKS."

"Besides, I now am hearing that neighborhoods are organizing for self-defense and calling themselves mini-ARKS. In this case I do want you to use profiling for your arrests. Our Behavioral Analysis Unit from the FBI has developed a profile of the personality predisposed to go ARK or join the Constitutional Resistance Movement.

"Listen to this: anyone who stands erect instead of slumping and anyone who looks you in the eye instead of looking down. Now that is a useful profile. I want to hear about hundreds of thousands of arrests by the end of the week. Don't worry about probable cause or habeas corpus. I suspended those today with Executive Order 11,267. Go!"

"Yes sir. Sir?" The President looked up, tilting his head back in his trademark "look down his nose at you" pose. "Yes, Madame Secretary?"

"Sir, are we authorized to use deadly force? That is, to shoot first and ask questions later?"

"Of course! Why do you think I authorized you to build up Homeland Security into a military force and buy up those billions of rounds of ammunition for all these years? After what happened in Salt Lake City, I think it's time to use *excessive* force."

* * * * * *

The next day all Federal enforcement employees were ordered to begin random arrests of citizens based on the behavioral profile. SWAT teams raided suburban homes whenever they could schedule coverage by the media. They arrested Americans at random. Fathers going to work. Mothers returning home from work. Parents in front of children. It was all on TV.

Grace and Isaiah were monitoring a broadcast from the communications closet at the Young farmhouse, via satellite feed.

"Amy Trammel here with a special report for CBC News. Vigilant Homeland Security Agents and other Federal Agents have begun rounding up suspicious Americans, those who might sympathize with the traitors of the Constitutional Resistance Movement. We have dramatic footage of one such arrest last night in Chicago."

The screen changed to footage of a business woman coming out of an office building with a briefcase and handbag. Two brown-shirted DHS agents seized her arms. A third agent jerked away the briefcase and handbag. "What is this? Who are you? HELP! Police!"

The two agents pushed her up against the wall and handcuffed her. "Lady, we ARE the police. Homeland Security. You're under arrest on suspicion of sympathy for subversive elements."

"But I have two children at home! I'm a single mother! Who will take care of my children? I have no relatives near by!" She began crying.

"Lady, we are the government. We know about your two children. Amy and Michael, right? Well, Amy and Michael are on their way to a reeducation camp for children of subversives. Our Child Reclamation Agents are telling them what a vicious traitor their mother is. The Agents are interrogating them about any negative comments about the government that you've made at home. We'll soon know all about your traitorous opinions, and we'll have two little eyewitnesses to testify against you! Let's go." The agents walked her to a black SUV.

Amy Trammel reappeared on the screen. "Homeland Security Agents have arrested tens of thousands of such suspicious suspects today in towns all across America. The message to Americans is 'Support your government, and your government will support you. Question your government, and your government will question you.'"

"In other news, the Federal Department of Food Assurance announced that this month's ration of potatoes would be cut by twenty percent per person. Their nutritional scientists tell us that this will make us twenty percent healthier."

Grace clicked off the feed on the computer monitor. "I can't stand it. That poor mother. Kidnapping her children. Arresting her on some flimsy pretense. What they really wanted was this footage. They wanted to strike fear into the hearts of every mother and father in America. Shut up, or your children go to a concentration camp for kids."

Isaiah looked grim. "They obviously aren't using warrants or probable cause to make their arrests anymore. Just profiles, tips, and rumors. Well, I think I can help them with that." He sat down in front of the computer and began typing. "Thanks to the Blivit Joseph and I deployed, I can now slip inside the federal computer network. Don't wait up for me, Grace. I'll be working late tonight."

Chapter Thirty-Nine

The next day in Chicago, the same three brown-shirted Homeland Security Agents were cruising the city streets looking for more people to make an example of. A cameraman from the local CBC affiliate station was riding with them to get more footage of arrests. All three agents got an "alert" tone on their phones. The agent in the passenger seat said, "I got this. It's those two in the black raincoats on the right. Pull up beside them. Ready?"

The black SUV screeched to a stop on the city street and the three agents jumped out with guns drawn, followed by the cameraman recording. "Hands up! Federal Agents! You're under arrest for subversion! Up against the wall!"

The two men in black raincoats yanked out badges and held them up. "You put your hands up! National Security Agency! You're under arrest for interfering with an undercover operation."

The leader of the brown-shirts spun one black raincoat and pushed him against the wall. "Where did you get those badges? Toys-R-Us? You'll get ten extra years for impersonating a federal officer. Put your hands behind your back."

Another black SUV screeched up and another three brownshirts jumped out, followed by their own cameraman. "All of you drop your weapons! Homeland Security! You're all under arrest!"

The first brownshirt leader yelled, "Are you crazy? We ARE Homeland Security. We're arresting these two subversives! Now back off! This is our bust."

The leader of the second contingent yelled just as loudly, "We got a warning about imposters! Badges, uniforms, official looking phones, everything! You'll get ten extra years for impersonating a federal officer! Drop the weapons!"

The two groups of brown shirts faced off with guns trained on each other. "I'm warning you one last time!" shouted the leader of the first group. He began firing. Shots rang out in rapid sequence as all six agents began firing. The two in black raincoats drew their own weapons and began firing. Brownshirts returned fire. After three minutes of continuous gunfire, all eight men lay inert and bleeding. The two cameramen stopped filming and walked up to each other.

"You get all that?"

"Yeah! Me too. That was intense! What a segment this is going to make! Say! Let's make a deal. You record the stand up for my segment, and I'll record the stand up for your segment. This is our chance to break into street reporting! Those snotty reporters never give us photographers a chance. What do you say?"

The other cameraman held out his hand. "Deal!" They shook, while eight people bled out around them. They began blocking out camera angles and where they would stand for their 'on the scene' reporting.

* * * * * *

All across America this scene was repeated. Armed federal agents of dozens of agencies tried to arrest each other. Trained to be suspicious and arrogant, and made paranoid by Isaiah's phony "bulletin" about officer impersonators everywhere, they did not accept each other's authority. The result was shoot-outs, death or injury by 'friendly fire,' or agents arresting and jailing each other.

Most of it was recorded and reported by the media. They had been promised a big story to run this week. And they got one.

* * * * * *

"Madame Secretary!" The President was furious. "You're making us look like fools!" The Secretary for Homeland Security looked down at the rug and shuffled her feet.

"Mr. President, with all due respect, the FBI, ATF, Secret Service, ICE and all the other enforcement agencies have been jealous of DHS for some time now. My department has grown faster than theirs and they resent it. I think this was a conspiracy to make me look bad by resisting arrest and trying to arrest my agents."

The Director of the FBI stood up. "Trying to arrest HER agents! Ha! My men were just defending themselves from her trigger-happy crew! In over eighty percent of the cases, her agents began shooting without identifying themselves as DHS. Besides, we all had the same advisory that there were impostors masquerading as Federal officers."

"Mr. President! You explicitly gave me orders to use deadly force in executing this round-up of subversive elements. You told me that it was time to use excessive force!"

The President, a trained lawyer, replied, "But did I give it to you in writing?"

The Secretary said, "Well, no! But you told me, right here in the Oval office. You told me!"

"Madame Secretary, whatever you think you heard, you mis-heard. Unless you have it in writing, I expect you to sign this resignation on my desk now. Otherwise you'll face a court-martial for failure to properly follow a presidential executive order. My press secretary will be denouncing your incompetence on national television in one hour."

Chapter Forty

CRM AGENTS BEGAN MOVING MORE FREELY AROUND THE COUNTRY. They were equipped with Isaiah's 'David's Sling' app, now patched to eliminate Alexander's security breach. They evaded government agents by detecting their "roach" icons on their phone maps. If any got too close, the CRM people activated the "I am a government bureaucrat" announcement at top speakerphone volume. In the resulting confusion, the CRM resistance fighters easily slipped away.

Isaiah walked into the capitol building through the employees' entrance. He wore a baseball cap that read "GSA." Special rubber patches disguised his cheekbones. They resembled scar tissue. If asked, he would say that he had been burned in an explosion in Iraq. The patches foiled the facial recognition software that would be scanning for him.

His government-issue khaki shirt and trousers profiled him as a maintenance worker. His ID badge identified him as a GSA employee (General Services Administration – the maintenance service for all federal buildings). The photo matched his new appearance, and the bar code would scan him in. He carried a tool case with IT component parts and the tools to install them.

After going through the metal detector at the security checkpoint, he waited while his tool case was searched. "This your tool bag?" asked the security guard. Isaiah nodded.

"May I see your maintenance work order?"

Isaiah unbuttoned the flap over his left shirt pocket. He withdrew a folded document and handed it to the guard.

The guard gave it a cursory look. "Repair House chamber projection booth AV equipment. OK. Up two levels. Then it will be ..." He flipped through several screens on a monitor. "... about the 3ʳᵈ door on your left. It's marked AV."

Isaiah could see the video feeds from security cameras being displayed on the guard's monitor. "Thanks," Isaiah nodded. He picked up the tool case and walked away.

He went into a men's room. When he finished, he washed his hands. Wiping his hands on a brown paper towel, he walked to the waste receptacle. As he did so he hid his right hand behind the wad of paper towels clenched in his left hand. He pulled his phone out of his waist band, but kept it behind the paper towels, shielded from the security camera.

He paused at the waste receptacle. He put both hands and the cell phone below the metal rim, as if pushing down accumulated paper towels. He looked at the phone screen and touched an icon. Then he straightened, palmed the phone into his pants pocket, and picked up his tool case. He knew the security camera would only see a man putting paper towels into the trash.

When he entered the door marked AV, he immediately took out some tools from his case and sat in front of an IT component frame box. He began disassembling and then reassembling some components.

After his mental clock said two minutes had elapsed, he pulled his phone out and verified the time. Then he opened a hidden app that hacked into every security camera feed in the building. Thumbing through screens, he came to the video feed for the AV room he was in. It showed him in three quarter profile, hands buried inside the IT component box. Satisfied that his 90 second loop was working, he went to work on Operation Writing on the Wall.

*   *   *   *   *   *

At the morning staff meeting, President Fletcher wrinkled his upper lip as if he smelled something bad. He was shuffling through the morning briefing papers. The news was not good.

The dilapidation and decay of Detroit had spread to most major

American cities. The rule of law was replaced by the rule of gangs. Packs of feral dogs roamed burned-out city centers. Often, packs of feral humans fought the dogs for scraps of food.

Food riots. He had issued orders for several National Guard units to be called up, but only a handful of men had shown up. He needed them to clear away the bodies of those who died of hunger and bury them in mass graves. He wanted to hide the evidence of the collapse of the delicate web of food production and healthcare services. Collapsing because his central controllers could not cope with the complexity.

He looked at the next report. Armed gangs roamed major cities – looting, raping and murdering. One report even mentioned cannibalism in some city centers where food deliveries had long since stopped. Just like the starvation and cannibalism in the Ukraine in the 1930s used by Stalin to exterminate the kulak peasant farmers.

Of course, there was also the Chinese seizure of Hawaii, but his people in the media had made sure that all commentators voiced enthusiastic agreement with the spin he put on it. He had, as usual, taken no action, but gave a speech on television.

"As part of our commitment to atone for the past sins of American imperialism, we welcome the repatriation of Hawaii to its rightful owners, the sovereign nation of mainland China. As I've always said, the original peoples of any land have the rightful historical claim to it. Since everybody knows that the Hawaiian people are descended from ancestors in China, it is only right and proper that the Hawaiian Islands be returned to China. The Chinese Ambassador has been gracious enough to present me with the very first entry visa into the Chinese Province of Hawaii, so that I can continue to spend time in my vacation condo there."

He had ordered the military commanders in Hawaii to surrender quietly. Only the top commanders of the Joint Chiefs of Staff knew that. All but the Chairman were hand-picked to be loyal to him. His foreign policy of weakness was inviting aggression from other authoritarian countries.

* * * * * *

The Chinese ambassador had demanded a one million dollar ransom for each American military prisoner of war in Hawaii. The President had declined. Fewer soldiers to get involved in wars of aggression abroad, he thought.

The Chinese then embarrassed him when they called a televised press conference in Honolulu. As further humiliation, the press conference was held on the viewing platform of the USS Arizona Memorial. Two dozen captured American sailors, marines, and pilots were lined up wearing prison garb. P.O.W. was stenciled on their orange overalls. The Chinese admiral stood in front of them in dress uniform.

The Chinese Admiral spoke. "The Chinese People's Republic is proud to stand in Honolulu harbor in our ancestral Chinese province of Hawaii. Now that we have regained our province from the Oppressive Imperialist American Capitalists Occupiers, we are prepared to offer humanitarian mercy to the conquered military prisoners here. We have contacted the families of the men and women you see standing here. We have arranged for the American media to broadcast the anguish and emotional pain of the families of these captured war criminals."

The various networks cut to scenes of weeping wives, husbands and children in their homes, watching the pictures of their loved ones on TV.

The Admiral spoke again. "The Chinese People's Republic generously offered to repatriate these prisoners for a reparation fee of one million American dollars each. Your President Fletcher has refused."

Once the White House saw how the Chinese were making an end run around the president to go directly to the American people, they signaled their lackeys in the mainstream media to switch back to regular programming. They all did so, except FACTS News.

FACTS News reporter Hal Enry, out on bail, continued broadcasting his interview of the wife of one American sailor. She wiped tears from her eyes.

"Mrs. Smith, your husband Joe is now a prisoner of war in what used to be his own country. He was captured when his ship put into Honolulu for supplies just before the Chinese invaded. This has been difficult for your family."

"Hal, our children, Marta, 8, and Joe Jr., 6, miss their dad. Joe has shipped out regularly on tours of duty since Marta was two. Marta, show Mr. Enry your crayola pictures?"

A solemn Marta held up a crayon drawing. It showed a figure in a tutu labeled 'Marta.' The next one showed a stick figure labeled 'Dad' behind the bars of a prison.

Marta said, "I used to show Dad my drawings when we did our Skype calls. We can't call him anymore." She looked down.

Mrs. Smith said, "Joe Jr. just started pee-wee ball. Didn't you, Joey?"

A small boy in a baseball cap ambled up. His mother put him on her lap. He looked at the camera.

"When will Dad come home? I want him to see me swing the bat at my game. Dad, I hit the ball two times last week!" He hugged his mother.

"Hal, the Chinese are deliberately mocking the families by letting us see our loved ones. They know President Fletcher won't pay their ransom, so they are taunting us in front of the world. Ever since the president began retreating around the world, the bully nations have been lining up like vultures to pick the bones of the United States. My Joe is paying the price for the President's cowardice. Mark my words, Russia will go after Alaska for the Alaskan oil next."

Hal Enry thought, They'll revoke my bail quickly after this, but it feels good to broadcast the truth one last time.

*   *   *   *   *   *

Fingering the reports about the Chinese annexation of Hawaii, President Fletcher thought, Now we won't be able to get involved in Asian wars. That's a good thing. No more bullying of smaller nations. It did not register with him that China, undeterred by the US Military, was now a bully on the doorstep of the west coast of America.

But on the mainland, America's descent into chaos could not be hidden anymore. Report after report lay on his desk.

Time to do what I do best, he decided. Time for a speech to the American people. Make it a speech delivered to a joint session of Congress. That will make good theatre and settle things down.

He pressed his intercom and said, "Send in my Chief of Staff. We have a speech to write."

*　　*　　*　　*　　*　　*

President Fletcher lightly gripped the sides of the rostrum as he looked out over the Congress, Cabinet heads, and Supreme Court Justices. All major media were there to televise his speech: FACTS News, CBC, PBS, BBC, NBC, ABC, Al-Jazeera and the new worldwide UNTV. His thugs at the Justice Department had brought pressure to bear on all satellite and cable providers. Every one of their 500+ channels would be showing the President's address. No one in the United States could turn the channel to escape it. The internet had also been rigged so that all browsers defaulted to White HouseTV.gov. All smart phone and pad apps had been disabled. They all defaulted to WhiteHouseTV.gov. You couldn't even make a phone call during the time the President would be speaking.

He raised his chin up in his trademark pose. He looked down his nose at his audience. In each television screen, you could look right up his nostrils.

"Members of Congress, Cabinet Heads, Supreme Court Justices, and my fellow Americans. We face an unprecedented crisis. Thanks to the greed of food companies, ordinary Americans cannot afford enough food to meet the minimum daily caloric intake as decreed by the Food and Drug Administration. Thanks to the greed of oil companies, ordinary Americans cannot afford enough fuel to drive to work all five days of the week. Thanks to the greed of utility companies, ordinary Americans cannot afford to light and heat their homes with electricity more than a few hours each day.

"I have directed Ben Wiemar, the Head of the Federal Reserve, to immediately print more money and deposit it into the bank accounts of every American below the fair share of wealth target level as defined by the UN and the Occupy and Abolish Capitalism protest groups. Effective tonight, 99% of Americans will see $57,000 added to his or her bank account. Then they can afford food, fuel, and electricity."

The Progressive, Socialist, and Democratic party members

of Congress rose to give a standing ovation to the President. The conservatives, libertarians, Tea Party and Republican members of Congress sat stony faced.

"Look at the stony faces of the opposition parties," smirked the President. Here, on cue, all cameras swiveled to show the faces of the congressmen and Senators who remained sitting. "They would rather let the people starve. In Matthew 9:13 Jesus said, 'I will have mercy, and not sacrifice.' If they were truly Christian, they would want to give more money to poor and middle class Americans." More applause.

"What would Jesus do? He would print more money, so the people can eat!" Applause.

"In the past, many of my initiatives to help the American people were stopped and sabotaged by the greedy special interests and their lackeys, the opposition parties."

More applause from the left.

"Today, in this unprecedented crisis, we cannot afford to allow these opposition groups to stand in the way of my initiatives. I have the best interests of the American people at heart, and, whether the people realize it or not, whatever I do is in the best interests of the American people."

His supporters again rose in a standing ovation.

"Accordingly, I, We, have today issued executive orders for these five things: One, We have dissolved the Supreme Court. We can no longer allow this small group of only nine people to stop our programs that help the American people.

"Two, We have appointed Federal Governors to run the fifty states. They all report directly to me. We'll have no more of this 'states rights' nonsense.

"Three, all opposition members of Congress have been replaced by my appointees from the Progressive Socialist Democratic Party. We can't afford endless debates and votes that go nowhere."

Another standing ovation from his party.

"Fourth, we have declared martial law and suspended the Constitution. Instead of three branches of government, we now have only one: my executive branch. I will control the government directly without waiting for Congress to fund it or pass enabling legislation.

Congress can still meet and discuss issues until they reach consensus about supporting my decisions, but what I say goes."

"Fifth and finally, we have suspended this year's presidential, congressional, and all local elections. Indefinitely. In such a crisis as this, we can't wait for the people to do the right thing. We know what is best for the American People, and we will tell them what is best for them. All government agencies, federal, state, and local, are now under my direct control." More applause.

Justice Thomas muttered, "The last vestiges of the old republic are swept away. The Jedi will have to go into hiding." Justice Ruth Bader-Ginsberg leaned over and said, "Shhh!"

At that moment, a huge 30 by 50 foot screen rapidly descended behind the President, the Speaker of the House, and the Vice-President. There was an immediate buzz and pointing from the audience. The President turned around to look where they were pointing. All cameras swiveled to show the huge screen.

An image of a stone wall was projected on it. A larger than life hand appeared and seemed to engrave letters with a forefinger. Shocked, the President stood open-mouthed, staring. The hand was withdrawn. These words were left, in letters two feet tall:

MENE MENE, TEKEL, UPHARSIN

The President turned around and looked at his chief of staff Sim Smyth. "What is going on? What is the meaning of this?" Sim shrugged and held up his hands in a gesture of helplessness.

Then a soft resonant voice came through the sound system.

"Mr. President, here is the meaning. MENE, God hath numbered your kingdom and finished it."

The Attorney General and many others gasped. They recognized that voice. It was Grace Washington.

"TEKEL, you have been weighed in the balances and art found wanting." Most of the Supreme Court Justices and members of the opposition parties rose. Then they silently turned their backs on the President.

"UPHARSIN, thy kingdom is divided, and given to the Medes and Persians."

There were gasps from the left side of the aisle, from those who vaguely remembered their Sunday School Bible stories. Many put their hands over their mouths. Several whispered to themselves, "The Book of Daniel."

The voice continued, "The modern-day Medes are the patriots and groups devoted to the Constitution. The ones that you attempt to intimidate and imprison. The modern-day Persians are those dictatorial and power-hungry outside forces and nations like Iran, La Raza, the Agenda 21 UN forces, China, Russia, and the various radical Islamist groups."

The opposition party members and the Supreme Court Justices with their backs to the President now began filing out of the House chamber of the Capitol building.

The President attempted to regain control, shouting, "Wait! Master of Arms, stop those people from leaving! You can't leave until after I'm done speaking!"

Justice Clarence Thomas turned back, looked him in the eye and said in a booming baritone, "Mr. President, you are done." Then he turned and walked out.

A military aide ran up to the President and whispered in his ear. "Mr. President, the UN Agenda 21 Enforcement Military Command has landed in New York City and taken control of the New York and Jersey City ports. The general in charge has issued a proclamation that he is in control of New York, New Jersey, and Delaware. Armed UN convoys are heading toward Pennsylvania and Maryland."

Stunned, the President collapsed into a chair near the rostrum. "Mr. President, there is a danger to you. We recommend that you evacuate to Venezuela. The neo-Chavez-ians have offered asylum."

The President looked up, angry now. "Retreat in our moment of triumph? You overestimate them. I have just seized total control of the entire United States! Those UN troops are our allies. We can negotiate with them. I've always said I extend an open hand. I have a deal with them to become the President of the UN and Czar of the whole world next year! This is just a misunderstanding!"

Chapter Forty-One

In the Pentagon at that moment, the Chairman of the Joint Chiefs of Staff was on a conference call with all theatre commanders. "As far as I'm concerned, you are all released from the chain of command. I hope that each of you is a patriot who loves our Constitution. Use your forces to do what you think is best to defend the American people. I took an oath to defend the Constitution of the United States from all enemies, foreign and domestic. I can no longer serve this President without dishonoring my oath of office, because he has now proclaimed himself a domestic enemy of the Constitution.

"Ladies and gentlemen, may almighty God, El-Shaddai, defend and protect us. May we do what is right for our Constitutional Republic, as God gives us to see the right. God bless America!"

Tears in his eyes, he put down the phone. A Federal agent from the Political Security Forces stepped into the room. The PSA was an agency recently created by the President to act as his personal enforcers. PSA agents were deployed to all key government and military commands, much like the political officers of the old Soviet Union.

"I heard what you just said, General, and it is treason, punishable by death on the spot under martial law." He raised his handgun. It had a silencer on the barrel.

The Chairman stood at attention and saluted. "I die a loyal servant to my commander-in-chief, but a servant of God and the Constitution *first*." The agent fired a round. Thwippp! It hit the Chairman in the forehead. He crumpled to the ground.

The agent removed a framed copy of the Constitution from the wall.

He broke the glass and placed the paper replica under the General's forehead. Then he took a picture of the General's face resting on the blood-stained document. "This will make a nice headline in the New York Collective Times tomorrow. And a good warning to other potential traitors to the New Order," he mused aloud.

Looking at the body for a moment, he said, "You decided to remain loyal to the idea that all men are created equal. I'm loyal to the most powerful man on the planet. You were a fool!"

*   *   *   *   *   *

Captain Adel Najafi crouched below a window of the guard house at the White House entrance. His finger was already on the trigger of his Heckler & Koch MG4 machine gun. He glanced back at his twenty-man squad, barely distinguishable in ninja black. A voice softly spoke in his earpiece, "Ten seconds out."

He eased up to look in the window. The two security guards had their backs to him, looking at the entrance from Pennsylvania Avenue. Headlights flashed through the window as the Presidential motorcade turned in. One officer stepped out of the guardhouse.

The lead car stopped. The passenger side window came down, and the Secret Service agent showed an identification symbol to the guard. The guard nodded and waved them in.

As soon as the gate shut behind the last car in the convoy, Captain Najafi keyed his mike and said, "NOW!" His team began firing at the tires of the cars, shredding them. He stood up and shot the two guards in the guard house.

As each car lurched to a stop, commandoes raced up from both sides and slapped plastic explosives to the bulletproof glass windows. Then they ran.

Within seconds, the charges detonated whoom! whoom! whoom! – shattering the windows. The occupants of the cars began to stumble out, deafened by the blasts and blinded by the smoke. Commandos reappeared and began firing at everyone except those in the President's car. Secret Service agents shook with the impact of the bullets, then fell. The commandoes raced up to shoot them in the head, knowing that many wore bullet-proof vests.

The President had been shoved to the bottom of his armored limousine by his Secret Service agents. He coughed from the smoke and gasped for air. One agent was on top of him. Suddenly that agent was pulled off. The President heard Brat! Brat! Brat!

"Agent Cromwell?" the President gasped out. "Agent Cromwell is dead, Mr. President," barked an unfamiliar voice. A hand grasped his suit collar and dragged him out of the car.

Two soldiers took his elbows and hustled him into the White House, where another commando unit had seized control. They took him into the Oval Office and stood him before his own desk. A soldier sat in his chair with his muddy combat boots propped on the desk.

"Who are you?" choked the President.

"I am Captain Adel Najafi, commanding a special forces unit of the UN Agenda 21 Enforcement Military Command. You are now a political prisoner. Do as you are told and you will be well treated. Resist, and you will regret it."

"You can't speak to me this way! I'm the President of the United States! I'm the Commander in Chief ! I am in charge! I am an ally of the UN Agenda 21 Agency! We had a deal!"

Captain Najafi rose and came around the desk. He backhanded the President so hard he nearly fell. "You are NOT in charge!" He struck the President again. "Who is in charge?" The President was dazed, a trickle of blood running from the corner of his mouth. The two soldiers held him up.

"But I'm the Commander ..." Another backhand to his face cut off the President's words. He stumbled back and fell to his knees.

"WHO is in charge?" shouted Najafi, learning down and grasping the President's shirt.

The President kept his eyes down and muttered, "But, but ..."

This time Najafi used his fist. He broke the President's nose. "Ahhh!" wailed the President. "Stop! Please! ..." Blood ran from his nose.

"WHO is in charge?"

"Y...You are," mumbled the President.

"Good," grunted Captain Najafi. He handed the President a cloth.

"You'd better get something for that nose." He nodded to the soldiers. "Put him on the couch."

The President leaned his head back, pressing the cloth to his nose. The pose was reminiscent of his trademark "down the nose" speaking angle.

One soldier turned on the TV set. The screen came to life with CBC commentator Kathy Coeur-Saignant speaking "… and the President had barely finished outlining his wonderful new program for national recovery when some counter-collective criminals somehow projected this cryptic message."

The screen showed the hand writing the first word: MENE.

The President stared at the screen. What did the voice say that meant? Then the broadcast continued with the voice from the Capitol chamber.

"MENE, God hath numbered your kingdom and finished it."

Part Three.
The Rainbow Option

*"If to please the people, we offer what we ourselves disapprove,
how can we afterwards defend our work?
Let us raise a standard to which the wise and honest can repair;
the event is in the hand of God."*
Washington's advice to the Constitutional Convention of 1787

*"... that we here highly resolve ... that this nation, under God,
shall have a new birth of freedom ..."*
Abraham Lincoln, The Gettysburg Address

*"And God remembered Noah ... And God said, This is the token
of the covenant which I make between me and you ...
I do set my bow in the cloud ..."*
Genesis 8:1 and 9:12 King James Bible

When God remembers us,
Will we remember God?

CHAPTER FORTY-TWO

GRACE AND ISAIAH WERE RELAXING ON THE PATIO OF THEIR HOME overlooking the harbor at Christchurch, New Zealand. A titoki tree cast a pleasant shade from the late afternoon sun. November was a warm spring day here in the southern hemisphere. A mass of soft purple Hebe flowers crowded over a low retaining wall on the east side of the patio. Grace smiled at the blossoms illuminated by the last low rays of the sun in the west. Isaiah was listening to a radio news feed from an app on his phone.

Isaiah sat up straighter. "Grace! Listen to this!" He turned up the volume and put it on speaker.

"This is the Constitutional Resistance Movement, with the underground news about the UN invasion forces. Yesterday, a UN armored brigade tried to move into North Carolina, coming down Interstate 95 with their tanks loaded on flatbed trucks. Resistance fighters of the CRM, backed by Ranger Units from Fort Bragg and detachments of Marines from Parris Island, used shoulder-fired rockets to stop the trucks and destroy the tanks. Several soldiers from the Ranger units recognized that the UN soldiers were speaking Farsi, so we can assume they are part of the same Iranian Revolutionary Guards who took over Washington D.C. and captured the President. Our losses were heavy, due to the air cover provided by Soviet Hind attack helicopters.

"The UN troops now control a corridor from Norfolk to Boston and extending about 100 miles inland from the coast. We have learned that the population there has been forced under Sharia Law, enforced by the UN occupying troops under Muslim commanders.

"In other invasion news, Navy sailors loyal to the US escaped with most of the fleet stationed in Norfolk, including aircraft carriers, and sailed to safe harbors in Wilmington, North Carolina, Guantanamo Bay and Charleston, South Carolina.

"There is bad news from the West Coast. When armed gangs overwhelmed most police forces, policemen deserted to stay home and protect their families. In the resulting chaos, the Mexican army, aided by armed elements of La Raza and the drug cartel gangs, invaded and seized control of California, Arizona, New Mexico and Colorado. We're told that the Texas National Guard held them at the Texas-New Mexico border and along the Rio Grande River. Many Air Force units were able to escape with their aircraft to airfields in Texas and Oklahoma.

Refugees from New Mexico are now reporting that the Navaho tribal councils refused to accept Mexican sovereignty over their reservations. The Mexican commander sent in drug cartel militias who slaughtered thousands of Navaho families. Those who escaped are now hiding in the backcountry of the Navaho Reservation."

"Signing off, this is the Constitutional Resistance Movement for Radio Free America. God bless America."

Grace sat limply, with tears running down her face. "Oh Isaiah! Those lives lost! Those soldiers, those young men and women. Dear God."

Isaiah got up from his chair and knelt beside her. With one arm around her shoulders, he leaned his head against hers and whispered, "Grace. I'm here baby."

After a few minutes, he said "Let's pray for those who died. Let's pray for help."

They both bowed their heads and Isaiah whispered "Lord, we know that all things are in your hands. We ask You to bless the souls of those brave soldiers and welcome them home to you. We ask You to send comfort to their families who miss them so much. We ask You to strengthen the spirits and resolve of those freedom fighters resisting the invaders from without and resisting those who seek to impose tyranny from within. We pray this as we were invited to pray, in the name of Jesus. Amen."

Wiping her tears with the handkerchief Isaiah gave her, Grace said, "I wonder ..."

"Wonder what?"

"I wonder if we should go back again, to help the freedom fighters." Tension lines were visible on her face. She sat up in her chair and clasped her knees.

"No. We helped build up the self-sufficiency and defenses of some of the Ark locations. We helped set up distribution networks for the vaccine and cure for the deadly EarthPurge virus. We made sure the knowledge was shared with as many Arks as possible. Now we can give them more help from outside the country than we can from inside."

"How? All we can do now is smuggle in the vaccine and my super seeds to help feed them, and rebroadcast reports about what's going on." Her face was unhappy.

"We can also analyze the reports to help suggest resistance strategies. Our old friend and mentor George T'Chaka Wright has already recruited ex-military Ark Pacific people to form a military intelligence and strategy group. I've got a dedicated team of software designers working on decryption, misinformation, and hack attacks on both the invaders and our own internal totalitarians, a.k.a. the Feds. We've made .ARK into an encrypted darknet so that we can communicate securely."

He put his mouth to her ear and whispered. "Since we have no 'cone of silence' here on the patio, and because I like kissing your ear, I'll tell you that my team has developed virus-borne software that makes our aircraft invisible to their radar. We've been resupplying the resistance fighters with high tech weaponry and electronic warfare gear."

Grace turned her head and put her mouth to his ear.

"Yes? You have something to tell me?" he whispered.

"No. I just wanted to kiss your ear. Thank you for loving me and giving me the strength to carry on in bad times."

*   *   *   *   *   *

Joseph Wakini looked through digitally enhanced binoculars at the valley before him. Interstate 25 made a nearly straight line, stretching south to Fort Collins, Colorado. The northbound lane was covered with military humvees, pick-up trucks, and armored personnel carriers. He estimated the convoy to be nearly an eighth of a mile long.

Lowering the binoculars, he noticed the red targeting slide switch and smiled. He remembered opening the box that Isaiah's people had air-dropped to his CRM unit. Isaiah had written a note to him. *For when you need more than blivits.* He raised the binoculars for another look.

A Mexican army unit plus a contingent of Drug Cartel militia, just as we were told. Looking at the first vehicle in the convoy, he touched a GPS coordinate lock button on his binoculars. He did this for the next four vehicles, then repeated it for the last five at the end of the convoy.

Next he activated the targeting activation slide switch. He shimmied back down from the crest of the hill. When he was out of sight from the south, he stood up and walked to where his second in command sat under camouflage netting, watching a laptop screen. He crawled in beside him.

"Got the coordinates?" He peered at the laptop screen.

"Yep."

"Use our liberated drones to attack the south end of the convoy. Use the GPS-guided Stinger missiles against the north end."

"Got it."

Joseph took another look at the aerial view transmitted by one of the drones he controlled. "OK. Now."

Richard Littlehawk's fingers flew across the keyboard, tapping out a syncopation of destruction. Joseph looked up to see five members of his unit rise from under their camp netting and point their shoulder-fired Stinger missiles south and over the crest of the hill. These were modified to be surface-to-surface missiles. Exactly three seconds later he heard five whooshes and saw puffs of rocket exhaust from the launcher tubes.

The rockets arced up and over the crest of the hill, seeking the GPS coordinates fed to them. Joseph looked back to the laptop display. The first five vehicles of the convoy exploded on cue. John shifted the view to the end of the convoy. Six seconds later the last five vehicles exploded.

Richard panned the view to the middle of the convoy. Panicked soldiers were turning their vehicles into the southbound lane and racing away. They were unable to regroup when their commanding officers were killed in the lead vehicles. The Cartel militia followed in their pick-up trucks, burning rubber as they accelerated around the slower moving army vehicles.

"Send the recall signal to the drones and our men. Let's get out of here. Mission accomplished."

Richard looked up and flashed a grin at Joseph. "Roger that." He tapped a few more keys, then closed the laptop and stowed it in his backpack. The others were packing in their camo netting.

A medic was looking at one man's shoulder.

"What happened?" asked Joseph. "Anything serious?"

The medic looked up. "Just sprained muscles in his shoulder. He braced his knees when he fired his stinger instead of bending them. The recoil bruised him a bit. He'll live."

The medic's stenciled name on her field jacket read, "Barnes, Audrey."

"Thanks, Medic Barnes." Joseph started walking north. Several SUVs were waiting for them under camo netting beyond the next hill. They would take separate back country roads and rendezvous at a safe house somewhere between Cheyenne and Laramie. They had to avoid detection by the remaining gangs in those cities. They were fighting enemies both foreign and domestic.

It's going to be a long war, thought Joseph.

*　　*　　*　　*　　*　　*

As it turned out, the Mexican Army units and the Cartel Militias had to live with their own answers. That shortened the war.

In the first town they took over in Arizona, a Cartel Militia staged a show of bravado and intimidation. They rounded up and publicly murdered four ranchers and their wives and children, to "show who was boss!" The remaining farmers fled to the countryside with their families.

The militia then went on a drunken rampage of looting, burning, murder and rape. By the second day of destruction, they were bored. They piled into their trucks and drove out to a ranch where they could stage a "bull fight."

Finding the corral where the bull was kept, drunken militiamen lined the rails, shouting, firing their guns in the air, and laughing insanely. One of them jumped into the corral and waved a blanket at the bull. When the bull charged, the "toreador" pulled out his handgun and emptied a clip into the bull. The hurtling body of the bull plowed a short furrow in the ground and came to rest ten feet from the gunman. Spilling over the fence rails, a drunken group posed on the carcass for pictures to post on their Facebook pages. Seeing some crops on their way out, they stopped their trucks and burned the fields.

This scenario was repeated in every town they invaded. The practice spread to the Mexican Army units, where what little discipline existed – evaporated under the chaotic example set by the drug cartel militias. Farming and ranching towns were laid waste across California, Arizona, New Mexico, and Colorado.

No crops were planted. No food was harvested. Untended cattle starved in the next winter. Stinking carcasses littered the landscape. The supermarket shelves were empty.

By the second year of the occupation, the Mexican Army and cartel militias had eaten up all the available food. Even where some cattle managed to survive, there were no calves for a new generation, because all the bulls had been shot in the popular "armed bullfights." No more beef for food.

Defeated by starvation, the Mexican Army units and Cartel Militias began to pull out and go back to Mexico. They had existed their entire lives by taking what they wanted at gunpoint. They had no idea how to raise crops or farm animals, or how to make things. There was nothing left to take by force. They couldn't eat AK-47s.

Chapter Forty-Three

"Grace!" Isaiah sounded out of breath. Grace looked up from her desk. The name plate on her desk read: *Dr. Grace Washington, Director of Research and Development, Nutritional Abundance Industries.* A flower pot was on her desk with a single wheat stalk rising from it. Ripe grains of wheat clustered at the top of the stalk.

Isaiah stopped abruptly. "What's this?"

Grace beamed. "The tenth generation of my wheat super-seeds. The grain you see here matured in 25 days. When you harvest the grain, more grows from the same stalk. We've been able to get 12 harvests in one year."

"Grace, that's incredible!" Isaiah reached out to touch the grain.

"And, the seeds reproduce, so that no one is forced to keep buying seeds from us. They can save their own seeds for planting."

"Wow! And you can still make money that way?"

"You bet! Car companies lure customers with newer and better models. Their cars don't 'expire' after one year. Customers buy because they want better – whether it's cars or seeds. We will continue to make better performing crop seeds year after year. Customers will voluntarily buy improved seeds every few years."

She stood up and picked up the pot, holding it up to the ray of sunlight shining in through her window.

"Isaiah, the time is coming when an affordable back yard greenhouse could feed a family of four year-round. Food self-sufficiency for anyone who wants to learn and do the work."

She put the pot down. Isaiah put both hands on her shoulders. "Let me just look at you. The woman who conquered world hunger. And I'm married to her. I'm so lucky!"

She smiled and kissed him. Thoroughly.

"Isaiah, what was your news?"

"Oh! The latest news from the formerly United States. Some localities are publicly announcing that they want help from the ARKS! These are folks who are <u>not</u> affiliated with the Constitutional Resistance Movement. So, they've had a change of heart. Could it be that the flood waters of control and coercion are receding?"

Grace frowned. "How will we know that it's safe to come our of our ARKS?"

Isaiah smiled. "Like Noah, we will release a dove of capitalism. If it's welcomed, we can take a chance and come out. If it returns to us – metaphorically – we wait, like Noah did."

Grace looked thoughtful. "What form can this dove take?"

Isaiah picked up a legal pad from her desk and sat down. "We can offer a covenant, a voluntary option for them to sign. When enough people in a given area sign the covenant, then you and I announce to our fellow ARK dwellers that in our opinion it's reasonably safe to re-enter that locality. It will of course be their decision to do so or not."

Grace sat at her desk and pulled over the King James Bible she kept there. Without opening it, she stared out her window and said, "And God remembered Noah … And God said, This is the token of the covenant which I make between me and you … I do set my bow in the cloud, …"

She looked over at Isaiah, eyes shining. "Oh Isaiah, the bow in the cloud! We can call it it the Rainbow Option. The rainbow was a symbol of God's promise never to flood the earth again. The Rainbow Option covenant will be a symbol of people's promise never to flood their fellow citizens with coercion and control again. Then, like Noah, some of us may come out of our ARKs and help rebuild the world. A promise, a choice, a covenant, an option … the Rainbow Option."

Isaiah reached out and took her hand. "Grace, that's perfect, that's it. The Rainbow Option."

He looked into the distance thoughtfully. Abruptly shaking himself, he said, "Let's write that covenant, shall we?"

*   *   *   *   *   *

Word went out via .ARK and the CRM underground network, and then was passed on to church groups, mutual protection groups, mutual-aid survival groups, co-op food groups, black market flea markets and the few remaining radio and television stations that were still broadcasting. A message was coming from the two Noah Option architects, the two who were the public face of the ARK refuge communities: Isaiah Mercury and Grace Washington. A day and a time was named, with assurances that it would be archived on .ARK for later viewing and rebroadcasting.

The title of the message was *The Rainbow Option: An Invitation to a New Covenant of Constitutionalism and Capitalism.* It quickly became shortened to "The Rainbow Option."

"Have you heard about the Rainbow Option invitation? You'll be able to see it on .ARK." "That Rainbow Option message you've heard about? You can hear it on The Don Smith Show on Blogtalk Radio on the internet." "Our local TV station is going to broadcast the Rainbow Option message from .ARK." "Our church is going to watch the Rainbow Option message in our social hall."

The day arrived. The title *The Rainbow Option* was on the screen, and an instrumental version of *God Bless America* played. Then the camera cut to Grace and Isaiah, standing with an American flag.

"Hello my fellow Americans. I'm Isaiah Mercury."

"And I'm Grace Washington. We have an invitation for you. We call it *The Rainbow Option: A New Covenant of Constitutionalism and Capitalism.*

"You may have seen or heard us nearly three years ago when we announced *The Noah Option.* The Noah Option was an invitation to hard working Americans to leave their homes and bring their families to places of refuge. Refuge from the rising flood of government coercion and control that was wrecking their lives and livelihoods.

"Many Americans did flee to the ARKs with their families. They live in these refuges now, living their lives cooperatively, without bullying one another or trying to mind each other's business. They are hard-working, smart, and productive. They are craftsmen, engineers, teachers, contractors, cooks, architects, small business owners, farmers, barbers, carpenters, electricians and grocers."

Isaiah spoke again. "They all have one thing in common: they make things or services that are useful to their fellow citizens. They sell their products and services to those who are willing to voluntarily pay for them. They do not ask for something for nothing. They offer value for value. They work.

"They left you because you allowed your society to become hostile to Makers and friendly to Takers. They were tired of working hard to make something, only to have government sanctioned Takers come along and take the fruits of their minds and their labor. So they left. They left you to live with your answers."

The right hand side of the screen showed scenes of gangs smashing windows, looting food from pantries, ripping clothing from women, slapping children, and setting homes on fire.

Grace said, "You have now lived with your answers for the past three years. When you said it was OK for the Takers to take, as long as they had government permission, they gradually grew to believe that they were entitled to take whatever they wanted, with or without government permission. These are the gangs that have stolen your food, burned your homes, farms and factories, raped your daughters and wives, and beat you and shot you and left you for dead."

Isaiah pointed at the pictures on the screen. "These are the gangs that you had to fight off with neighborhood self-defense groups. You have disintegrated from a 21st century society to a 14th century feudal society where you spend less time making and producing and more time defending yourselves from the barbarians. The result is that you now live a subsistence lifestyle, working sixteen hours a day just to survive. There's no time for art, entertainment, or making products to improve your lives. There's no more 'going to the mall.' Indeed, you risk your life by going to the burned-out and deserted malls. Only packs of feral dogs and packs of feral humans roam the malls of America today."

The picture changed to a pack of wolves. Grace went on, "Those of you who studied ecology know that when the prey, the food supply of the predators, is used up, the predators begin to die off."

The picture changed to a family: a woman, a man, and two small children under six, a girl and a boy. "You were the prey," said Grace, "and these were the predators." The screen showed gangs, outlaw Homeland Security squads, and a SWAT team wearing Kevlar vests with the letters EPA. They were burning a farm field.

Isaiah continued, "Unlike defenseless deer, rabbits, or other prey, you learned to fight back. Now, from the reports we hear, the ratio of people in predator gangs has dropped to about one in twenty. If you keep resisting and defending yourselves with deadly force, you can expect to reduce that further. Like all predators, if they can't capture new prey, they will starve. So, resist them and starve them out."

Grace spoke, "You and hundreds of millions of Americans have lost their loved ones to starvation, disease, murder by gangs, slaughter by the Mexican army and Cartel gangs, and execution by occupying UN troops enforcing Sharia Law without your consent. A greater number of Americans have died than in the Civil War, our bloodiest war up till now.

"You're starting to rebuild your lives and you are taking responsibility for your own survival. So, Isaiah and I offer you an invitation, an option. It's your decision whether or not to accept."

The right hand screen showed the graphic: *The Rainbow Option: An Invitation to a New Covenant of Constitutionalism and Capitalism.*

Isaiah explained, "In the Bible story of the flood, God promised Noah that He would never again flood the earth. As a symbol and reminder of His promise, He "set His bow in the cloud." The Rainbow.

"But God didn't send this flood of coercion and control that caused the collapse. *You did.*

"You raised the flood level a foot every time you gave more power to your government in the name of minding other people's business. You are now living with the results of your agreeing to, tolerating, and permitting such a political system of centralized power. You are living like refugees. You are living like North Koreans, with barely enough to eat and in continual terror for your lives.

"*So, we want you to promise never to do it again.*

"We're asking you to sign an agreement that you will not initiate force against your fellow citizens. We're asking you to promise to support only limited governments that will protect life, liberty, property and the pursuit of happiness. We're asking you to promise that you will mind your own business and allow your neighbors to mind theirs. We're asking you to return to the constitutionally limited government and free market capitalism that produced the greatest abundance the world has ever seen.

"Like any contractual agreement, you are required to sign two copies and keep one for yourself. It is your personal promise, and we will hold you to it. This is not a 'collective' agreement that you can hide behind. Once you sign, we expect you to keep your promise, whether the majority of your fellow citizens sign it or not. Freedom is an individual and personal responsibility. You can't hide behind a group. Wives can't sign for husbands. Husbands can't sign for wives. You have to stand up as an individual. When children become adults, they will be expected to sign for themselves.

"Everyone living in the ARK communities has signed this covenant. Some who came to the ARKs decided not to sign. Their option, their choice. We believe in minding our own business. They are no longer a part of the ARK community.

"A covenant is an agreement between two or more parties. What Grace and I offer is this: if eighty-five percent of the inhabitants of any state of the formerly United States of America can get signatures of agreement to this covenant, then we will offer our personal recommendation to ARK dwellers that it is reasonably safe to return to that state.

"No ARK dweller is obligated to return, and no ARK dweller is obligated to take our word for it. As self-responsible adults, we encourage them to do their own due diligence and not just take our word for it. And, as adults, they don't need to wait for our say-so. They can decide to return whenever they want to, covenant or not.

"So, whenever eighty-five percent of the people of a state voluntarily agree to this New Covenant of Constitutionalism and Capitalism, Grace and I will invite ARK dwellers to exercise their own *Rainbow Option*: the option to return to a world they left. It will be their option to return and help you rebuild your flooded world. It will be their option to trust you to keep your promise.

As a sign that you have agreed to this covenant, we are suggesting that you display a rainbow icon at your place of business and your home. It will signal that you have signed the covenant. It will signify that you respect the right of others to be responsible for their own lives and that you expect others to respect your right to be responsible for your own life.

This will be our "mezuzah" of constitutionalism and capitalism. All who see it will know that you respect the rights of others.

"Will you do it? Will you promise not to do it again? Will you show us a Rainbow? The ball is in your court. It is your option now. Your Rainbow Option."

Grace smiled. "And now we leave you to read the covenant for yourselves. It will scroll up the screen and it will be available for download and printing on the internet domain .ARK. There are instructions for how to get signed copies back to us. We will not accept any modified versions with exceptions, loopholes, and excuses. As you have learned the hard way, reality and the laws of nature offer no exceptions, loopholes, or excuses. We hope to hear from you. We pray for your safety and well-being. May God bless you."

Isaiah looked at Grace. Then he smiled as he looked back at the camera.

"If you choose *The Rainbow Option*, if you promise to abide by the principles of freedom and respect for individuals in this *Covenant of Constitutionalism and Capitalism*, then we have the chance that Noah and his family had: the chance to rebuild a flooded world. A chance, as Abraham Lincoln said, "that this nation, under God, shall have a new birth of freedom."

The document began scrolling up the screen.

The Rainbow Option
A New Covenant of Constitutionalism and Capitalism.

A legally binding agreement. I voluntarily agree to this covenant with my fellow citizens.

1. *I agree to never seek to control, coerce, dictate to, or force my fellow citizens to do what I want. I will use verbal persuasion and voluntary agreements with my fellow citizens.*

2. *I promise to give my consent only to government that is limited to protecting life, liberty, property and the pursuit of happiness.*

3. *I agree to organize and give my support only to a government whose sole purpose is protecting citizens from those individuals or groups who initiate force or fraud against us, be they foreign or domestic. Domestically, this includes robbers, con-men, assaulters, rapists, and murderers. From abroad, this includes terrorists, attackers and invaders, whether in uniform or not.*

4. *I agree to use force to defend myself and others only against those who initiate force against me and others. This is my right to defend my life, which can be shared with government, but can never be taken away by government.*

5. *I agree to never use government to interfere with my fellow citizen's business or property, unless it materially harms me. In the case of material harm, I will sue and/or bring criminal charges for remedy and restitution under liability, contract, and/or criminal law.*

The list went on, but it was short. There was one space for a signature and a date.

Chapter Forty-Four

Joseph Wakini spoke sharply to Judge Block. "Judge, it's not safe for you to go! There are still some gangs lurking around Cheyenne. When they hear of you appearing at a public meeting to answer questions about the Rainbow Option, they'll target you. They don't want this new Covenant to succeed!"

"Joseph," said the Judge, "I know there are risks. I am the last one to run unnecessary risks. That's why I got out of San Francisco and came here. When the local gangs, drug cartel militias and Mexican Army units began to run the city like a war zone, I knew there was no hope. But when this many Wyoming citizens ask for my help, how can I not go? This may be our best chance to rally public support for the Covenant."

"Judge, in one more year, I predict that those gang members will all be dead, either by starvation or shot down by vigilante groups defending themselves from gang attacks. Then it will be safe for you to go. Is one more year too much to ask?" Joseph was red in the face.

The Judge thought, *He's gun-shy after losing Cathy to a drone strike.*

He took a deep breath, then said, "I'll be armed and I'll wear a Kevlar vest. CRM commandoes will provide security at the meeting and be my bodyguards. Nearly every grown man and woman is armed whenever they leave their homes now. Only suicide assassins would attempt something in a meeting where every last soul is armed. And the punk gangs you describe are not religious martyrs. They're just gangs wanting to survive by stealing from others.

The Judge looked earnestly at Joseph. "But the time is now. Grace and Isaiah offered The Rainbow Option only two weeks ago. These folks want to sign, but they have a few doubts. That's natural. If I can answer their doubts, it's worth the risk."

Taking his own deep breath, Joseph said, "I can't stop you. It's your decision. But I don't like it."

The Judge put his hand on Joseph's shoulder. "I don't like it either. But sometimes you've got to do risky things in order to make a difference. You have. You've led military raids. You stopped the Mexican army raiders, rapists and looters at the Colorado border. You made a difference. Now let me try to make a difference."

* * * * * *

Nearly everybody at the meeting wore a side arm or a shoulder holster. Many also carried rifles. Reloading ammo was one of the fastest growing cottage industries in the state of Wyoming. The faces of the men and women were weather beaten and lined. Everybody spent time outside growing food, standing guard over their gardens and livestock, or hunting game. All looked grim. All were survivors.

Someone introduced Judge Block as a member of the Constitutional Resistance Movement and personally acquainted with Isaiah Mercury and some ARK dwellers. The judge stepped up to the podium.

"You are all survivors of the collapse. You all have adapted to wild-west conditions of lawlessness. You have all used lethal force to defend yourselves and your families from ruthless armed gangs. You all experienced first hand how a power-hungry and predatory government treated you as cattle to be herded. Now we have a chance to tame the wild west a second time, a chance to cage and restrain ravenous government. The Rainbow Option is our second chance."

The Judge looked over the crowd. "What would you like to know?"

A pale-faced man in his fifties stood up. He wore eyeglasses and "dude" hiking pants. He had been an EPA land-use regulator. His daughter and her two teen-age children were supporting him with a large back-yard vegetable garden. He did not help to tend the garden, pleading ignorance. His daughter loved him and did not press the issue, although it irritated her.

"This agreement seems to call for a government that is no government at all! There is no protection for the environment or welfare for poor people."

Judge Block peered at him over his "half" reading glasses. "What part of the environment do you own?"

"I don't, but I live with my daughter who owns an acre. We have a vegetable garden that might be contaminated by our neighbor's pesticides. Those pesticides should be regulated and controlled by the government."

The Judge answered, "This covenant calls for strict liability laws for that kind of a problem. If your neighbor's pesticides blow onto your property, or hurt your tomatoes, sue him for damages. This covenant calls for a court system to settle such disputes."

"But our neighbor shouldn't be allowed to use pesticides at all!"

"Why? Has it hurt you?"

"No, but it might."

"And you might commit murder. Should we put you in prison?"

"That's ridiculous!"

"I agree. Next question."

A gaunt woman in her forties stood up. "This says the government will only use force against those who initiate force. What about the drug dealers? They cause harm, but they don't force people to buy from them. Before the collapse, I had one son who died of an overdose. Drug dealers should be outlawed."

"Ma'am, I sympathize with your loss. My aunt died from an overdose of prescription pain killers. The drugstore was the drug dealer who sold her the pills. Should we outlaw all pharmaceuticals in order to save the lives of those who misuse them? Many people are cured and given pain relief by drugs. Many die of alcoholism. Once we start deciding what drugs other people ought to be allowed to have, then other people will decide what drugs we are allowed to have."

"Then how can this problem be controlled?"

"Self-control. I'll control me and you'll control you. We will guide and set good examples for our children, but once they become adults, they control themselves. As long as they don't initiate force against others, they have the right to life, liberty, property, and the pursuit of happiness, even if we don't like the happiness they are pursuing."

"Well, I don't agree."

"Then don't sign the Covenant. I respect your right to control yourself, and I won't try to coerce you."

When the meeting ended, all but six people had stepped forward to sign the Covenant.

* * * * * *

"April in Dallas," breathed Grace, as she and Isaiah strolled through the park along the Trinity River. She stopped to touch a flower. "So many prairie flowers. Bluebonnets everywhere."

Leaving the park, they strolled back toward the downtown area. A house caught Isaiah's eye.

"I've always admired Craftsman architecture. So simple, such clean lines. And that porch! Couldn't you picture yourself in one of those rocking chairs, sipping a cool drink?" He turned and did a slow 180-degree scan of the street. "Reminds me of the Craftsman style homes in Ansley Park, in Atlanta. I remember cruising through there during Freaknik one year. When I was young and foolish. Good times, though."

"Yes. I went with some girlfriends myself one spring break. Oh, to be young again! But not foolish." She looked up at him with a twinkle in her eye.

"Speaking of foolish … did you see the list of attendees for the Constitutional Convention for the United States of Liberty? All the usual suspects, all the usual grievance groups and special interest groups, from sexual orientation to AARP to ethnic origin. Didn't we learn anything from the collapse of the United States? I thought eighty-five percent of the people of these states signed the Covenant of Constitutionalism and Capitalism?

Grace let out a big sigh as she continued walking. "We have just gone through a phase change politically. In physics, a phase change from ice to water means that the rules have changed. Many of these folks don't realize that. The things you could do with ice don't work with water. You can stack ice cubes. You can't stack water.

"Good analogy," said Isaiah. "Water adapts to flow around anything, and capitalism flows out to meet all needs. Unless it's frozen in place by central control."

Grace replied, "The Federal Government grew like a cancer, until, like a cancer, it killed the host. It seized all the wealth and then proclaimed it would 'redistribute' the goodies 'fairly.' Naturally, all of these grievance groups demanded their 'fair share.' And it worked – they were given goodies. So they were reinforced for making demands – to be given something taken from others. We do the behaviors that get reinforced; the behaviors that worked for us in the past. So naturally these groups are doing what worked for them in the past: demanding goodies and special rights and privileges. That was our previous political phase, the ice cubes."

She shivered in the warm Spring air.

"So if I follow your analogy, under centralized ever-growing government, the ice cubes were grabbed and stacked up in one central location by the Feds, to be given out to their chosen crony groups. Under constitutional limited government and free market capitalism, it is water, flowing out to nourish new growth."

"Exactly! If we can create a more strictly limited constitutional republic this time." She paused, remembering Ben Franklin's comment after the first Constitutional Convention. "And if we can keep it."

Grace sighed again. "It seems that every generation has to learn that lesson all over again. I wish so-called 'political science' were more like real science. We scientists don't have to rediscover the laws of physics every generation. Instead, we use previous knowledge to create new discoveries and new inventions."

Isaiah nodded. "And to riff on your analogy a bit more, under a huge central government, daily life and business is frozen. Nothing grows in winter. Like Narnia, where it was always winter, but never Christmas." He frowned.

Grace smiled. "Yes. And now political spring has come to these Covenant states. Every new law and regulation is like a winter storm, freezing all activity. If we can hold back, restrict, and cage the power of government, then the snow and ice will melt. As snowmelt waters nourish new plant life, the flowing waters of capitalism will nourish new entrepreneurs, new inventions and new prosperity for everyone."

Isaiah's face was still grim. "Well, the icy grip of central control still reigns in the Northeastern states. Those pitiful people are starving and getting by on two hours of electricity a day, like the North Koreans. But they can't let go of control, even when there is nothing left to control!"

They were now back in the downtown area. They looked at the modern glass-faced buildings lining the wide street.

Grace looked up at one of the buildings, all mirrored glass and angles. "I'm so glad Dallas was spared major destruction. The looters and gangs smashed street level windows, but didn't manage to do much harm higher up. Some fires, but the whole city didn't burn."

Isaiah brightened up. "Amen to that. I think it's fitting that this Constitutional Convention for the United States of Liberty be held in Dallas, a city known for business. Or 'bidness,' as real Texans say."

Grace turned to look at their hotel. "Well, I want to go to our room and make more notes for the new constitution. I'm getting some good ideas from Mark Levin's book *The Liberty Amendments*."

Isaiah offered his arm. "Shall we?" She took his arm. Together, they strolled into the hotel lobby.

CHAPTER FORTY-FIVE

THE NEXT DAY AT THE DALLAS CONVENTION CENTER, JUDGE BARRY Block gaveled the Constitutional Convention to order. There were representatives from each state that had signed the Covenant, nineteen in all, stretching in a crescent from Idaho and Montana down through Utah, Texas, Oklahoma, and Arkansas, across to Georgia and the two Carolinas.

Florida had formed a Maoist government under Chairwoman Wasserwoman. The West Coast states still could not decide whether to fight the Mexican Army or to welcome them. The mid-Atlantic states and New England states were feudal areas under the control of various local war-lords and UN protectorates. The midwestern States were run by union bosses who made private property illegal and rationed everything. Their capital was Detroit. What was left of it.

Clearing his throat, Judge Block began. "We have a committee writing a first draft of our new constitution, patterned after the original. The original Declaration of Independence contained some principles that are fundamental to a free society governed by a constitutionally-limited government. So, they have used some of the principles and language from the Declaration. Mr. Mark Levin is the chair of the writing committee. Sir, would you read us the preamble your committee has drafted?"

Mark Levin rose and walked to the podium with one page in his hand.

"Mr. Chairman and fellow delegates, here is our Preamble:

"We hold these truths to be self-evident, that all men and women are

created equal in self-sovereignty and dignity, that they are endowed by their Creator with certain inalienable Rights, and that among these rights are Life, Liberty, Property and the Pursuit of their own Happiness, so long as their pursuit does not infringe on the exercise of those same rights by their fellow citizens. That to secure these rights, governments are instituted by mankind, deriving and given their enumerated powers by the consent of the governed.

"That whenever any form of government becomes destructive of these ends, it is the right of the people to alter or abolish it, and institute new government, laying its foundation on such principles, and specifying, enumerating and constraining its powers in such form, as to them shall seem most likely to protect their Lives, Liberties, Property, and their right to Pursue their own Happiness.

"Protecting our lives, liberties, property, and our right to pursue our own happiness is the one and only proper function of government. Government is not instituted to guarantee equality of outcomes or take from some citizens to give to other citizens. Government is an arbiter of disputes about rights. These inalienable rights are freedoms from coercion by their fellow citizens, foreign powers, and their own government. These rights are not entitlements to be given anything by government; not goods, services, special privileges or monopolies.

"By its nature, government produces nothing to give, except protection of your rights. To give anything else, the government has to take from some to give to others. This we explicitly forbid government to do. The government exists to protect everybody equally, not some more than others, and not to accord special rights and privileges to some groups. Government exists to protect liberty for all.

"That's it. Four paragraphs. You will notice, ladies and gentlemen, the addition of the right to property, the enabler of all other rights. Property was included in the original Virginia Declaration of Rights written by George Mason. It was the model for the Declaration of Independence. You will also notice that we do not say that the purpose is to promote 'the general welfare.' It is the people's responsibility to provide for their own welfare, not the government's responsibility. This concludes my reading."

The delegates broke out in applause, whistles, and stomping. Many patted Mark on the back as he returned to his seat.

Judge Block took the podium again. "I will now take comments from the floor. Each delegate is limited to five minutes. In the interest of getting a Constitution written and ratified, I suggest that you make suggestions for changes, not lengthy criticisms of what you don't like."

An auction-style paddle with a number was held up. "I recognize Delegate … " the Judge's assistant consulted a numbered list and handed a card to the Judge, "Delegate DelMonte from the great state of Louisiana."

Ms. DelMonte rose and opened her jacket to reveal a t-shirt that said 'Go Bio!' "Mr. Chairman, I wish to give the floor to my friend from the Bio-Diesel Producers Association."

A man in the seating section for the public stood. "On behalf of the Bio-Diesel Producers Association, we move to include an article that requires all citizens drive diesel cars, and that all fuel is required to be bio-diesel. Bio-diesel is recycling and renewability at its best! Bio-diesel is good for the planet!"

Banging his gavel, Judge Block said, "As a point of order, when this Constitutional Convention was called, each state was to elect delegates representing all the people of that state, not some special interest groups. Therefore, no delegate may give the floor to a non-delegate. If a delegate wants to speak on behalf of some right or privilege that applies to *all* the people, you may do so. I again recognize Ms. DelMonte."

Ms. DelMonte again took the cordless microphone. "Mr. Chairman, I object to this high-handed exclusion of a citizen exercising his free speech rights. You have no right to do so!"

"Objection noted. Now then, Ms. DelMonte, you are a duly elected delegate, and you have …" he squinted at a stopwatch, "four more minutes to say whatever you wish. Proceed."

"Well! I never! When I think of the disrespect and prejudice endured by the Bio-Diesel community, it infuriates me that …" She ranted on for three minutes, then Judge Block held up his hand. She stopped.

"Ms. DelMonte," said Judge Block, "you have one minute left. Do you wish to propose an article to this constitution granting special rights and privileges to the Bio-Diesel Producers Association? You have the right to propose articles to the constitution."

"Well! I never!" she spluttered once again. After taking a breath, she said, "I move to include an article to the constitution making it mandatory that every citizen drive diesel-powered vehicles, and that all fuel is required to be bio-diesel."

Banging his gavel, Judge Block said "So moved! Like any other article or amendment, this is subject to ratification by eighty percent of the delegates, and then by every one of the nineteen state legislatures. Delegates, when you vote, ask yourself: does this grant a special privilege to some but not to all people equally? Does it confer a monopoly on fuel to bio-diesel producers? Next speaker!"

A placard went up from another Louisiana delegate. Judge Block recognized him.

"Mr. Chairman, speaking on behalf of Ms. DelMonte, I wish to state that no vote of a majority changes the scientific fact that bio-diesel is renewable fuel. Her article should be included in the Constitution without a vote!"

Judge Block responded, "Since our basic political principle is consent of the governed, *everything* we put into the Constitution will be voted on by you, the governed. Including the Preamble. If you want her article in, persuade your fellow delegates to give their consent. You have four and a half minutes left."

Flustered, the second delegate sat down without speaking. "Next!" barked Judge Block.

The next delegate waved a flag with the letters BRA. "Mr. Chairman, I speak on behalf of my constituents who belong to the Buddhist Respect Association. For over two hundred years, Buddhists in North America have not gotten any respect! I offer an article that authorizes any Buddhist the right to make a citizen's arrest of anyone who offends them, disrespects them, refuses to associate with them, or refuses to do business with them! With the presumption of guilt until proven innocent by a jury to be drawn exclusively from the BRA community. Penalty upon conviction: 10 years in jail and a $50,000 fine!"

Judge Block raised one eyebrow. "I thought Buddhists believed in passive acceptance?"

"Mainstream Buddhists do, but the BRA split off. We are tired of being dissed!"

So it went all afternoon. Special pleading, special entitlements, special privileges for groups, businesses, and industries. The last gasp of grievance groups and crony capitalism, clawing for government coercion on their behalf.

After a break, Grace raised her placard to be recognized. "The chair recognizes Delegate Grace Washington from Alabama." The hall grew hushed. Everyone knew her role in creating the ARK refuge communities.

"Mr. Chairman, I move to include seven articles. First, that all laws passed by Congress expire at the end of three years. By that time the people will know whether it's a good law or not. If it is good, their representatives will pass it again.

"Second, that all senators and congress members be limited to one term in office. We need to revive the self-correcting principle of citizen-legislators, not career politicians.

"Third, that Congress shall be in session for only three months every other year, so that all senators and congress members shall be classified as part-time jobs and so compensated. They'll have to make a living like the rest of us during the rest of the time, and live with the answers they impose on us. Parkinson's law states that the work (and the mischief) expands to fill the time allotted to it. Three months is long enough to deal with the important issues, but short enough to keep out the trivial ones.

"Fourth, that Congress and all other members of the government shall be subject to the same laws and regulations that they inflict on their fellow citizens. No exceptions. Period.

"Fifth, that Congress shall meet in rotating locations for each session, to include the state capitals of each state and one other location chosen by each state's legislature. This may not eliminate permanent lobbyists, but it will force them to be mobile. It will also increase the visibility of the proceedings to the citizens. Make the government come to them.

"Sixth, that all bills passed by Congress must cite the Article, Section and Clause of the Constitution that enumerates the power to take the action that the bill specifies.

"Seventh, that all members of Congress must certify by oath that they have read every word of each and every bill they vote on, whether voting yea or nay. Failure to do so, or perjury under oath, triggers automatic dismissal from Congress. Any citizen of the state and district that elected them may quiz their member of Congress about any portion of any bill that they voted for. Failure to answer accurately triggers an automatic recall vote."

"Thank you, Mr. Chairman." Grace sat down.

The assembly broke out in applause. Someone touched her shoulder. Looking around, Grace saw Audrey Barnes. She leaned down close to Grace.

"How's that finger?"

"As good as new, thanks to you, medic Audrey." Grace held up her finger for inspection.

"Glad to hear it. Wish I could disinfect away some of the intellectual infection I'm hearing here. I'm a delegate for Wyoming." Audrey straightened up, smiled at Grace and returned to her section.

The Judge gaveled for order. He banged his gavel for the next fifteen seconds before the applause subsided.

"So moved. These will be debated and voted on." Isaiah raised his paddle. "The chair recognizes Delegate Isaiah Mercury, also from the great state of Alabama."

Rising, Isaiah said "Mr. Chairman, I move for two articles. First, Congress shall make no law regulating Commerce, excepting for patents, trademarks, and copyrights. These are forms of property to be protected under the Constitution. Congress shall not regulate commerce within a state, between states, or with foreign nations. Nor shall the states regulate commerce between states or with foreign nations. Commerce shall be governed by established contract law and liability law. Citizens and corporate entities shall use criminal and civil law to settle disputes involving commerce. Voluntary agreements between consenting adults shall have the protection of contract law, and shall not be subject to prior restraint or ex-post facto regulation.

"Second, I move that Article II, Section 4, the impeachment clause of the Constitution, shall be amended to include that failure to adhere to, uphold, and stay within the Constitutional limits of his or her authority, or taking any action not specifically enumerated in the

Constitution, shall also be grounds for impeachment of the President. The House shall bring articles of impeachment against the president by a simple majority vote, and the Senate shall act as jury. The Senate can vote to impeach and remove the President by a five eighths vote, rounded down from any fraction."

"Thank you, Mr. Chairman." Isaiah sat down. Again, applause erupted. This time, Judge Block did not attempt to stop it. He just waited.

"I believe the delegates now have over eighteen articles to discuss among themselves in order to prepare for floor debate and a vote. That's enough for one day. This convention is adjourned until tomorrow morning at nine a.m." He struck his gavel.

Isaiah approached the Judge. "So many proposals for entitlements, regulations, and control! I'm worried that we'll end up right where we were before the collapse."

The Judge smiled. "Keep the faith. These people have been through a lot. I trust them to ratify only the proper functions of government. Remember, 'the event is in the hand of God.'"

"Amen, brother, amen."

CHAPTER FORTY-SIX

JOSEPH WAKINI LAY IN HIS SLEEPING BAG AND STARED UP AT THE stars. The Milky Way. *As if God had taken a handful of diamonds and scattered them across the night sky. So beautiful. So abundant. I miss you, Cathy.* He cried aloud, "I miss you so much!"

His horse nickered in response. She was tethered twenty feet away. Joseph turned his face in her direction. "It's all right, girl." He and the horse were alone. The embers of his campfire still glowed. He was camped next to the bomb crater where Cathy had died. By starlight, he could see the wooden cross with her neckerchief tied to it. Her grave.

Joseph was on a pilgrimage, a spirit quest, back to the scene of Cathy's death. *I know I need healing. Spiritual healing. Dear Lord, please help me. Sweet Jesus, please help me. I can't stop thinking about Cathy and it hurts. It hurts so much.* He closed his eyes and drifted into sleep.

He turned in his sleeping bag and saw a shadowy figure standing beside the faint embers of the campfire. The figure put some brushwood branches on the embers. Flames flickered up. He could make out the face. Blond curls under a straw cowboy hat. *Cathy!*

She took a step to where he lay and knelt down beside him. Her face was serene and shone by the fire glow. "Joseph. My sweet Joseph."

"Cathy! Cathy, I miss you so much!" He struggled to get his arms out of the sleeping bag and reach out to her.

Her hand caressed his face. Her fingers were so soft and warm. He stopped struggling and relaxed.

"I know, I know. I miss you too. I want you to know I'm OK. I'm safe. We'll see each other again." Her fingers smoothed his brow. He looked into her eyes.

"Joseph. I know you hurt. I'll always love you. I've been sent to release you from your pain so that you can go on with your life. I've been sent to heal you." Her palm cupped his cheek.

He stirred a little. "Sent? Who sent you?"

"The One Who healed the sick and cured the lame. He cares for you so much. He sent me."

She leaned over and kissed him on the lips. Her lips were warm. "Be healed, my darling. Be healed."

He woke up to the nickering of his horse. The morning sun was warm on his face. He touched his lips. *A dream?*

He pulled on his jeans and boots, then stood up. He walked over to the cross on Cathy's grave. He touched the faded neckerchief tied to it. *It all seemed so real. Was it just a dream?*

He walked back to the campfire circle and picked up some split kindling to rebuild a fire for his breakfast. As he bent over to place the kindling on last night's ashes, he saw some brush twigs half burned.

I didn't put brush on my fire last night. I had split wood for the fire. Then he remembered the dream.

Joseph felt pure joy wash over him. He fell to his knees before the ashes and bowed his head. *Thank you, Lord. You are Lord of all healing. Thank You for sending Cathy to let me know she's OK and safe in Your arms. Thank You for sending Cathy to heal me. Thank you, Cathy, for sending me a sign.*

He raised his face and looked up. Up into the clear blue sky. He again felt the warmth of the sun on his cheek. He felt a calm serenity. He smiled for the first time in a long, long time.

I'm healed. I'm healed!

*   *   *   *   *   *

Three months later, Grace was humming happily as she mixed the ingredients for Isaiah's prize-winning barbeque sauce. With a secret ingredient of her own added. *I'm so glad Kansas was one of the states that signed up for the Rainbow Option,* she thought. *If they ratify the new*

Constitution, Isaiah will be able to enter his barbeque sauce at the Kansas City American Royal, the world's largest barbeque competition. It's the only competition he hasn't won yet!

It was his birthday, and she had left work early to prepare a surprise for him. She glanced out the window. It was another beautiful day in Christchurch. A soft sea breeze blew through the open window.

A loud "HONK!" came from the driveway. She put down the mixing spoon and went to see who it was. Isaiah was behind the wheel of a sleek touring sedan. An electronic key dangled from his upheld hand. She squealed and ran to him.

Laughing, he got out of the car and hugged her. "Oh Isaiah, it's beautiful!" She let her hand caress the smooth metallic blue finish. "This lacquer looks a meter deep. Is this your mid-life crisis car?"

"Nope. It's a present to you on my birthday. And a present to the world! Look at the nameplate on the front."

"Moore? I've never heard of that brand of car."

"That's because this is the first one off the assembly line. Get in. Let's try your new ride."

After stopping at the end of the drive, she accelerated onto the country road. "Oh!" she gasped, "This baby is fast! Why isn't there any engine noise?"

"Because it's all electric! You remember that I partnered with a South Korean firm for some research and development? They were working on high capacity batteries. My team was working on software to boost the performance of the batteries. The result of that partnership is that this car can travel one thousand miles on one charge, carrying a family of four. You can fully charge it in two hours. Fifteen minutes, and you're good for one hundred twenty-five miles."

Grace expertly took a succession of S-curves at speed. "And she corners like she's glued to the road!"

"Wahoo! We partnered with some investors and bought a factory from a Korean auto manufacturer. You are driving VIN number 000000001 of a flood of three hundred thousand cars about to hit the world markets. Next year, maybe a million."

Grace pulled into a spot next to a beach. "It drives like a dream. Why the name Moore?"

"To honor Gordon Moore, who predicted that the computing power of chips would double every two years. And as the capacity of chips went up, the cost came down. Which gives you a hint as to the best thing about this car."

"Which is?"

"It only costs twelve thousand dollars! The average family can afford it. Grace, when entrepreneurs are freed up to do their thing, there is another kind of flood, a flood of innovation and low-cost abundance!"

"Wow! That's great! I see it has internet access on the dashboard screen. Let's look for some music and see just how good these speakers are." Grace worked the controls on the touch screen.

Music began playing, but was quickly interrupted by a 'ping' which signaled a call from Isaiah's phone link. It was a Skype call from Judge Block. "Greetings, Isaiah and Grace. Good news! A new nation was born today. The United States of Liberty! All but one of the states ratified the new constitution, so the remaining eighteen voted to form the new republic. Some good news for this tired old world. Be well, my friends." The call ended.

Isaiah laughed, and tears of joy streamed down his face. "Free at last, free at last! Thank God Almighty, we have a free nation again." He clasped Grace's hand. "Dear Lord, thank You for letting us live to see this day. Thank You for giving strength to the people of the Constitutional Resistance Movement and the ARKs to go on through the dark days. We ask You now for Your blessings on our new republic. And send us the wisdom to keep it this time. Amen."

"Amen! Now that calls for a celebration! Let's dance!" Grace worked the screen. Ben E. King's *Stand by Me* began playing. They both got out, kicked off their shoes, and began a slow dance in the sand. A soft sea breeze caressed them as they swayed together. The sounds of the ocean surf blended with the rhythm of the song.

"You stood by me when they imprisoned me in Guantanamo," Isaiah murmured to her.

"And you stood by me when they arrested me and put me on trial in D.C.," she murmured back.

She sang the refrain softly in his ear, "No, I won't be afraid, Oh, I won't be afraid, just as long as you stand, stand by me."

Isaiah squeezed her hand. "Lord, thank You for standing by us."

"Thank You, Lord," said Grace.

Putting her mouth to his ear, Grace whispered, "You got a new car and a new nation for your birthday, brother man, but I've got the best present of all for you."

"What's that, sister woman?" he whispered back.

"We are going to have a baby!"

He stood back, his hands on her shoulders. A happy grin split his face. For once, he was speechless.

The End.

The Rainbow Option is the sequel to Michael McCarthy's first thriller,

The Noah Option. To order, go to www.TheNoahOption.com

Printed in the United States
By Bookmasters